CAROUSEL OF PROGRESS

Katherine Tanney

# CAROUSEL OF PROGRESS

A Novel

Villard New York

SECTIONS OF THIS BOOK WERE ORIGINALLY PUBLISHED IN *TEXAS THOROUGHBRED* MAGAZINE AND *PUERTO DEL SOL.*

GRATEFUL ACKNOWLEDGMENT IS MADE TO HAL LEONARD CORPORATION FOR PERMISSION TO REPRINT THE FOLLOWING: AN EXCERPT FROM "SCENES FROM AN ITALIAN RESTAURANT," WORDS AND MUSIC BY BILLY JOEL. COPYRIGHT © 1977, 1978 BY IMPULSIVE MUSIC. ALL RIGHTS RESERVED. INTERNATIONAL COPYRIGHT SECURED. AN EXCERPT FROM "BRASS IN POCKET," WORDS AND MUSIC BY CHRISSIE HYNDE AND JAMES HONEYMAN-SCOTT. COPYRIGHT © 1979 BY EMI MUSIC PUBLISHING LTD. TRADING AS CLIVE BANKS SONGS. ALL RIGHTS FOR THE UNITED STATES AND CANADA CONTROLLED AND ADMINISTERED BY EMI APRIL MUSIC INC. ALL RIGHTS FOR THE WORLD EXCLUDING THE UNITED STATES AND CANADA CONTROLLED AND ADMINISTERED BY EMI MUSIC PUBLISHING LTD. ALL RIGHTS RESERVED. INTERNATIONAL COPYRIGHT SECURED. USED BY PERMISSION.

LIBRARY OF CONGRESS CATALOGING-IN-PUBLICATION DATA
TANNEY, KATHERINE.
    CAROUSEL OF PROGRESS : A NOVEL / KATHERINE TANNEY. — 1ST ED.
      P.   CM.
    ISBN 0-375-50537-7 (ACID-FREE PAPER)
    1. CHILDREN OF DIVORCED PARENTS—FICTION.   2. BROTHERS AND SISTERS—FICTION.
    3. CALIFORNIA, SOUTHERN—FICTION.   4. TEENAGE GIRLS—FICTION.   I. TITLE.
    PS3570.A556  C37  2001
    813'.6—DC21                                 00-053132

VILLARD BOOKS WEBSITE ADDRESS: WWW.VILLARD.COM

PRINTED IN THE UNITED STATES OF AMERICA ON ACID-FREE PAPER
9 8 7 6 5 4 3 2

FIRST EDITION

*Book design by Barbara M. Bachman*

For Hans & Freda,

Greasy & Flaky,

Everett & Judith


For Dina

IS IT PROGRESS IF

A CANNIBAL USES A FORK?

—*Stanislaw J. Lec*

1978

APRIL

They had put my father in an orange driving suit and a helmet and shown him how to get inside the cockpit of a Formula Ford racecar. Being tall and broad-shouldered, he didn't exactly slide right in, feet first. Rather, he had to stuff himself into the ground-hugging vehicle by tucking and compressing his body in ways that made me wish for a giant shoehorn.

"At least we're getting a tan," said my mother, to my left. Her oiled midriff was turning deep brown. The smell of cocoa butter made me hungry.

It was my father's turn to work on cornering, the technique explained in the classroom that morning. Instead of lying out by the hotel pool a second day, my brother and I had tagged along with him. Sonoma was the pits—Peter and I renamed it Sominex—but driving class turned out to be an exception. The instructor, a cool, soft-spoken ex-racer, drew pictures on the chalkboard and talked about getting on the right line when driving into blind curves. From the driver's head he drew an arrow way across the track to a tree, and told the class to aim their wheels at the tree if they wanted to come out with any speed. They had to quickly unwind their steering wheels, too, to regain lost speed. There were a dozen things to remember.

After my father's fifth revolution, the other drivers started getting in their cars and zooming onto the track. The swarm of them would soon be like giant hornets going round and round, sawing my head open with the sound. "I'm broiling out here," I said. "Can't we go back to the hotel?"

"Don't complain, Meredith. It's boring. And tuck in your chin, please. You look like a monkey."

According to my mother, who was sexy and exquisite without trying, I stuck my chin out all the time, especially when I was in a bad mood. I wasn't aware of doing it, but according to her it was extremely unattractive. Peter's racecar noises, on the other hand, didn't bother her a bit. My little brother hung from an imaginary steering wheel to my right, jerking his shoulders violently whenever my father's car went into a turn. I elbowed him and said cut it out.

"Men." My mother sighed. She'd been doing it a lot lately, talking— complaining, really—about the problems between men and women.

"There's a woman out there, too," I said, removing my camera from my neck. The weight of it made me slouch, plus there weren't any good pictures to take from the bleachers.

"She doesn't have a family. She can do what she wants," my mother said.

"How do you know she doesn't have a family?"

"Meredith, you are being argumentative. I'm not in the mood, honey."

Those of us not enrolled in driving school were getting grouchy. How had my parents imagined that watching my father have all the fun would be an enjoyable family vacation?

Peter revved up. "I'll bet he's at four thousand RPMs!"

"Could be," my mother said.

We continued following the bright-blue car, number seventy-three, around the track, even though all we could see was his helmeted head peeking out the top as if it belonged to a mannequin. I decided not to speak for the rest of the trip. They could beg me, trick me, tickle me, but no more "argumentative" words would pass my lips. I let Reese Phillips's gorgeous face take over my mind. I had seen it for the first time just days before, at school, and immediately made him my new fantasy guy. All I needed was the face. I could take it with me wherever I went, whenever I needed something good for myself. Substituting Reese for my father in the orange suit and helmet, I imagined I was watching a high-stakes race. I became the sexy girlfriend in the stands, following the action with the knowledge that if Reese lost, Tom Saucer (my former fantasy guy, and racing kingpin) would have him killed and I'd be sent back to Tom, who still wanted me and hated Reese's guts for stealing me away.

"You want a Tab?"

It was my mother. She was holding out the can for me. Luckily I remembered to say nothing.

"You want one?" I took it from her and looked at the far green hills. I wasn't Reese's woman. I was just me, miserable and petulant. "You're welcome, Miss Sourpuss."

I didn't know why I was being this way. My mother smoked her cigarette and stared at the sky. Peter belched.

Those days, I was studying fashion models, looking for faces that were sort of like mine because my mother had promised me a nose job that summer. I stood in front of mirrors, pressing my nose flatter, thinner, pointier. I thought I could have any nose in the world and that it would change my look completely. Not that I was so bad. I was blessed with my mother's clear olive skin and blue eyes, and her pale, full lips which always looked thirsty. The main problem was my father's big nose, slapped in the middle of everything.

"A penny for your thoughts?" my mother said. I could feel my heart beating faster. It was hard to be so mean, but I pretended not to hear her.

She said, "Have you ever heard of the mother's curse? Because I'm going to put it on you if you keep up this behavior, Meredith."

I pictured Amy Sloane's face. The nose of noses, kindest girl in the school, and the best singer. I had taken loads of pictures of her for the yearbook. Amy's mother was dead, hit by a car the year before while aiding a stranded motorist. The tragedy gave her a certain glamour, I thought. She had palpable pain and people ached to reach out to her with their sympathy. Everyone felt sorry for Amy. Something BIG had happened to her. "When I was thirteen," she'd still be saying when she was old, "I lost my mother." It would always be a conversation stopper, maybe the most interesting thing that would ever happen to her. When my mother heard the news, her only comment was, "All good deeds will be punished."

"The mother's curse, for Meredith Jessica Herman: I hope someday, my daughter, that you have children, and that they grow up to be just like you." My mother's mouth was pursed in a sarcastic little smile.

"Ha! That's a curse? It sounds more like a beautiful blessing to me, so thank you very much."

I had spoken. She'd won her little war and she knew it. Then Peter screamed and pointed at the track. Number seventy-three slid hard into the barrier, buckling like an empty pop can.

---

MY FATHER PUT a giant piece of steak in his mouth. "So much for my professional racing career." Then he whipped his head back to clear the hair from his eye. His foot had gotten stuck under the brake pedal and he couldn't wedge it loose before crashing. The entire incident exhilarated him. He drank a bottle of red wine with his steak and was more talkative than I had ever seen him. "At least I remembered to take these off the wheel before impact." He lifted his hands. "See? No broken wrists."

My mother played with her celery stalk. She was having Bloody Marys for dinner. We got to order whatever we wanted, no questions asked, on account of my father's brush with death. I got a fancy shrimp cocktail and garlic toast, and a hot fudge sundae for dessert. Peter had a plate of fries, a plate of onion rings, and unlimited Cokes. "We're celebrating," I told the waitress, because she didn't seem to like us very much. In a circular booth at the hotel restaurant, the four of us sat curled in like fingers of a hand. My father had emerged from the wreckage unscratched and I told myself we were special, a great family. Only my mother was sad. She fiddled with her straw and stared at the three of us as if we were strangers in a dream she was having.

Now, of course, I can imagine what was going through her mind. A theory was being hatched—one she'd grow increasingly determined to prove come summer—that my father no longer loved her. The fact that he preferred death in a racecar to another bland day of their marriage was her evidence. Or maybe she no longer loved him. Maybe she sat listening to the loving details of his impact and was stung by the realization that she didn't care whether he lived or died. All I know is, my parents sat side by side without being necessary to each other anymore. Not that I understood any of this at the time—least of all why, the very next morning, she did what she did.

My father was suited up again, strapped inside of a brand-new car. The exuberance of the previous night had worn off and there was only apprehension among us, stunned disbelief to find ourselves back at the track. "What about his feet?" Peter said. "I thought they were too big."

"Come on," said my mother, walking away.

I didn't argue, for a change. I grabbed Peter's hand and the three of us headed back to the hotel. When we reached the dark hall in front of our rooms she told us to go in and pack everything up.

"What about Dad?" I protested.

"He'll find his way home." She didn't look at me. "Peter? I don't want you to worry about Daddy. Daddy's a grown-up. He's a good driver. He'll be fine. We're going to go home and wait for him there, okay?"

Peter nodded slowly. He felt the need to put his trust in someone just then, and my mother's timing was perfect.

Back in our room, I put out the DO NOT DISTURB sign and threw myself on the bed. My mother's curveballs were a standard part of every vacation. Normally she refused to go out to dinner with us, or pretended not to know us. Already she'd threatened to run away with a strange man just to prove that she could.

"What are you doing?" I saw Peter emptying a drawer. He carried an armful of clothing to the bed, then looked at me.

"Packing."

I went into the bathroom and attempted to trick the mirror into showing me my profile. My hope was to turn my head quickly and catch the earlier side view still there in the glass. I knew how reflections worked, of course, knew all I needed was a second, handheld, mirror to easily look at my profile, but I actually believed the laws of nature might bend for me one day like they did for people on *The Twilight Zone*. My father's nose stared back at me, head-on.

"Stop looking at yourself and pack." Peter stood watching, so I lifted my toothbrush from the holder and dropped it into the wastebasket, followed by my comb, a barrette, and my wet bathing suit, just to see what he'd do. Then I picked up the wastebasket and walked past him, saying, "I think I'll take this home as my new carryall."

He followed me back into the room. "You can't do that. Mom'll get in trouble."

"No she won't." I pulled it away from his outstretched arm. It was too easy to get Peter worked up, but I felt like arguing and he was the only one there. When the phone rang a moment later, I dived for it to warn my father of our impending departure, but it was her. She was on the other side of the wall, and I thought I could hear her distantly and close up at the same time.

"You kids almost ready?"

I didn't know what to say.

"Meredith?"

"Yes?"

"What's your brother doing? Is he packing?"

"Yes."

"Good. Hurry up, both of you. I'll be over in one minute." I didn't really think she was serious. I figured we'd make it as far as the car before she called the whole thing off.

"One minute," I told Peter. He started moving twice as fast. He knelt on the floor and checked under both beds, then he was at the dresser, banging every empty drawer. Finally he noticed I wasn't moving.

"You better start packing."

She knocked on our door, two bumps with the side of her fist. Peter picked up his suitcase and let her in.

"Got everything?" she said.

I was still standing in the middle of the room, holding the waste-basket of stuff. She moaned. "What is taking you so long, Meredith?" That's when I told her I wasn't going.

Peter let out a cry of frustration.

"Fine, then. Bye-bye." She continued looking at me another second or two, then turned her attention to my brother, as though I no longer existed.

As their footsteps faded on the carpet I expected a feeling to grab hold of me, telling me to run after them, but it never came. None of it seemed real. Eventually, the maid rolled her cart in front of the door and looked at the wastebasket in my hand. I smiled—her presence signaled a spell-breaking return to order—and requested she come back later.

Over the years I have wondered about this day again and again. Could I have done more? I know I considered rushing back to the track like it was a major emergency, but the thought of my father's worried face as he ripped off his helmet and saw me standing alone, waving my arms at him, stopped me. I feared he'd get back in the car after hearing the news. Perhaps he would have come back to the hotel with me and rubbed his face all day until he decided what to do. Mostly, though, I wanted to outsmart my mother. I remember trying to determine what she expected of me so I could do just the opposite. In the end what I did was this: I got back in my nightgown, pulled out my magazines, and turned on the TV. Sooner or later, I decided, my father would come to me. I turned the pages and changed the channels, and the burden of responsibility became a speck floating somewhere far behind my eyes. It dulled the sharpness of the world, but only slightly.

At noon the phone rang seven times, then stopped. I wrapped one arm around my waist and pulled the pillow to my face with the other. Reese wanted me, bad. We rolled around the bed, our lips pressed tight. He pinned me beneath him. "If you ever leave," he said, "I'll come after you. I'll bring you back, and my men will watch you night and day." I bunched up my nightgown and rolled onto my stomach, rubbing against the material until the familiar shock waves of pleasure carried me high above the roof of this world. When I woke up, it was almost two.

I had an idea about divorce, that kids had to go to court and say on the stand who they wanted to live with. In my case, the decision came down to fun (my dad), versus duty (my mom), but more than anything I saw my father, sad and alone if they divorced, and Peter and me forgotten in the gulf between them.

The hotel room was oppressive. I was sick of old movies, so I took my swimsuit out of the wastebasket and slid it, cold and damp, over my warm skin. Posing like a model in front of the mirror, I realized I was quite hungry. When the phone rang again, I picked it up and lied to my father, saying we were all down at the pool.

"I just came in to use the bathroom," I said.

He had eaten lunch with the group and was about to start the afternoon session.

"What time are you coming back to the hotel?" I said.

"I want all of you to come to the track at four-thirty. We're putting on a demonstration, then there's a little party for the graduates. Tell your mom it will be fun."

"Okay."

"Bye-bye, sweetie."

EVERY PERSON HAS his or her way of getting into a swimming pool. Some people take five minutes. They work their way, joint by joint, into the gentle swirls of water created by their own movements. Others stand erect, pinch their nostrils shut, and drop themselves like message tubes into the watery chute. Given a diving board, there was only one way for me to get into a pool at fourteen: a single bounce on the end of the board, followed by a midair somersault with just enough time before immersion to straighten out my legs and point my toes. It was my way and I was good at it, the way some people were good at the crawl, which I hated.

The pool at the hotel was crowded. I took a chaise longue in the sun and opened my new *Cosmopolitan*. If ever there was a magazine to make you wish you had big beautiful breasts, it was *Cosmo*. I was flat as a boy, but according to my mother there was still plenty of time for me to develop. I opened to the quiz, "How Honest Is Your Guy?," and made sure Reese and I scored pretty high as a couple. Then I got up and stepped onto the diving board. At the tip, I looked down into the clear blue water, where white snakes of light shimmied along the surface. Reese's men were everywhere, stationed around the pool, thinking I didn't notice them, while Reese himself, in bathrobe and swim trunks, smoked a cigar and counted his money. I jumped into the air. The board absorbed my weight and flung me back out. I tucked my head and knees into my folded arms and spun myself around like a ball, releasing when the pull of gravity tugged me down to the water like a speeding arrow. Piercing the water's skin, I felt time slow way down. My velocity softened. Little bubbles tickled and encircled me as I waited to be pushed back up by the space around me closing and filling.

When I was back in the sun, my body streaked with beads of pool water, I thought of my mother. Was she thinking of me? She had completely ruined the weekend, but what else was new? I watched two girls with curvy, seventeen-year-old bodies walk to a table where lunch was served. The waiter flirted with them, then brought two big bowls of rich clam chowder, which they signed for. I wrapped my towel around me and went to a table.

"Clam chowder," I announced, like I was royalty and there was no question I had the authority to sign for it.

At four-thirty I headed back to the room, where I discovered the maid had thrown away all my toiletries, which I'd forgotten to take out of the wastebasket. Luckily, there was hotel shampoo and soap. I got in the shower, still wearing my swimsuit. A few minutes later the curtain opened, which is when I screamed, even though I could see it was my father in his orange driving suit. I had been singing at the top of my lungs, and the embarrassing sound of my voice still clung to the walls.

"Where's your mother?"

I thought about lying, saying she was still at the pool, but obviously he had been there, and to his room, from the look on his face.

"They went home."

He yanked the curtain shut, creating a gust of cold air.

-------------------

"THERE'S A LADY in the class, name's Catherine. I'm going to ask her to give us a ride to San Francisco. Then you and I will catch a plane home, all right?"

I remembered the female driver, and the disagreement my mother and I had over her. It seemed a long time ago. My father and I were walking down the path that led from the hotel to the racing school. He'd showered and changed into street clothes and a suede jacket. I was concentrating on the sound of the gravel beneath our shoes, specifically its resemblance to the daily sound in my head made by chewing breakfast cereal, when he said, "I should be mad, but, truth is, who can blame her? Your mother got a dose of it yesterday. She hasn't got the stomach for it." He squinted as he spoke, as though his thoughts had sharp little points.

I couldn't believe he was letting her off so easily. He seemed to think she'd abandoned him out of love or something. He was a good-looking man, with thick dark hair worn longer than most dads, a rebel strand usually falling in his eye. I watched him count the money in his wallet. "And listen to me, if Catherine asks what happened to Mom, just tell the truth. Say she went home early."

"What if she asks why?"

"She's not going to do that, trust me."

"How do you know?"

" 'Cause she's a smart lady. Want to bet?"

"No."

"Hey, I'm glad you stayed. I want you to take some good pictures of your old man with his racing buddies."

I wanted him to understand that my mother meant to do him harm. The night before, he'd practically had to carry her back to their room after dinner, she'd had so much to drink. He held her and moved her through the corridor with her eyes closed, her head resting on his chest, all the time saying things to make her laugh, but did she remember that?

As soon as we arrived under the canopy, several people shouted "Bigfoot" at my father. They came over and slapped his back and said things to me, like did I know my father was the missing link? I started taking pictures immediately. Someone gave my father a drink. More people came over, each making an almost identical joke to the ones that had come before. Through my viewfinder I watched my father as I would any stranger, saw the pleasure he took from being part of this group. They were mostly like him, people with regular jobs, there for a pricey thrill. I noticed there weren't any other kids at the party, and only a few wives or girlfriends. My mother would have hated it.

Catherine arrived wearing a crash helmet and a homemade sash that said TOKEN WOMAN. Everyone hailed her arrival, as they had when my father and I showed up. They called her Cha-Cha. It referred, I found out later, to a famous woman racer. She made a big fuss when she saw me, shouted to my father that she knew right away I was his daughter.

"And she's got a camera! Oh, sweetheart, would you mind taking a picture of your father and me? I'm going to write 'Cha-Cha and Bigfoot' underneath it in my photo album."

Her brashness made me shy. I lifted my camera to my face as she threw her arms around my father's neck.

"Oh wait! Wait!" She was in a mad panic, letting go of him to adjust her sash for the camera. Then she reattached herself and posed like one of those girls who shows up to be photographed on the arm of the winner. My dad went along with it. He put his thumb up and winked like some guy in an advertisement. As soon as I took the picture, Catherine ran over and gave me a little hug and said thank you several times. She told me I was gorgeous and whispered, "Just like your father," before running off to throw herself at other people.

My father asked if I was having fun, so I said sure. Then he told me to wait while he went to ask Catherine about the ride. While his back was turned I downed a cup of champagne. Across the way, I saw her remove her helmet so she could hear my father, and beautiful long gray hair spilled out over her shoulders. It went a long way toward balancing her plump physique. She was actually sort of pretty. Catherine looked at me then, so I smiled and started to wave but she looked away as though she hadn't really seen me. I took the opportunity to empty another cup of champagne.

"We're all set," my father said when he came back. "She'll meet us in the lobby in forty-five minutes."

----

I TOOK A PICTURE OF the hotel room before leaving. It was the kind of photograph you know is a waste of film even as you click the button. The drugstore would send back an underexposed image of a nameless room with sickly green walls. I thought all this as I framed the shot, yet I wanted it anyway.

Catherine was in the lobby, chatting with my father and nervously picking fuzzballs from the big coat draped over her arm. She tugged one out, then smoothed the spot, as though meaning to be done with the activity. Then the cycle started over. She was introduced to me as Mrs. Stone but said to hell with that, I should call her Catherine.

"My own daughters do, so why shouldn't you?" The first thing I thought was that I had been right. She *did* have a family.

Catherine talked faster than anyone I had ever met, and this allowed her to fit twice as many words into unsuspecting silences. On the way to the car, she finished my sentence for me three times. I wondered what my father thought about this, but he avoided eye contact with me once we joined up with her.

The car was a two-seater with an area beneath the hatchback the shape of an isosceles triangle. Obviously, I was supposed to fit there, squeezed in with all the bags.

"Good thing you're so skinny," Catherine said. Her hand felt strangely heavy on my shoulder and the heat of her skin annoyed me. Then she was dangling her keys in front of my father. "How about it, Robert?"

I couldn't help thinking she just wanted a man to drive her, a rare occurrence she didn't want to miss out on. She made a joke about the car my father had wrecked, then winked at me as if we were in on something hilarious against him. I smiled politely, trying to convey a glimmer of the dislike I was starting to attach to her. Not that she noticed. She talked constantly, and too loudly, considering we were only inches apart in her cramped car. It was her tireless cheer I minded, her whole style, really. Her clothes were drab and loose fitting, more like sheets with buttons than clothes. The only makeup she bothered with was a heavy black line all the way around her grayish eyes. What did she think she was doing putting those thick rings on top of that washed-out skin? I had never been around a woman like her before. Even just sitting in the car, she could barely organize herself.

My father made the wheels sound like a tortured animal as we left the parking lot. His right arm sliced the air with the stick shift as though, beneath the car, corresponding patterns were simultaneously being carved into the earth. He treated driving like nothing else in life, pretending to dominate the road, the car, everything. He kept his head straight, his shoulders rigid, and his eyes fixed ahead, rapt. All emotions flowed through his arm to the knob on the stick, which he gripped with surprising nonchalance.

I was used to it. I thought it was pretty funny how he jerked and thrusted like a busy robot. I don't know what Catherine thought. Whatever it was she kept it to herself, unlike my mother, who had to threaten to get out of the car sometimes to make him stop. One time, he actually called her on it. He pulled to the side of the road, leaned over, and unlocked the door for her. We were about six blocks from home and it was late at night. My mother got out in an instant and slammed the door behind her before walking off. We sat and watched her for a few moments, then my father drove up beside her and rolled down the window.

"Get in the car, Leigh."

She told him to go to hell. We shadowed her in the car a little longer. She was moving fast and probably didn't even mind the chilly night air.

"Goddamn it, Leigh."

"Fuck off," she told him.

It had been weird that time to come home without her, as though we'd forgotten something at the store. We unloaded the groceries, turned on the lights, but until my mother walked through the door eight minutes later, we moved around like blind fish.

Now Catherine was talking about her daughters.

"How come they didn't come with you?" I said.

She swatted her hand at the air. "What, are you serious? They're home with their friends. Hanging out with Mom is, you know, extremely uncool."

I could envision her, the wisecracking divorced mom. Her relationship with her kids was probably free-form, more like roommates, and completely different from what went on at our house.

It was growing dark out. Lying there with my heart to the mat, I felt every bump in the road, like a balloon drifting down again and again into the savage, uplifting blows of a crowd.

My father and Catherine got on the subject of Las Vegas. "Vegas," they called it, like it was someone they both knew.

"It's a state of mind," he said. "Vegas is all attitude."

"Absolutely."

I had a great view of her face, her constant smile and the deep lines it etched into her cheeks, like parentheses, as if she'd spent her whole life listening and smiling, and nodding up and down, going "Uh-huh, uh-huh" every few seconds.

"In Vegas, money is just paper. It doesn't mean a thing."

"Yep, no place like Vegas."

"Except Vegas, of course."

"Naturally." They laughed.

"So, you're Scorpio, right? Just a guess," Catherine said.

"Here we go." My father sighed. "Wrong."

"Rats! I was sure of it, especially after what you said about Vegas. Okay, don't tell me, don't tell me. I'm really good at this."

"You're wasting your time. I don't believe in that crap."

"The good ones never do. I'm going to guess Aries or Libra. It's got to be one of those, right?"

"Aries."

She clapped her hands. "I knew it. See? I told you I'm good. It's my job to know people. Seriously, I've gotten to the point where I can read a person in two minutes. They call me the high priestess of human resources at work."

"You're at William Morris, right? I'm on the phone to you guys all the time."

"Well, sure, you would be. Sheesh, you must be a glutton for punishment, working in PR."

"Right."

They seemed to be talking in shorthand, understanding one another perfectly. I was hazy from the champagne. Human resources turned into human remains in my imagination, body parts being tilled like fresh earth. I readjusted my position so I was on my back, looking up through the glass at the sky, which was interrupted by traveling reflections of lights, and once in a while by the shiny glint of my own eyes.

"Look at us, we're talking shop, Robert."

"You started it."

"Oh thanks, thanks a bunch. Okay, tell me what you'd really like to be. I mean, if you weren't a copywriter."

My father hummed, giving it some thought.

"C'mon. You know. I know you know."

I knew the answer. My father wanted to write books. He liked the idea of being a best-selling suspense author. He cut articles out of the newspaper sometimes and kept them in a notebook. My mother would say, "You're never going to do it. You'd have to give up watching sports first, and you're never going to do that."

"I really don't know," my father said.

"The man doesn't know. Okay, like I believe that one. Well, I'm not afraid to tell. I'm going to write and produce a television series. I hope. I pray. It's not such a pipe dream, you know. I mean, look where I am. Do you know how many agents I'm friends with? See, there's a method to my madness. I've already shown my stuff to one agent and she said it was better than most of the material she sells! No kidding, that's what she said. Plus, I'm learning so much about the business. It's only a matter of time."

Being around her made me tired. At some point I gave up following the endless ribbon of words falling from her mouth. Her brassy voice was an irritant, but one I could bear as long as I reminded myself we would lose her at the next stop and I would fly home, side by side with my father.

---

THE SIGHT OF all those people in front of the airport made me smile, because the journey was finally over.

"We'll have to have lunch sometime," she said. "I'll be back in L.A. on Thursday. Your office is, like, five minutes from mine."

"I'll give you a call." My father sounded exhausted, too, and who wouldn't be after an hour with Catherine Stone?

"Be sure to say thank you," he muttered to me as I stretched out my aching limbs. Catherine got out and the three of us stood over the hatchback, sorting out the bags.

"You sure were quiet back there. Did you fall asleep?" Catherine rubbed my back vigorously.

"Almost." I dreamed of saying, How could I talk when you wouldn't shut up for a minute?

My father thanked her. "I don't know what we would have done without you."

"Oh please, don't even think about it."

"Yeah, thanks a lot," I said.

"You take good care of him." She was suddenly holding me in a totally one-sided hug. I was speechless. She moved on to my father, squeezing him more formally, like a loaf of bread. Then his hand cupped her butt. I watched in amazement as he gave it an encouraging pat. Catherine, thrilled, hurried back to her car, yelling good-bye and waving nonstop until she drove away.

Male chauvinist pig. My mother called my father that now and then—not often, because he oinked at her. "Suey!" Peter would holler to get in on the action, and then I'd have to roll my eyes to show my female support. But it was faddish, in my opinion, something my mother said to be hip, to show she was up to the minute, the same way she bragged about having smoked a "marijuana cigarette" once. She wanted people to know she was groovy. I suppose I inherited my lack of moral certitude from them both, because my father's hand on the ass of Catherine Stone, far from stirring easy condemnation, prompted me to consider several possible readings: he was just being "nice," trying to make her feel good because she'd helped us out; his hand simply came to rest there and he was so out of it and exhausted and concerned about getting home that he didn't even realize it was her ass; he was on more intimate terms with

Catherine Stone than I had previously realized; he was just a male chauvinist pig.

I had never flown at night. Alone beside my father it seemed glamorous, as though we were the kind of people whose lives you could snap your fingers to, jet-setters moving from one fast vehicle to another, leaving curious onlookers like Catherine in our wake. My father had given me the window seat because he knew I liked to look out and ponder the altitudes, but the sky and earth were coated in darkness, and again I saw my own reflection in the glass.

"I keep thinking about the look on your mother's face when we're already home and unpacked with our feet up, watching TV. She and Peter are probably wiped out from driving, stuck in some hotel room in the goddamned middle of nowhere."

The front door of our house had become a finish line for him, the object of our lives to cross it first and claim victory. I tried to imagine it, too, my mother walking in, her body stiff from all those hours in the car. She'd look at me with disdain. Selfish brat. That's what she'd think when she got home.

"Can I try your drink?"

He was drinking bourbon and soda with his airline peanuts. The liquor smelled sweet, a smell I imagined had everything to do with grown-up sophistication. The cup was passed and I took a sip.

"Interesting." Disgusting was more like it. My mouth stung with a taste resembling ground coins and flowers.

Twenty minutes later they collected our cups and then there it was, Los Angeles, a boiling pot of lights spilling over the landscape as far as I could see.

"You see the Coliseum? And the Sports Arena?" My father was leaning over my shoulder and pointing. "Let me know if you see Luciano's down there. We'll wave to our pizza."

"Oh sure, Dad."

"You do want pizza, don't you?" Our ordeal was nearly over. We had returned to the familiar and everything was going to be all right.

At the first pay phone my father called the restaurant. He wanted everything. Salad, garlic bread, pizza, spaghetti. He timed it for a nine-thirty pickup, which gave us no time to get our bags or find a taxi. "Don't worry," he said, "this way the food'll be ready when we get there. I don't want to wait tonight."

Our bags hit the carousel just as we arrived to claim them, then a taxi pulled up as we came out to the curb. A conductor seemed to be orchestrating life just to suit us. I ran in to get the food while my father waited in the car. Naturally, it arrived at the take-out counter the same moment I did. Then Reese Phillips and his mother walked into the restaurant as I was leaving. I was so shocked to see his face for real that I stared like a goon. He was probably used to it.

"Hi," he said, flashing me a smile worth suffering for. It was a long hi, and he looked into my eyes the whole time he said it, as if he really was glad to see me. I reenacted it several times on the way home, prolonging the precise moment our eyes had met and he had smiled and spoken. I replayed the questioning glance from his mother, his unbelievably perfect bone structure, how much taller than me he was, just every little detail I could remember. It immediately replaced the old picture of him in my mind.

As soon as we turned onto our street I saw the blue and red lights ahead, but for some reason—probably I was still dazzled from seeing Reese—I was slow to react. My father repeated our address to the driver, but his voice lost its force as we approached and he realized something was going on. Mrs. Jordan from across the street was standing at the curb with her arms crossed. A policeman stood with her, writing on a pad. The jumble of things both strange and familiar made me feel like a spectator. The police radio was up loud, dotting the air with fuzzy, incoherent noise, and all the lights were on in our house. The Mercedes was in the driveway, which meant my mother had made it back after all.

"Stay in the car." My father got out to join the cop and Mrs. Jordan.

Maybe I was motherless, I thought before I could stop myself. It was the beginning of a string of thoughts that fanned out in my mind like a morbid deck of cards. Murder: my mother with her throat slit. Suicide: my mother with an empty bottle of pills. Maybe she had accidentally murdered Peter, knocked the blow-dryer in his bath, or maybe they'd both been finished by roving psychos. And somehow I had known to stay behind. Now it would be just me and my father with our terrible story for the world to pity us by.

I found my thoughts disgusting and wished I could erase them.

"Tell your old man the meter's still running," said the driver. I was about to get out when my father returned.

"Everything's okay. The house was robbed, but nobody's hurt. Probably didn't even happen today. They just took stuff. Let's go in and see your mother and Peter." Together we gathered our belongings, then he sent the driver away with money.

Of course nobody was dead or even hurt. These were things that happened to other people, people in the newspaper or on TV. In our lives things were never that dramatic. I followed my father into the house where he immediately called my mother's name. Peter came running down the stairs with a startled, excited expression.

"Dad!" He threw his arms around my father's hips and squeezed tremendously.

"Hey, kiddo. What happened here?" Peter stepped back and looked at us with wonderstruck eyes.

"Robbers. They took the TV and the stereo and your camera and Mom's diamond earrings, and, and, whoosh!" He crossed his arms in the air just like the one who waves the winner across the finish line.

The house looked normal to me. You had to look twice to notice certain things were missing. A man's voice came from upstairs. He was saying that an officer would come and dust for fingerprints in the morning.

"So we shouldn't touch anything?" It was my mother's voice.

"If you can help it," the cop said, as though he didn't expect to find anything. The two of them came down the stairs.

"Welcome home," she said, sarcastically. She barely looked at me.

"Evening, sir," the policeman said. I saw from his name tag that he was a sergeant. He had an enormous gun strapped to his hip, with a fat wooden handle I was dying to grab.

"What's that?" my mother said, taking the food from my hands. "As if I don't know. Looks like you and your father were going to have yourselves quite a party."

She had a way of making everything I ever did alone with my father sound suspiciously romantic. When he and I did photography together she called us "the shutterbugs." If we went to a basketball game together she called it "a date." I followed her into the kitchen, where she put the food on the counter.

"You know what?"

She didn't answer. She was looking through the bags, starting to organize the meal.

"You remember the woman in Dad's racing class? The one you said could do what she wants because she doesn't have a family?"

"Meredith, don't talk now. I'm tired, I'm hungry, and I'm still very annoyed with you about this morning."

"Well, it turns out she does have a family. She has two daughters." My mother stopped moving but didn't turn around. "So, there. I was right. Do you want to know how I found out?"

"Did you hear me?" She suddenly turned. Her face was pale and contemptuous. "I want you out of here. The sight of you makes me sick.

I don't want to hear you, I don't want to see you, do you understand? Now *move.*"

I should have run away fast, but the thought of the sergeant seeing my hot, red face as I passed him in the foyer kept me from budging. He couldn't have missed overhearing her attack. He probably figured I deserved what I got. Meanwhile, my mother had taken over the food, ripped it away from me as if it were hers to control, and all I could do was stand there, watching her and fighting back the swelling in my throat. She always won in the end, was always better than me, smarter, more powerful. The tears started to flow, followed by helpless gasps for breath.

She watched me awhile, then told me to wash my face with cold water, that it would make me feel better. She said that sometimes I pushed it too far, that I asked for it. She wondered did I have any idea how hard it was to be the wife and mother all the time? Then, finally, when I wouldn't stop, she held me and stroked my hair. I closed my eyes and tried to pitch myself into the darkness and warmth, but couldn't shake the feeling I was an imposition on her.

I started putting dinner on the table and returned to thoughts of Reese and his mother at Luciano's, eating the same food we were about to eat. Was there a chance he was thinking about me?

"Babe?" My father entered the kitchen, slipping his arms around my mother's waist, his chest to her back. "How you doing?" He nuzzled her cheek.

"I don't know." She closed her eyes and relaxed into his embrace. How was it the only person anyone was mad at was me?

"Poor Leigh-Leigh. The bastards got your diamond earrings." His lips pressed into her skin.

"Anyway"—she pulled away from him—"you don't have to baby me. I'm not a child, Robert." He stood there, looking lost.

At dinner my father reviewed the insurance coverage, saying "beautiful" and "terrific" between mouthfuls of pizza. I assumed this meant we were covered. For some reason, Peter decided it would be an excellent time to demonstrate his fake epileptic seizure. "In case I'm ever attacked," he explained. He'd been perfecting it forever. "I'll freak 'em out by going into convulsions and making noises so they think I'm about to die. Check it out."

My mother smiled patiently at him, her good child, the one who didn't argue when she told him to do things like ditch his father in Sonoma, but I could tell she was disturbed by his surprisingly convincing display. My father put down his paperwork to have a look.

"I think I've still got the receipt for those earrings," he said, as soon as Peter got off the floor and put his tongue back in his mouth.

"Well, thank God I won't have to go very long without real diamonds on my ears." I thought she was trying to be funny, but my dad didn't get that. He tossed his pizza crust on the plate, disgusted. My mother made a face at him. "I mean, is that all you can think about, Robert?"

His head was pointed down, but his eyes were fixed on her. "What should I be thinking about, Leigh?"

"Well, let's see." She looked up, as though the answer were pasted on the ceiling. Peter and I pressed our knees together under the table. Their arguments always began this way, with my mother making fun of my father, treating him like an idiot. He took it, too, fuming silently as she talked. "Today your wife left you completely stranded for no apparent reason, and then, when you came home, your house was burgled! Just another day in the life of Robert No-Sweat Herman, I guess. There's always another way home, another pair of earrings. I mean, does anything get to you?" She was leaning forward, her chin on her hand. My father cleared his throat, but didn't speak. Finally, in an extremely soft voice he said, "Right."

"What was that? Did the great one speak? Please, great one, grace us again with your monosyllabic pearl. Share it with us."

"I said," he spoke in a clear, composed tone, as though none of her bitchery affected him, "right, yes, things get to me."

"Such as?" my mother instantly demanded. The terrible thing about being the child is seeing what's going wrong without having any right to comment. Couldn't she tell he was like a sponge swelling bigger and bigger?

"That's all I have to say." My father uncrossed his arms. "I suggest you save the rest for Betsy. You kids are excused."

Betsy was my mother's therapist—"My shrink," she called her, as in, "My shrink wants me to write a book," or "My shrink thinks I'm the only sane one." Though I'd met Betsy once—an attractive, middle-aged woman—whenever my mother said "My shrink," I immediately imagined a cold white sheet blowing wildly on a clothesline in the middle of nowhere. It was pretty clear a lot of my mother's recent ideas about men being pigs who kept women back had come from Betsy.

Peter and I left the room and climbed the stairs, stopping on the fifth one to listen to the rest of their conversation. The legs of a chair scraped the dining room floor. My mother told him not to leave. She threatened him, actually said if he walked away he could pack a bag and get out. "Not everything is so easily replaced, you know," she continued. "Did it even occur to you that if you had died on that racetrack, the kids and I would be left alone?" There was a long silence. "I know. That's not the way you think. We've all got to go sometime, right?" Another long silence, then "Don't touch me, Robert. It's too easy for you."

He shushed her, told her, "That's enough."

"Stop it, goddamn it," she shouted. "Get your hands off of me." He quickly left the room, so we hurried up the stairs. "I'm not a goddamned car," she screamed. "Stop trying to drive me into the ground!"

"She's crazy," Peter said, once we closed ourselves in his room. I didn't agree. I was beginning to comprehend that my father—and I—had failed a test of our love. She'd wanted to win for once, but nothing had gone according to plan. He hadn't rushed home to beg forgiveness or, even better, express outrage at being abandoned by her. No, he'd finished his racing course, attended his graduation party in my company, easily found a ride to the airport, and showed up in remarkably good spirits with a raging appetite. He hadn't fallen apart or gotten angry. The only thing he was guilty of was trying to understand and forgive her.

Over the years I've replayed, again and again, my shining moment of misplaced heroism. It begins with my mother's surprise and disappointment when I refuse to leave the hotel. I watch her say "Fine then," and turn away, handing me over to that strange place without a penny, without a thought. It hadn't occurred to either of us before then that we could do without each other. Surely the shock of it blinded me to her pain? She discarded me like someone else's mess, and so, naturally, I retaliated by concealing her absence from my father for as long as possible. Am I to blame, then? If I'd run right back to alert my father, would he have taken immediate steps to stop her? If I'd gone along as she asked, would it have saved their marriage? What if? Peter used to say it all the time. "What if I paid you five hundred dollars? Would you stand up and sing really loud in a crowded movie theater? What if I made it a thousand? Would you do it topless?"

y mother was standing over me, beautiful as always. Her warm hand brushed the hair from my face. "Don't," I said, turning away. She had interrupted the best dream of my entire life. I shut my eyes in a last effort to go back, and for a second he reappeared—Reese but not Reese, part David Soul, part Robert Redford—a deeply pained expression of love in his eyes from caring about me so much he could hardly stand it. I remembered the feel of his arms around me, how it had been to be a woman and not a young girl, but I couldn't reenter the dream.

My mother ran the tip of her finger along the length of my nose. "You know what day it is?" She smiled. Summer had come and I'd trained myself, in anticipation of my nose job, to fall asleep on my back. Each night I nodded off with the idea my nose was a butterfly that quietly opened its wings, then closed them, open, close, in a slow graceful manner that lulled me to sleep. Soon the butterfly would take off and I'd never see it again.

We sat in our nightgowns in the sunny kitchen. Peter was at day camp and my father had already left for work. As usual, all my mother ate for breakfast was half a grapefruit and dry toast. "Let's get dressed up for your consultation so Dr. Zubeck can see how pretty you are. I want him to see all the possibilities. Then we can go out to lunch afterwards. We can make a day of it," she went on, "go shopping, or we could see a movie. Let's be bad girls and eat whatever we want. Let's try on expensive shoes and dresses; maybe I'll even treat us to manicures at Elizabeth Arden."

She was in her jubilant, life-is-wonderful mood, which I hated, because it generally prefigured her life-is-hell-on-earth mood. Anything could trigger the change, any contradiction of the rosy film playing in her head. One time, a quadriplegic rolled past us in the supermarket and the rest of her day was ruined. She became sluggish and sighed a lot, then railed against the "idiots" who believed in God. Wretched bastards, she called them.

"You know, you might start thinking about having your eyebrows shaped." She leaned forward to examine my brows and I found myself looking at the bra beneath her nightgown. It was a little trick she'd learned in college. She wore an underwire bra to bed every night and swore it was the reason for her nice firm breasts at thirty-six, despite two kids. I thought of braless Ms. Jolly, who'd been my history teacher that year. Not only were her breasts much smaller than my mother's but they drooped like squashed tubes of paint beneath the knit tops she wore each day. Ms. Jolly was the least jolly person I had ever known. Jittery and turbulent, she told us she was a feminist, "capital F," and addressed us as "people," not "ladies and gentlemen," or "boys and girls." "C'mon, people," she would say, "listen up." Every year on her birthday, which coincided with the anniversary of Martin Luther King Jr.'s assassination, Ms. Jolly set up a phonograph at the front of the room and played a recording of the song "What the World Needs Now Is Love." The song was mixed in and out with speeches by John F. Kennedy, the "I Have a Dream" speech by Dr. King, something from Robert Kennedy, too, I think, and the awful live coverage of the shootings, then more of the song until it was so gut-wrenching that some of the students broke into uncontrollable sobs, at which point she pulled a brassiere off her desk, held it over the wastebasket, and set it aflame, shouting, "Women are not chicks! Black is beautiful! Power to the people!" Then she ran out of the room and class was over. It was such a powerful display and had become so controversial at the school that kids were given consent forms at the beginning of the year for their parents to sign.

"I can't believe you'll let me have plastic surgery but you won't let me get my ears pierced." I fastened one of my mother's pinch-your-flesh clip-ons to my earlobe. We were in her bedroom now, the two of us wearing cotton sundresses and sandals. She'd come up with the idea of dressing alike.

"Let me do your hair." She plugged in the curling iron. I had a Far-rah Fawcett cut, like everybody else in the world except my mother. She had Julie Christie hair, frosted and flipped under at the bottom with long, sexy bangs across her forehead. She could make the bangs disappear when she wanted a dressier, elegant look.

A *look* was what I wanted more than anything, but I lacked the discipline to acquire one. You had to buy the same kind of thing again and again, until every article, even your makeup, sunglasses, and haircut, adhered to the concept of the *look*. My look was a confusion of concepts. Leslie, my best friend, who would know, said I was a fickle shopper, that I liked everything equally. I blamed the fashion industry for constantly changing things and creating so many different looks to choose from.

In any case, I arrived for my first consultation with Dr. Jay Zubeck, plastic surgeon, looking like a junior version of my mother. This was enhanced by her wanting us to hold hands all the way from the car to the doctor's office.

"Remember to tuck in your chin," she said, before we went in.

I expected a dark, cramped office full of people with protuberant features. I imagined them looking up as I entered, and zeroing in on my honker. Instead, the waiting room was a bright, plush place full of leafy plants and long, softly upholstered benches. On the walls were large, black-and-white photographic panels, before and after pictures of presumably satisfied customers. To my surprise, the woman in the nose-job display was not dramatically improved. In fact, I preferred her face in the before picture, though clearly she looked pleased with her new nose. It seemed to me most of her personality had been smoothed away.

As my mother filled out papers, I studied the chin augmentation photos. The girl in the before photo had a recessed chin like Laverne De Fazio's. There was a sweetness about her. Now, of course, she just looked like anybody. I couldn't love her. I had the same reaction to the eyelid job. Why had the woman bothered? It hadn't made her look younger or prettier, just more alert. As for the face-lifted woman, she went from looking like a soft, juicy peach to a mean baseball. Surprisingly, none of this had a negative effect on my decision to get my nose done. I had seen a version of myself in the dream and she was beautiful. Reese, or whoever it was, adored her.

"Why don't you start by telling me what you don't like about your nose, Meredith."

Dr. Zubeck was another surprise, young and cute, with curly dark hair. It was easy for me to talk to him.

"Well, for one thing it's too big for my face." I turned so he could see my profile. "It sticks out too far. I mean, it comes up too high, you see what I mean? It's like a bowling pin, it's kind of hookish, like too Jewish or something. The whole thing curves into a hook shape."

Dr. Zubeck had positioned himself behind my chair and was pressing his fingers against the bones in my nose. His hands smelled of lotion, and he had a nice gentle touch. After this little examination he sat down again behind his desk.

"I'm going to tell you what I see. I see a very pretty girl with a distinctive nose. That's not necessarily a bad thing." I looked at my mother. She shrugged. "Don't get me wrong," he continued. "I'm not in the business of dictating how other people should look. What I do is try to work with my patients to achieve a look that *they* will be happy with. In your case, it's my job to tell you that at fourteen, you may be wise to wait a few years. Today you hate your nose. All your friends have 'normal'-looking noses." He indicated quotation marks with his fingers when he said the word *normal*. "You think your nose 'sticks out,' so to speak. In a couple of years all that could change. You might meet a guy who tells you the thing he loves most about you is your nose."

I was confused. It seemed to me Dr. Zubeck didn't want to do my nose, that he was trying to make me change my mind.

"So, you're saying I'm too young?"

"No, I've performed rhinoplasty on kids your age. I just want to be sure that you're sure. That you're not being pressured into this by Mom or your friend 'Susie' "—again with the quotation marks—"or by anyone or anything. This has to come from you. You know, at fourteen your face isn't fully developed. That's something else to consider. It may balance out to your liking in a few years."

"Right," I said. There was a long silence, then my mother spoke.

"Meredith, all the doctor wants is to be sure you know what you're doing and that you're ready for it."

"I don't see what the big deal is. I know lots of girls who have done it."

Zubeck looked at my mom and smiled. "Why don't we leave that subject for now, and you tell me your expectations of the surgery, in other words, how you think having your nose altered will affect your life."

"Well, hopefully I'll feel prettier, less aware of my nose. I'll be able to look in the mirror and like what I see."

"That's good. Very good." I felt I was being graded, that someone was listening to our discussion from another room and counting up my points. "I see you've already done one of the assignments I ask my patients to do after the first meeting. Did you bring in some magazine clippings to show me?"

I handed him my folder. He looked through the glossy pictures with a studied eye. "Uh-huh. Very good." Then he came to one, I couldn't see which. " 'Fraid this one's overly optimistic." He turned it around and I found myself face to face with the wide-open stare of a chimpanzee. Zubeck grinned. I had no idea how he worked it into my stack, but I was won over by his prankster soul.

We went in a room where he took photographs of my face from several different angles. He said I would come back in a few days and he would show me, using the photos, exactly what he could do for me. Then if we were in agreement he would schedule me for surgery.

"He was cute," my mother said when we got to the elevator. I felt a powerful need to be alone, just me and a mirror. The elevator doors opened and we joined the other people already standing inside. I wondered how they felt about my nose.

"Did you get the feeling he was flirting with me a little?" she went on, as soon as we got out. "I noticed he wasn't wearing a wedding band. Divorced, or possibly never married. He *is* pretty young—what do you think?"

I decided I could wait until we reached the restaurant, then use the bathroom mirror. Maybe I was more interesting-looking than I thought. Perhaps all I needed were new clothes and a different haircut.

"Honey, I'm talking to you."

Maybe I was pretty *because* of my distinctive nose and just couldn't see it. I thought about those before and after photos in Zubeck's waiting room, and an episode of *The Twilight Zone* popped into my mind, about a society of pig-faced people who kept operating on a gorgeous woman to help her look like everyone else. I started to feel hot and slightly queasy.

No one was helping me decide what to do. My parents didn't seem to care if I ruined my face, but then, I had hounded them for over a year to give me a nose job.

"I don't know what to do now," I finally said, after my mother started the car.

"That's okay." She patted my hand. "We'll have some lunch and some girl talk and just don't think about it anymore for now."

I imagined socking her, hard. I wanted to think about it. It was the only thing I could think about.

"Look at it this way," she said. "Pretend you're a reporter doing research for a story. It's just information. You may use it or maybe not. There's plenty of time to make a final decision."

"No." I stamped my foot into the car floor. "You don't understand." The more she tried to be cheerful, to brush it off, the crazier I felt, like I was going to start screaming and beating my fists against the dashboard until she understood me. I was way beyond worrying about her mood.

She turned off the engine. "Meredith, do you want to go home right now? Because that's where I'm going to take you if you don't sit up and start acting like a young lady this instant instead of a spoiled baby."

"Shut up."

"All right, that's it." She slapped me hard, once on the arm, once on my head. "You are spoiling the whole day. I wanted to have a nice lunch with you and an afternoon like girlfriends, but now you're going to have to go home and stay in your room."

Tears rolled down my cheeks. I studied the flowers on my dress, really seeing them for the first time. They weren't flowers at all, but little bits of yellow, green, orange, and pink arranged in ways that suggested flowers. In my bedroom closet was half a bottle of strawberry wine, so what did I care if she took me home? Peter would be home in a few hours and I could talk to him about my nose. We could take a walk and look in other people's windows, or play Yahtzee.

"It's still not too late," my mother urged. "You can start behaving like a young lady and we'll have a nice afternoon together or you can go home and sit in your room."

"Can we go to the Elbow Room?" I was still staring at my lap. The shards of color jumped back together. All I could see were flowers.

"Your mother, who doesn't care for you and doesn't love you at all, already made a reservation."

The Elbow Room had giant long-stem strawberries served with sour cream and brown sugar for dipping. The manager, Oscar, always remembered me and made a fuss. I wiped my eyes and apologized.

On the way to the restaurant, my mother pulled up to a pay phone and begged my father to join us. "We're lonely. Come take us to lunch." The Elbow Room was only ten minutes from his office. "Jesus, Robert. So reschedule it. Do something impulsive for once. I really need you." Obviously, she couldn't face the idea of lunch alone with me. The happy mood was fading. So much for being girlfriends. My father must have turned her down, because she slam-dunked the receiver, then called it a prick.

When we were seated she closed her eyes, took a deep breath, exhaled slowly, opened her eyes again, and smiled at me. "Now, let's start over again."

"I have to go to the bathroom," I said.

I took my time loitering in front of the mirror. Since I was the only one in there, I got real close and studied my face. The longer I stared, the more it seemed the person looking back knew more about me than I did. Knew everything. I began to feel scooped out, as though *I* were the reflection, when my privacy was interrupted by a well-dressed old woman. I said hi, casually, so she wouldn't think I was doing anything strange. She didn't really look at me, just smiled timidly on her way to the stalls. I remembered my purpose and shifted my attention back to making an honest appraisal of my nose. I moved my hand in front of my face, then lifted it quickly. I turned my back to the mirror, whirling suddenly around in an effort to surprise myself with my face. I played with my hair to see if perhaps a different style would do the trick, but when I heard the toilet flush, I quickly took out my pocket comb and acted as though I'd been combing my hair all along. The lady stopped a few feet away from me and pulled a lipstick from her bag. I watched her carefully drag the greasy pink stain across her parted lips, stretched in a tooth-concealing smile.

"Can I ask you a question?" I said. Her eyes roamed to meet mine in the mirror. She pressed her lips together, spreading the color evenly, then smiled. "What I want to know is, if you were me, would you get a nose job?"

"Oh, precious," she said, sweetly, "I don't have my glasses with me. I can't see a thing." She put her lipstick away, shaped her hairdo with her hands, and said good-bye.

Over lunch, I told my mother about Leslie's dad, and another friend's father, both divorced, and super-nice to their kids since they only saw them on weekends. She had a pasted-on smile and glassy eyes that looked at me without seeing or hearing.

"You're so lucky to be growing up today, with all the choices women have. Don't make the same mistake I did." She was holding up a pretty glass of white wine. "You're beautiful and bright. You've got your whole life in front of you. Be your own person. Don't go looking for someone else to take care of you."

The words were clear and simple enough, but I found them staggering coming out of her mouth. My mother had never talked that way before. Usually, she commented on my flaws. I wanted her to say more, not about the mistake she'd made, which presumably referred to my father, but about my glorious future as a bright, beautiful woman. I waited.

"You want the strawberries?" she said, finally. She looked bored, ready to go.

If my mother envied my freedom, I secretly coveted her life. Many were the mornings I sat in school, yearning for the leisure of her days. Who wanted to work when you could goof off all day, play tennis, go out to lunch, and shop? She talked of the power and opportunity that awaited me, but the only power I hoped for would make boys fall madly in love with me so I could have a life much like hers.

"Is everything okay, Mom?" I said.

She tapped the last few drops of wine into her mouth and looked at me. "*Mom* . . . Is that all I am to you?"

--------------------

THAT NIGHT, MY MOTHER, Peter, and I sat in the kitchen eating hamburgers and artichokes. She ate hers without a bun, of course.

"These are neat." Peter scraped the soft flesh from a leaf with his front teeth.

"We've had them before," I said.

"Not me," he insisted.

"Yes you have." He was building a neat stack of discarded leaves on his plate.

"Have not," he said softly, defiantly.

"Have so, have so, have so," I practically sang.

"Babe?" my father called from the top of the stairs. He was watching baseball in the bedroom. "Leigh?"

My mother ignored him, her nostrils flaring, her eyelids heavy with insolence. "Can someone get me another ginger ale?" he yelled, then went back into the bedroom. She rolled her eyes, waited a minute, then slowly got up. Peter quickly removed the discarded leaves from her plate, and continued constructing his tower.

"Why are you doing that?" I finally said. It was becoming ridiculously tall and unbalanced, muddy green and smelly.

"It's fun." He acted like he was a genius architect, onto something with his stack of old food. He took a few leaves off my plate.

"If you don't stop, I'm going to knock it over."

"Okay, I'm done." He crossed his arms, sat back, and presided over his accomplishment.

"It's going to fall," I assured him.

"No it isn't."

We waited. I sat back, too. The tower, at least a foot high, held. Five minutes must have gone by. My mother didn't return.

"See," Peter said. "Wrong again."

He was twelve now, and though I could still push him around, it was getting harder to pin him to the carpet in Fighting Rink, one of our many games. Over the years we'd proudly invented Monster in the Rug, The Understanding Mugger, Sudden Vampire, and The Commercial Game. Even our parents, who hated TV commercials, played that one. It should have been called Screaming Match, because the point was to yell out the correct product before it was shown or mentioned in the commercial. The first one with the right answer got a point. Mostly it came down to speed, to whoever had the fastest reflexes. We had seen the commercials before. You could feel the collective tensing and mental positioning during the half-second of black between show and advertisement, then

Me: "Crest!"

Peter (a split-second later): "Crest. Damn!"

My mother (playing it safe): "Colgate."

My father (ever the gambler): "Ding-Dongs, what the hell."

It was actually more fun if we didn't know the answer, if the car speeding along the country road turned out to be an ad for cheese instead of Chevrolet. Then we sat together in silence, straining our imaginations.

Another game Peter and I played from time to time revolved around a made-up private detective from south of the border whom our parents knew nothing about. His name was Frank Sanchez. I didn't have a name.

You could say I was the dispatcher. I suggested assignments for Sanchez and assisted him in his work, which consisted of eavesdropping on our parents, searching their dresser drawers, examining their mail, her purse, the desk in the den. Most of the time I played lookout, listening for footsteps on the stairs, cars in the driveway. I memorized the way things were before we moved them around, and put everything back just right. "Give it the treatment," Sanchez would say when he was done investigating, and I'd go to work erasing our tracks. It was our secret game, the point of which was to find out other people's secrets.

One afternoon we uncovered a major stash in my father's nightstand: a sexy book stuffed behind a box of Ramses on top of a *Playboy* magazine! Peter examined the magazine while I checked out the book, called *Chloe and Daniel.* Its cover photo showed a man and woman embracing in a bay. Their bodies were darkened, nearly silhouettes against the glittering water. I flipped through the pages, skimming for something juicy, until I read:

> Ray was a hot-blooded creature of the night, driven by a
> wild carnal pulse. He thought of Chloe on the beach that day,
> could taste the salt of her undoing, smell the season of her
> trembling as if she were there, naked before him, which she
> soon would be.

Pretty sexy. I noted the page number for another time and place.

Peter was the one who discovered the diary in my mother's underwear drawer. We were looking for anything unusual, anything the slightest bit raunchy, and then Peter pulled out this black book that said *Daily Diary* on the cover.

"The plot thee-kins, amigo." He displayed the book at various angles for me to see.

"Let's put it back." I realized I didn't want to know my mother's private thoughts, although knowing she kept them in a book made her seem less like my mom somehow, more like a regular woman.

"Aren't we gonna check inside?" he said.

"Uh-uh."

"One page?"

"It's wrong, Peter."

He grabbed his throat and began choking and coughing. "Like, we're in her bedroom, Mere, looking at her underwear." Then he landed his fist in the center of his forehead to conclude his exposé on my stupidity. "I say we check out one lee-tul page."

"If you do, I'm not playing Sanchez ever again." Not that he needed me. Peter really did have the makings of an alley-slinking professional. He enjoyed the quiet, clever methods of the trade, the seeing while remaining unseen. Most of all he knew how to sniff out a good secret.

I could see him trying to decide what to do. Then, in brilliant Sanchez form, he let the diary fall to the carpet while making it appear he had accidentally dropped it. The book landed open and a page stared up at us.

"Oops." He smiled.

"Very smart," I said. He was learning things from *Columbo*. I felt I had no choice, so I pushed him into a long row of suits hanging at my father's end of the closet, and quickly bent over to get the book. I heard Peter tumble and fall.

*She can have him.*

The words seemed to jump out at me from the book, though I'd tried to see my mother's handwriting as just scratches on a white background. I'd seen the page for less than a second but there it was: *She can have him.* Not nearly enough and already too much. The words traveled like wind through my mind, blowing open doors, getting into tight spaces.

Peter picked himself up, complaining he'd bumped his head. "You hurt me." He raised his arm to sock me but I held him back and we struggled for a while. He was extremely cute when he huffed and puffed, when he wanted to break through but couldn't. I started laughing, he was so earnest and feisty, but it weakened me and that's when he hit my nose. All I felt was the pain. My face was a bell ringing with it.

"You broke it!" I covered my nose with both hands. Yet even as I accused him I was pressing on the bones with my fingertips, convincing myself of just the opposite.

We heard the front door open downstairs. My mother called for us to come help her unload the groceries from the car. Forgetting about my nose, I told Peter to go, then I gave the area a quick treatment.

"What have you two been up to today?" my mother asked later, when we were sitting at the kitchen table eating a snack. Peter calmly told her we'd been playing games. As soon as she left the room, we erupted in tuba bursts of suppressed laughter. Peter said, "Hey, how's your nose? Should I call the paramedics?"

"Ha, ha, ha."

*She can have him, she can have him, she can have him.*

---

LESLIE AGREED my father could be having an affair.

"Then again," she said, "it might be nothing. Can't you read some more?"

There was nothing Leslie and I couldn't talk about, including masturbation. She did it lying on her back with her finger stuck inside, a thin, silky blanket spread over her breasts. I was an animal by comparison. Her way sounded exotic, pretty. I did it face down, rubbing against a bunched-up sheet, or my clothes. I was quick about it.

If anyone knew about marital cheating, I figured it was Leslie. Her father had fallen for his secretary six years before, and gave up the house, the car, and nearly everything else to move to a boat with the secretary, whom he eventually married. I'd been down there a couple of times for dinner on the water, and both times, when we arrived, Leslie and her father behaved like people who hadn't seen each other for ages, who'd been separated as if by war. They squealed and hugged, and slobbered over each other with slurpy kisses and loud pats on the back. I figured it was a divorced thing, and it made me both envious and mistrustful of their relationship.

"So, you think I should read the diary." I was sitting on the floor of Leslie's decorator bedroom. The wallpaper matched the bedspreads and curtains, and, like the rest of the house, Leslie's room was always spotless. It was hard to imagine her father ever living there.

"Definitely," she said.

With that, I began waiting for my chance. I'd been so high and mighty about reading it in front of Peter that it was now necessary to keep my plan secret. This made it hard to carry out, because when my parents were out, I was usually Peter's baby-sitter. Even if we were in our own rooms, or had friends over, I knew only too well how hard it was to put one over on Sanchez.

Days went by. I grew eager to hurry and have a look, so, one night I declined the after-dinner walk to 31 Flavors for ice cream, a treasured family ritual of summer.

"You're not going?" Peter said. I acted like it was no big deal, said I'd had ice cream at Leslie's house earlier in the afternoon. I immediately regretted it. Like the rest of my family, I relied on ice cream for a sense of well-being. Now I couldn't even ask them to bring me one back.

"Robert, honey," my mother said—the two of them were trying hard to be considerate of each other—"I left a couple of overdue library books next to the bed. Would you mind going up? I must have climbed those stairs a dozen times today."

"Where are they?" He was already climbing.

"They should be next to the bed on my table. Oh, and while you're up there, grab my white sweater, will you? It's in the closet." I waited patiently, imagining myself in that same closet as soon as they left.

"Where?" he yelled from the bedroom.

"In the closet," she hollered back, adding, with thinly veiled anger, "the same place it always is."

"I can't find it," he yelled, then, "I found it."

She rolled her eyes. When my father came back she sweetly thanked him. "No problem," he said.

"You sure you don't want to come along for the walk?" my mother asked me.

I said I wasn't in the mood. Finally, the three of them set off. I watched as they marched down the driveway and into the street, my family minus me.


JANUARY 12, 1978

*Betsy wants me to keep a journal of my thoughts. This diary was her Christmas present, and so my New Year's resolution will be to try to fill it up. Blah blah blah. My mind's a blank. I'm not used to writing how I feel.*


So far, my mother hadn't done a very good job of filling up the pages. The diary was mostly blank, except for a handful of entries near the front. It was a wonder that when Peter dropped it the book actually opened to a used page.


JANUARY 14

| | |
|---|---|
| *½ grapefruit* | *40* |
| *dry toast* | *60* |

| | |
|---|---|
| *ice cream sundae* | *650* |
| *chicken breast,* | |
| *dry salad,* | |
| *corn* | *350* |
| *wine* | *400* |

*1500 calories*

FEBRUARY 14

*I really hate the idea, the assumption, that just because I want to try something new, like TM or a floatation tank, well then I must be having a midlife crisis. It's like when men say, "Oh, she must be having her period." "Oh, it must be a midlife crisis."*

*Of course, people in their 20s who do this stuff—or in their 50s—are allowed, but people in their mid-thirties, especially women, are freaking out!*

*It's such an obvious rationalization by Robert, who is threatened and uptight, and needs a way to feel superior. He dismisses what he can't understand. What he fears. Besides, isn't thirty-five a little early for a midlife crisis?*

FEBRUARY 17

*Tonight's the night. I'm going to ask Robert to go to a marriage counselor with me. Wish me luck!*

The infamous Bernie Schneider, who saw my parents a grand total of five times before my mother refused to go back. The best thing to come out of their sessions with Bernie were the hilarious impersonations my mother did of him. She would put on a cardigan, sit hunched forward, make chipmunk cheeks, and in a whining voice, say, "Leigh, how does that make you feel, what Robert just said? Could you talk about it?" She thought he was an idiot.

FEBRUARY 24

| | |
|---|---|
| ½ grapefruit | 40 |
| ½ banana | 40 |
| dry toast | 60 |
| salad bar | |
| w/diet dressing | 350 |
| crackers galore | 140 |
| 2 slices pizza | 700 |
| rainbow sherbet | 250 |
| vodka & tonic | 220 |

1800 calories

MARCH 2

Today I sat in Bernie's office and listened to Robert talk about his unpredictable childhood, and why it is he's so afraid of change. As soon as I could, I brought up his thrill-seeker side, and the fact that he loves to take risks, gamble, go fast, and all that. That's different, he said. He meant in his relationships. But why, why, why? Or how? How can he enjoy danger and be afraid of trying new experiences with me? At that point, Bernie seemed to take Robert's side. He called the risky behavior Robert's "pressure valve," said it was a more or less safe way for Robert to express his deepest yearnings. What do I expect from a man? They're all crazy for fast cars.

MARCH 8

*Crazy thought: taking the kids and moving to Greece.*

MARCH 10

*Bernie says that anger is unexpressed hurt. He asked if I was angry at Robert. I said it was beyond anger, that mostly I felt sarcastic or depressed. He said depression is anger turned against the self. It seems everything is something else.*

MARCH 13

*Weird Dream: Peter and Meredith and I are in a dark museum in another town, looking at tiny, dried-up people that have been arranged in dimly illuminated exhibits. The settings show how this ancient culture used to live and work. Then we can't find Peter, so Meredith and I split up to look for him. It's getting late and I have lost both of them now, and our bus leaves in less than an hour. I walk through a door that leads me outside, where a film director is talking to an actor in front of the camera. He sees me and pulls me into the shot, and tells me I will be the costar. I look at the actor and realize it's Paul Newman! Paul Newman and I are going to be in a movie together!*

MARCH 18

*Bernie suggested that I'm rebelling against my mother's early death and the need for security it aroused in me. Probably. The problem with Bernie, for me, is that even when he's right, it doesn't change anything.*

APRIL 17

*Driving home with Peter through the San Joachin Valley. Mile after mile of hot, desolate road and dull brown scenery, playing car games, listening to tapes, me trying to stay awake, thinking about Meredith. She stayed behind, asserted her individual rights. You're wrong, Mom, she seemed to be saying. I won't have any part of you. So she sided with her father. No surprise there. It's fun to get back at Mom whenever possible. Mom = policeman. Mom = rules, expectations. Mom = the drag, the complainer. So I decided fine, she can have him. For once I won't be the enforcer. I renounced that role. I figured she's old enough, she knows her way around the hotel. Let her be there to cushion Robert's shock, to make me look like the bad guy. It's just that once in a while I'd like a little of her sympathy, too. Betsy says it's natural at M's age to rebel against Mom and worship Dad. It's the age they start thinking about boys and worrying about their bodies. Mom seems square, the keeper of old-fashioned ideas, the permission-giver, but Dad—well now, he's hardly ever around. His life's a mystery, and besides, he's got that anatomical advantage. Dad's got the penis.*

What did that idiot Betsy know about me? I couldn't believe she got paid to say that bullshit. I was tempted to get a pen and remark on her ridiculous theory right there on the page, but of course, then my mother would know I'd read her diary. Part of me wanted her to know how mad I was. Didn't it ever occur to her that I hadn't agreed with her decision to leave Sonoma? Why did she have to chalk it up to some "typical" hidden worship of my father?

I decided to keep on reading, and see what other ideas my mother had formed about me. Then it hit me. I had become so caught up in the content that the famous words flew right by, unnoticed. *She can have him.* It was me. I was the she.

APRIL 30

*Crazy thought: Having my own apartment and some silly job to go with it. Being someone else, being poor, starting over, learning Italian, studying something important and useless, growing things in little pots everywhere, smoking pot, meeting a man who would expand my mind.*

JUNE 4

| ROBERT | ME | SPLIT |
| --- | --- | --- |
| *mechanical stuff* | *living room furniture* | *art* |
| *tv* | *all antiques* | *bedroom furn.* |
| *stereo* | *pots and pans* | |
| *most of the clocks* | *dishes* | |
| *games* | *dining rm. stuff* | |
| *records* | *Turkish rug* | |
| *den sofa* | *house plants* | |
| *typewriter* | *green chairs* | |
| *filing cabinets* | *fixtures* | |
| *desk* | | |
| *coffee table* | | |
| *nice wine* | | |
| *cameras* | | |

JUNE 16

*Scary thought: What if I gave a party and nobody came? (Or got a divorce and never met anyone better than Robert?) What if there really aren't any men like Saul Kaplan? (The character Alan Bates plays in* An Unmarried Woman.*) Fear of failing. Fear of flying.*

JUNE 28

*Robert asks me how I feel all the time now. How my day went, what I did with myself. He's making an Effort, capital E, under-lined twice! He rubs my back and offers to clear the table. Why doesn't it make me feel better? What on earth is it I want? The harder he tries, the sorrier he looks to me, and the worst thing is I have to be nice to him to encourage his "good" behavior. It just seems put-on to me, so very hangdog, tail between the legs. It makes me feel guilty, like I'm his mother. He sees I don't like him like this either, and it must make him feel hopeless. I guess I want us to want the same things, to care about mutual interests. It's always such an effort. Do we have anything left in common other than our children?*

That's all there was. The last entry had been written earlier that day. I felt ashamed of myself.

"Interesting reading?" Peter asked a few days later, smiling. "Did you get to the part about moving to Greece?"

How in the world did he know? He'd probably booby-trapped the diary somehow. "I don't read other people's diaries," I said, adamant. There was truth to this, I could feel it, despite all the evidence to the contrary.

------------------

"WE WERE WRONG," I told Leslie. "He's not having an affair." We were standing in front of the mirror in her bedroom.

"Well that's good, isn't it?"

"I guess." I didn't want to talk about what was in the diary. "I'm having my nose job two weeks from tomorrow."

She looked at me in the mirror. "I'm trying to imagine you."

"Just think of my mother, but with darker hair."

"You wish." Leslie inspected a pimple on her chin, then squeezed it bloody. She said, "Why can't I get a boyfriend?" I didn't like her very much at that moment. Her bleeding face grossed me out, and I blamed her for my decision to read the diary.

"Who do you want?" I said.

"Lars Hoffman's pretty cute."

That did it. Lars Hoffman was a slimy, greasy-haired pervert. How could anyone dream about him when there were guys like Reese Phillips in the world? It was clear to me that I possessed the finer instincts, and that my life was going to be vastly more interesting than Leslie's because of it. "I think I have to throw up."

"What? You don't think he's cute? Fine, who do *you* like?"

Feeling suddenly superior, I decided I had nothing to lose by telling her about you-know-who. This was a mistake. The minute I thought of Reese's face, I smiled shamelessly.

"Whoa! Meredith's in love."

"No I'm not."

"So who? Who is it, already?" I looked at her. She was grinning like a clown.

"Reese Phillips." I said it fast, like it was medicine I had to swallow. The name didn't register. I could see her reaching for a connection. She said the name a few times, but nothing. Then she walked away. The next thing I knew she was sitting on her bed, looking up his picture in the yearbook.

"Him?"

I sat beside her. "That's a terrible picture."

"Eh." She was reserving judgment.

"Trust me. He's gorgeous."

"He's not bad. He's just not my type."

In minutes we were looking for his number among the scores of Phillipses in the phone book. I didn't know a thing about him, not his parents' first names or what street he lived on, but Leslie was already dialing a Dr. Ronald Phillips on Mandeville Canyon Road.

"Uh, is Reese home?" Her voice was higher when she got nervous. "It's Cindy. I'm a friend of his from school." She flicked her hand impatiently, like how dare they ask so many questions.

At this point I latched on to the receiver so we could share it, whispering, "I can't believe you got him."

"Hullo?" His voice was deep and froggy.

"Reese?"

"Yeah." It cracked that time.

"It's Cindy. Do you remember me from school?"

"Cindy who?"

"Cindy, silly. I can't believe you don't know who this is. We were in English together." Leslie was pouring it on. There was a long pause.

"Yeah?" he said, finally.

"Anyway, I just called to say hi and ask you a question, Reese."

"Shoot," he said.

"It's about your dick?"

I lost it. I pulled away from the phone and Leslie pinched my arm to shut me up. I managed to stop laughing and put my ear back to the receiver.

"Well, anyway, me and my friend Debbie here are doing our own taste test, you know, like which one tastes better, Coke or Pepsi? Are you still there, Reese?"

"Is this Megan?" A cold fist entered my chest and seized my heart.

"Who's Megan?" Leslie teased, as if she deserved to know. There was another long pause. "So anyway, we want to know what flavor it is. Your dick, that is."

"Yeah, well, I gotta go now." He was taking it all in stride. He didn't seem mad or anything. He was a nice guy, I could tell.

Leslie hung up and opened the phone book again. "You want to call Chad Newton?"

"You think Megan's his girlfriend?" I said. She was busy looking up Chad's number. "Did you notice how calm he was?" I muttered. "Like girls call him every day and ask him about his dick. He probably does get lots of calls." Whoever Megan was, I already hated her.

"No answer at Chad's."

The spell had been broken. Megan had entered the picture and changed everything. In my mind, her name now traveled with his. It was the same number of letters. Megan and Reese. The summer was only half over and I'd just lost my fantasy guy.

I was floating around our pool on my father's raft when the heater clicked off, allowing me to hear my mother and her best friend, Judith. They were standing in the shallow end, smoking cigarettes and drinking diet grapefruit sodas.

"Did you see *An Unmarried Woman*?" my mother said.

"Oh, I loved it."

"What did you think of Alan Bates?"

"Oo-la-la." Judith's voice was full of innuendo. *"Et tu?"*

"I dreamed I was living in London and he was my lover. It was so great, I didn't want to wake up." I could tell she had a piece of ice in her mouth. The words sounded melted. "Could you believe Jill Clayburgh didn't go with him in the end? Right. She lets a man like that go. Uh-huh. I really believed that."

Judith argued with her, saying that was the point of the movie, that she wasn't going to deny her own life anymore for the sake of a man, not even a great man like Alan Bates. "I thought it was great," Judith said. My mother grudgingly agreed, then lowered her voice, to a level she assumed I couldn't hear.

"Do you ever think there's another man out there who you're really supposed to be with, you know, instead of Roger?" Judith didn't say anything. "Someone more sensitive, more alive, more . . . European, you know what I mean? Like an artist type."

"Not really," Judith said.

"Oh c'mon. Someone you could really talk to about things, who made breakfast in the morning after great sex, and helped cook dinner, and really looked at you when you talked, and listened, and even cried once in a while!" They broke into crazy laughter, as though that would be the wildest thing they had ever seen.

Judith said, "Unfortunately, I think they're all pigs. It's not their fault. I blame their parents."

"I don't know," my mother persisted. "I keep thinking about Alan Bates in that movie." She was really hung up on Alan Bates. I wondered if my dad had any idea he was competing with a character from a movie.

"He was pretty nice," Judith admitted. Her voice got much softer, so I couldn't hear what she said next. All I heard was my mother's response.

"The same. He makes a half-assed effort when I threaten to leave, but what he really thinks is that I'm just going through a 'phase,' that it's going to pass." After more murmuring from Judith, she said, "Are you kidding? That would require more initiative than he's got. Besides, he'd be lost without me." The heater switched back on and I lost the sound of her voice, but I could see my mother standing close to Judith, confiding. I closed my eyes and imagined Reese watching me from a patio chair, Megan at his side. He smiled at my jealousy as if to say, "Megan is nothing but a cheap imitation of you. A floozy. Purely second-string. She's a groupie, my love, but you are up there onstage. The lead singer. Megan worries about you, not vice versa. She's pathetic, a charity case, you got that? Now get in the water. I've got an important assignment for you."

I put on my mask and fins, and pretended to be a secret agent working for Reese. I swam from one end of the pool to the other without coming up for air, my bare stomach slithering along the bottom, away from the bad guys, against a ticking time bomb that only I could dismantle.

---

THE NEXT TIME I saw Dr. Zubeck, I was lying on the operating table, stripped to my underpants beneath a white paper smock. He was looking down at me.

"I love this nose. Nice nose. You're sure you want me to break it?"

"Uh-huh." I was smiling. He cupped my cheek in the palm of his hand. There wasn't a doubt in my mind. The assistant put a needle in my arm and taped it there.

"May God forgive me," Zubeck said, stretching rubber gloves over his hands. A mask was placed over my nose and the assistant told me to breathe and count backwards from one hundred. I was staring at the hot lights. I could hear myself counting. Ninety-five sounded like a mouthful of cotton. I don't remember ninety-four.

"Meredith." The word brought me back to the world. As if dead people remember their names. Nothingness. That's where I was, where I wanted to stay.

Mother of death. The nurse was wide awake in her white brightness, dressed in white, her wet teeth parting to make that sound, that funny name that belonged, in principle, to me. Her luminous gargoyle face bobbed above mine, a powdery mask of painted-on emotions. Had I been able to talk, I would have let her have it to the depths of my black being.

"Wake up, Meredith. Attagirl."

More and more, I inhabited the brightly lit recovery room, a waking coffin of right angles and clunky metal furniture. As the boggy waters of unconsciousness drained, I was left with a deep and abiding despair. Every object confirmed the ugliness and futility of human existence: the fixed grid of the gray blinds, the repetitious black holes in the ceiling tiles. I found the slow sad weight of things, their obeisance to the law of gravity, unbearable.

Having succeeded in wrenching me from my blissful, nebulous state, the nurse propped me up and hurried away. Outside I could hear people and cars—imagined all of it flooded with sunlight. What was the point of getting up, getting busy, worrying about stuff, being nice to people, then going to bed so I could wake up and start all over again? It was heartbreaking. Though my nose was packed, I began to cry. The sight of my mother did not make me feel any better. She helped me to a vertical position, and I discovered I could walk, though it required enormous effort and concentration.

Sunshine was the worst of all, going outside into it. We put the seat back so I could recline and close my eyes. My mother reached over and smoothed the hair from my forehead. I had to choke back the urge to cry again. I couldn't forget the way I'd been pulled back into the world—from where? The slow way my identity had reclaimed me, but from what? The end, was all I could figure, the end of Me. Me and all my pathetic little worries: Was I pretty? Did people like me? Was I smart? Was I special? All answered with total darkness. With absence. All gone.

From our car I glared, squinting, as the world passed by at thirty miles an hour, mile after mile of it. Glass and stone and paint and heat. The buildings rose up and receded like dominoes. I saw a child being dragged across the street by his mother and closed my eyes, beside myself with unhappiness. My own mother was listening to the radio. A woman was slowly listing the ingredients for a casserole. I didn't belong here. It was all a mistake.

In my quiet bedroom I climbed between the sheets. The worst was over. I had made it through surgery and was home again, uncomfortable but not in pain. I surrendered to the familiar, slipping back into velvet nothingness.

Leslie came over the next morning with flowers and a funny booklet she'd made for me using cutouts from fashion magazines. The title was "Meredith's New Life," and it was one gorgeous, happy-looking model after another with a story written by Leslie of how I get everything and more, thanks to my new face. On the last page she put a picture of a sexy male model and wrote: "His name was Reese, and he was brokenhearted because Meredith was so popular she never came to school anymore. In fact, she was last seen on the ski slopes with Al Pacino. The End."

Later that day, my mother said, "I'm taking you to see *Gone with the Wind.*" I had no desire to go, but she said it was four hours long and I could hide my face in the theater just as well as at home, so off I went to be forever changed by Vivien Leigh's dark hair and green eyes, and her perfect heart-shaped face. When she got Ashley alone while the other girls were napping, in order to declare her love, all I could think about was Reese. I woke up then and there to the possibility of doing such a thing myself. It didn't go so badly for Scarlett, meaning he didn't laugh at her or put her down, or even tell anyone else. In fact, he told her he loved her back, in his way. I couldn't get it out of my mind afterwards. If you loved someone, you had to let them know, because they might not realize it and their whole life could go by when you could have changed it.

I also admired Scarlett's method for handling bad news. "I won't think about that now, I'll think about that later," she said. Wow. It made sense, the best way to keep those awful moods and feelings from taking over. She was so beautiful and smart, and men adored her, and she knew what she wanted. "I think Charles Hamilton may get it," she cooed when the men were competing to fetch her dessert.

"Do you like it?" my mother said during intermission. It was the lowest point for Scarlett yet, after she'd returned home, dirty and hungry, with Melanie and the baby.

I couldn't even speak. I just opened my eyes really wide and nodded. I could still see all those dying men on the ground with Scarlett walking around them, looking for the doctor. Then I said, "This is the best movie I've ever seen in my entire life."

In the lobby, she smoked a cigarette and I bought a giant Nestle's Crunch for us to share. "This is fun," I said, before we went back to our seats.

She nodded. "The first time is very special."

Walking on Shady Lane, where the towering eucalyptus trees transformed the narrow street into a sharply scented arbor—though I couldn't smell it because my nose was still packed—it occurred to me beauty was partly a state of mind, a sort of equilibrium that said to others, "Catch me, I'm free." I almost never felt like that.

I concocted a picture of the me I wanted to be come September, when I would start high school. For starters, I would wash my hair no matter what. No more ponytails and baseball caps because I was too lazy. I would take time each Sunday night to coordinate a good-looking outfit for each day of the coming week. Also, I would make an effort to think nice thoughts instead of mean ones about the other kids in my classes, because, more than anything, I wanted to be a kinder sort of person, a Melanie Wilkes type in a Scarlett O'Hara body. These were the main things: work on a look, keep my hair clean, try to be nice to everyone, and maybe, just maybe, tell Reese how I felt about him.

-----------------

WHEN ZUBECK REMOVED the packing, my brain felt like a ball of yarn being unraveled through my nose. It kept on coming, long bloody strings of stuff from inside my head. I thought I would go crazy. Then he took off the splint and had a look. My mother stood next to him, studying me, but their faces revealed nothing. Finally I was handed a mirror.

My nose would never again be the thing you noticed about my face. Except for the bruising, which would fade in another week or two, it had become unassuming, perfectly polite and unobtrusive, calling new attention to my other features. I looked at my face but I didn't know it, didn't know how or where to concentrate my attention. I was so used to staring at my big nose, but it wasn't there anymore.

"It's amazing," I said, growing slightly more familiar each moment with the sweeter, prettier face looking back from the mirror. I was going to be pleasing, I could see, pretty and sweet, but not particularly interesting. Interesting was over, but that was okay. Pretty was worth it.

"Very nice," my mother commented. "A lovely balance."

Zubeck led us into the room where photos were taken. There was a large mirror mounted on the wall so I could now see the entire upper half of my body. There she was again, that pretty girl. Pretty, pretty, pretty. I started to like it a lot. My face had something new to say to the world, something closer to how I really felt inside. It was a truer face, more approachable, less impatient.

Zubeck took some pictures. He told me the swelling would recede over the next few weeks, and that I'd see more contours in my nose as time passed. There were lots of rules I had to follow. I got a sheet of them on my way out. At the bottom it said my nose would become thinner and more refined over the course of a year!

"Congratulations," my mother said, "you look great." There was something halfhearted about the way she spoke. I'd seen pleasure in her face earlier, but I'd also seen a certain shock, as though she hadn't counted on this moment actually coming to pass. She said, "It's just, you don't look like your father anymore. All your life, you looked like your father. Now you don't. You don't look like anybody." She sounded annoyed about that, not at me particularly, but in general.

I answered her in my head, thinking I should say it and expecting myself to, but never finding the right tone of voice. I look like me, I thought.

My mother enrolled in assertiveness training. She said it was for women who wanted to be taken more seriously. Peter called it a class for women who wanted to sound like broken records. Rather than argue with my father as she'd always done in the past, my mother calmly "asserted" her position now, over and over again until she prevailed. One night, she sat next to my father when he was watching football and, staring at him, said, "Robert, I need you to turn off the TV and talk to me."

"What's up?" He answered without even looking at her.

"Robert." She took a breath. "I need you to turn off the TV and talk to me."

The central feature of the technique was its faith in robotic repetition. If stated enough times, the theory seemed to go, the desired end could be achieved. The trick was in keeping the upper hand at all times, which meant staying calm and focused.

"It's almost a commercial," he said.

"Robert, I need you to turn off the TV and talk to me."

My father finally looked at her, sighed, and said, "Shoot. I'm all ears."

"The TV," she reminded him.

"Go. Talk. I'm listening."

"Robert, I need you to *turn off* the TV and talk to me." It was okay to accent certain words as long as you remained emotion-free. The TV went off. The room was quiet. My father, heeding his instructions, talked.

"Why are you doing this, huh? You agreed I could watch two games a week, so what's the problem? Are you going to give me shit about it anyway?"

The thing about assertiveness training was, once you got your objective, the rest was up to you. My mother stared at him, either so full of things she wanted to say she didn't know where to begin, or else so stunned by her victory she was unable to think of *anything* else to say. Her chin started to tremble, and her large eyes filled with tears. The next thing you know she was sobbing into his chest. "I don't know what's the matter with me. Why can't I be happy?" He put his arm around her and rubbed sympathetically, but from the way he did it, and the expression on his face, you could tell he really wanted to finish watching his game in peace. At moments like these, I found my mother ridiculous. Here she had this great way to get my father's attention, but what did she do with it? Nothing. As soon as she had him, she broke down and cried. It was as though she didn't want to be taken seriously, not if it meant angering my father. I mean, she was willing to anger him, but then she'd make a joke, or apologize, or cry in order to restore the old balance. She toyed with her power, but was afraid to really use it.

I thought a lot about assertiveness training, wondered how I could apply it to the problem of Reese Phillips. He now sat opposite me during first-period English, thanks to an unusual seating arrangement that placed one-half of us in full view of the other, yet demanded we strain our necks to see the teacher. I preferred to relax my neck and see Reese.

Throughout class I treated myself to long, adoring glances at his glorious head, which he kept lowered toward his desk, where he doodled endlessly in a notebook. For days I waited for him to notice me. I even worked his detachment into my fantasies, made it part of his hot-and-cold mastery over me. Finally, out of frustration, I came up with an assertiveness campaign of my own. It was small and manageable. All I had to do was say hi every day for a week as we filed out of class into the hall.

Do it, I told myself the first day, then choked. It didn't seem like enough. How would he know I was talking to him? We spilled into the crowded, noisy hallway, me staring at the back of his head, my heart throbbing. "Hi, Reese Phillips," I finally called out. My timing couldn't have been better. The words came out just as he stopped at his locker, turning to see who had spoken. With a wave and a smile, I glided through the double doors into the cold morning air. Mission accomplished. Four days to go.

Like my mother, I wanted attention, wanted to start something and see where it led, but unlike her, I wasn't afraid to see it through to the end. The plan went well. After two days, I caught Reese checking me out during class, though he quickly averted his eyes when I looked up. It wasn't until later, when I said the magic words to him in the hallway— "Hi, Reese Phillips"—that I realized something was wrong. He eyed me suspiciously, frowning. I raised my hand to wave and saw his annoyance. That pissed me off, which wasn't the way you wanted to feel as an assertive person. You had to be in control, confident. I followed him, almost sneering.

"I *said* hello, Reese Phillips," but he simply ignored me. "Your name is Reese Phillips, isn't it?" He stopped at his locker. I had ceased to exist in his universe. He didn't even turn around.

I joined Lars and Leslie on the sunny quad, a big tight knot in my stomach. They'd fallen madly in love at the start of the year and were making out, as usual. They were always touching and whispering things to each other. I didn't know how much longer I could stay loyal to her before finding another best friend.

"You cold?" Lars said as soon as he saw me. It was a brisk morning, but I answered no. Leslie slapped his hand, kiddingly. "Could've fooled me," he said.

Lars was big and tall, but there was something permanently immature about him, as though he rushed home after school to play with Hot Wheels. He had a pudgy face and a wheezy voice, like Mickey Rooney. When Leslie told me later he'd been referring to my hard nipples, which were showing through my shirt, I got a creepy feeling. I imagined the three of us, Lars's fingers on me, sticky from picking his nose, while Leslie watched, grinning. She grinned all the time now. I wanted to tell her about my fiasco with Reese, but she was just too damn happy to bear.

The teacher handed back our first tests the next day. While I had been busy thinking about you-know-who, it turned out he'd been listening closely to the teacher. Reese received the highest score in class, while I ended up with a C-plus. Angry, I started administering my obnoxious greeting at every opportunity. I even practiced it when I was alone. "Hi, Reese Phillips. Hi, Reese Phillips," I nattered like a talking bird. I went a little crazy, congratulating myself for being free of him at last, when in actuality I had finally managed a relationship with the guy, albeit a sick one. He wasn't ever going to forget Meredith Herman, the weirdo in the hall. Then, he was suddenly there one day, standing over me on the quad.

"What gives?" he said. It was the nearest to him I'd ever stood. I watched his mysterious Adam's apple rise and fall. There was a flake of sleep in his eyelashes. I smiled like an idiot.

"I don't like being made fun of," he said, "especially when I don't even know you." His voice was deep and creaky, like it had been on the phone. I imagined saying something outrageous, telling him I was madly in love with him, but his buddies walked over and asked if he was coming. "Guess I'll see you in class." He shrugged, and walked away.

I wore a strange expression as I stood there alone, trying to look above-it-all. For whom, I have no idea. Nobody was looking at me. A couple of years later, drunk on beer at a party, I finally did tell a guy I loved him. I did it Scarlett O'Hara style, got him alone in a room to deliver my grand confession, made him sit cross-legged on the floor beside me. "I love you," I said. "I've never loved anyone the way I love you."

He smiled sweetly, generously, the way one does at a child. "You don't know what you're talking about," he said. "You hardly even know me." He did have a point. The main thing I knew about him was that he was seriously interested in someone else, someone who was at the party, but I truly believed if I could convey the depth of my love to him, he would be swayed.

I was slightly humiliated but also grateful for his understanding response. He basically dismissed the whole episode as an unfortunate, though charming, mistake. The problem was, it made me love him even more, until Leslie—going on her third year with Lars—came up to me at school to ask about a rumor she'd heard that I had given the guy head. Apparently that was how he explained our time alone together at the party.

"You wild woman!" Leslie grinned.

Definition of the sexual revolution: the moment in history when giving a stranger a blow job became an accomplishment, and confessing romantic love, an embarrassment.

ur family went to see *The End*, with Burt Reynolds, about a guy who tries to kill himself because he's dying. Afterwards, at the ice cream store, my mother said if she only had a few months to live she'd kill other people, not herself. We were sitting in the store, feverishly tonguing our usual flavors. My mother's was French Vanilla, which for some reason cost fifteen cents extra. The act of consuming apparently required our full attention, because no one responded. "I'm serious," she said. "I've already got a list of names." The idea struck me as brilliant, much better than Burt's.

"That's lovely, dear," said my father, in a dismissive way that would have infuriated me.

My mother, ever the calorie-counter, tossed her cone in the trash and reached into her pocket for her cigarette purse. Peter immediately started fanning the smoke in an exaggerated fashion, pretending to choke. "Five more minutes," he announced, referring to the amount of time that particular cigarette was subtracting from her life. Once, he'd opened all the packs in a carton and drawn halfway marks on every cigarette because he'd heard the last half was the most dangerous.

"What about you, Robert?" she said. "Have you ever considered what you'd do if you only had a few months left?"

"Nope."

"Oh c'mon. Not ever?"

"What's the point? You don't know what you'd do until it happens."

"Well, just for fun, then."

"It's not fun to me."

"Just make something up." She sounded mad again.

My father stopped licking his Rocky Road, and just like that they were in the middle of another fight.

"I mean, you're the one who dreams of writing a book," my mother said, as though exasperated by his failure to do so. "How can you actualize that dream if you don't exercise your imagination once in a while?"

He didn't look at her. He didn't have a snappy comeback. He briefly considered the surface of his ice cream, then quietly resumed eating it. "Well?" she said. "How *can* you?" No one said anything. Why she wanted him to write a book if he didn't want to was beyond me. Their arguments were always the same now. My father was guilty for *not* doing something, *not* being someone she wanted him to be. If he loved her, she insisted, he'd at least try to change. I think she really believed she'd succeed with this method, that my father just needed prodding. She noisily smoked her cigarette—"I'm still waiting for an answer, Robert"—and he silently finished his ice cream.

My mother picked on him the rest of the way home, said he was passive-aggressive and anal-retentive. She told him she was on to him, that she knew it gave him pleasure to make her crazy. "You do it on purpose," she said. "You're a classic withholder."

I looked out the car window and tried to compose my own hit list. Though plenty of people came to mind, I found I didn't hate anyone enough to actually kill them, though Lars Hoffman was right on the borderline. I moved on to famous people—the band Foreigner, for instance. Yeah, but how would I ever manage to do it? My mother continued complaining. "I don't know why I put up with it, Robert." I closed my eyes and imagined the quiet of the car without her in it.

The next day, my mother informed us that my father wanted to take Peter and me to Hollywood Park to teach us about Thoroughbred racing.

"But I'm supposed to go to Westwood Village with Kerry Brooks and Teresa McNeal," I whined.

"Tough shit," my mother said, boning a chicken. "You're going to Hollywood Park with your father." Then she pointed the boning knife at me. "I don't want to hear another thing about it. Take it up with your father. Let him see how charming you are when you don't get your way."

Instead of going to see him, I went out front and sat on the lawn. The whole thing was so preposterous I could hardly believe it. Since when did they dictate how I spent my Saturday? I thought about Kerry and Teresa in Westwood. They were new friends and I didn't trust them not to talk about me behind my back. "My dad needs me to go to the racetrack with him," I imagined saying over the phone. "I'm his lucky charm. . . . Yeah, every time I go, he wins a bundle." At least that would make me sound cool. What choice did I have? If I told the truth, said I had to go, it would make my father sound creepy, like he didn't have any friends, or anything better to do on a Saturday.

I assumed my mother had bullied him into it, insisting he finally make good on his promise to teach us about racing. "You can't write that book, goddamn it, but you can sure as hell take your kids to the racetrack like you've always said." I could imagine her accusatory voice, and felt sorry for my father without even knowing if it was true.

We left the house about noon. I looked out the window of the car and thought about dollars, lots of them, being handed to me at the track.

"We going to Westwood?" Kerry had said over the phone, adding,

"Teresa can't go. She's grounded. Her mother found a joint in her drawer."

"Well, I can't go either," I said. "I have to visit my grandma's grave. Today's the day we always go. I just forgot."

"Wow, that's heavy."

At the end of the conversation she said, "Have a good time," as if I were going to a movie or something, and like an idiot I'd thanked her, which was not how someone going to a cemetery would have reacted. Now I would have to bring it up with her the next time we talked, say she offended me just to show I hadn't been lying. Unbelievable.

"C'mon, c'mon," my father said to the car in front of us, which was going slow, keeping him from speeding around the way he liked. "Move it, will ya?"

Traffic was heavy. There wasn't anywhere for the car to go. Then he honked. He just leaned the heel of his hand into the horn and left it there. Peter and I looked at each other in shock. It was something our father never did. He didn't believe in honking at people just because you didn't like the way they drove. You were only supposed to honk if they were about to hit you, in self-defense. At the light, we ended up next to the car, of course. None of us had the guts to look at the woman behind the wheel, whom I could feel shaking her head at us. "What's your hurry?" I heard her say, but the light changed and my father floored it.

When we got to Hollywood Park, Peter complained that he was hungry. "Hold your horses," my father said, and Peter thought that was the funniest thing.

"Get it?" he said, several times. His laughter was forced and obnoxious.

"Enough, already," I finally had to say.

The parking lot was endless. We had a long walk to the entrance. "What if we can't find the car later?" Peter said. He was behaving like a little child.

The place was a lot nicer than I expected. While my father bought the *Racing Form*, Peter and I quacked at the swans, who were quick to move away from us, and we tried naming each of the countries the flags represented.

"What's that for?" Peter said about the *Racing Form* as soon as my father joined us. He was starting to drive me crazy with his questions.

Opening his paper after we sat on a bench, my father said, "First thing, you want to remember that a long shot is just that, a horse that's highly unlikely to win. If the odds are much longer than five to one, you're talking long shot."

"Five to one," Peter said, and looked at me like I was stupid or something. My father went on to explain the different types of bets and what you say when you get up to the window.

"A safe bet is to pick one or two strong horses to place. You may not win big, but you win, and that's the important thing your first time out." Then he told us to open our programs to race number one.

As my father explained what the different graphs meant, and what we were supposed to look for in the blur of printed information, I only pretended to pay attention. What caught my eye were the horses' names, like Sonny's Heart, Momentary Boy, Solid Gone, Jet Trail. They either grabbed you or they didn't. My father finished his calculations and advised us that San Berdoo was a good, safe bet. My least favorite name.

"I like Jet Trail," I blurted out.

"No, sweetie, he's a long shot. Remember what I said."

But I had a gut feeling. "That's the one I want."

"You and your mother," he said, sorry for us.

We spread out around the paddock as the horses entered. It was as if I'd never seen a horse before that day, had never realized how breathtaking they were: tall and lean and muscular and shiny, with high-stepping gaits and sweet, sensitive eyes. One of you possesses the speed to win, I thought, searching their hides for clues, forgetting temporarily that they were animals and not athletes.

"Look, Mere!" Peter pointed. In the center of the grassy oval, a man emptied a bucket of ice over a horse's back. Its sinewy veins stood out underneath its coat. Like a movie camera, my eyes racked focus all of a sudden, and across the paddock, beyond the horse, I saw my father staring at the ground. His head was lowered as in prayer, or headache. I made my way to his side, passing behind men who hollered wishes of luck to the jockeys. "Counting on you, Mikey," one guy barked, a shadow of threat in his voice. My father hadn't said anything about the jockeys. Were they just as important as the horses? When I reached my father's side, he was still bent over, his head resting on his forearm.

"Dad?" He didn't look up, so I tugged on his sleeve. "Are you okay?" His face was pale and sleepy and far away. It took him a moment to recognize me, or so it seemed, to remember who I was and who he was to me.

"A penny for your thoughts," I said, trying to sound sweet and look adorable so he wouldn't be sorry I was his. But I was locked in my daughter role. I knew he wouldn't tell me what was really the matter.

"Sorry, not for sale," he said, finding his usual smile. It was all an act, my father's easygoing nature. I'd never seen it so clearly before, had never thought about it at all, in fact. He was locked into Dad.

A bugle sounded and the horses left the paddock, so we headed up a dark flight of steps into a dingy area that reminded me of a giant bus station. A group of mostly black men sat clustered in blue plastic chairs bolted to the ground. They didn't talk. They read their *Racing Forms* and watched the changing odds on TVs high up near the ceiling. Not too many females around, I noticed, though plenty of down-and-out types. Luckily, their attention was focused on the races and not on me.

"Feed me," Peter moaned. "I'm hungry."

It was decided I would hold a place in the long line of people waiting to bet while my father took Peter to get a hot dog. In front of me was a small man wearing a big Hawaiian shirt bursting with purple and yellow flowers. He looked Japanese, with gray stubble for hair and deep creases in the back of his aged neck. He must have felt my eyes on him because he turned around and smiled.

"I like number three." He jabbed his program with the tip of his pen. Momentary Boy. I smiled politely. "I been watching this horse for a year. He gonna do it today, mark my word." The man's nose twitched, full of excitement.

We were moving quickly toward the window. A year? That was a long time. Perhaps he knew something my father didn't. Then I started to think my usual *Twilight Zon*ian thoughts: Maybe it was meant to be, my getting in line behind him, so I could receive his message.

My father and Peter returned just in time. The Japanese man, who was at the window, stepped away, shaking his ticket at me and smiling. All around, people were calmly placing bets. "You ready?" my father said. What did it matter, I told myself, but the truth was, I couldn't imagine anything worse than picking the wrong one, blowing my chance to win. It was the first race of the day, and I felt if I lost it would be a bad omen.

My father put twenty dollars on San Berdoo to place. Peter, the copy-cat, had my father put half his money—we'd each been given ten dollars to play with—on the exact same bet. I looked at the man sitting behind the window in his white shirt and black necktie. His face said it all. He didn't give a damn which horse I bet on.

I told my father to put two dollars on Momentary Boy. The second it was out of my mouth I regretted it. He asked was it to win, place, or show, but by that point I didn't even care. I said place. He handed me the stub and I walked away, resolved at least that I had certainly picked a loser, but my father called it an "interesting" bet, very interesting, and looked at me as though he were impressed.

"Hey," I said, "how come you're playing it safe today? I thought you liked to take a chance."

"Me?" he kidded. "Not in mixed company. Wouldn't want you to think I was playing with your college education."

"Oh yeah," I kidded back.

"Every day," Peter joined in.

On a bench in front of the track, my father kept to his *Racing Form* and looked ahead to the next two races.

"How come Mom didn't come?" Peter said.

"You have to ask her." My father didn't look away from his graphs and ranking charts. "She used to like it a lot."

I was thinking that if Momentary Boy won, I'd make close to six dollars in profit. And if I bet on four races that day, and made at least six dollars each time, I'd go home with twenty-four extra dollars.

Three tones, like a doorbell, sounded, and the announcer said the name of each horse as it went into its starting gate, which was on the other side of the track. I didn't even realize the race had started until it dawned on me that all the stuff the announcer was saying—none of it intelligible—was the actual race in progress. It was completely confusing. People suddenly stood and started yelling. I finally saw the horses then, coming toward us around the final turn. The crowd moved to the fence without taking their eyes off the race. The screaming became deafening as the horses neared the finish. I looked for my horse, number three. There he was, halfway back in the pack. San Berdoo was out front, of course, but another horse took the race, coming up fast to the front and winning by a fraction of a second. Number seven, Jet Trail.

"Give me five, my man." My father slapped Peter's hand.

I was seething. If only they had let me alone. But no, they had to sway me with their "expert" opinions and advice. If I had only followed my instincts, listened to what my own voice told me, I would have made so much money. Jet Trail, Jet Trail, I knew it was you. I would have put five dollars on that horse and walked away with fifty! I wanted to kick myself, pull my hair out. I'd had a little tickle, a fluttering sensation. That's the one, it was trying to tell me, that's the winner.

"I was going to bet on that horse," I told my father on the way to the window where he and Peter would collect their winnings.

"What's that?" he said.

"I was going to bet on Jet Trail, but you told me not to because he was a long shot." I didn't even try to hide the brattiness in my voice.

"Long shots don't win, percentage-wise."

I stopped walking. "HE JUST DID!" I screamed and threw my arms out in front of me. Then I was crying. My poor father. It must have been a nightmare for him, everything going out of control. He looked confused, panicked. People were looking at me. He came back and leaned over.

"What is going on?" That's when I saw the Hawaiian shirt step up to the window and get his palm licked with bills. My father looked where I was looking. "What? What's the matter now?" I was speechless. Had the little man done it intentionally? Misled me so that later on he could laugh out loud about the gullible young girl he had convinced to bet on that shit horse number three? There had to be racetrack weirdos like that, who enjoyed helping others get knocked flat on their butts, but I couldn't believe it. I knew he had been sincere. Perhaps, like my father often did, the man had hedged his bet with another, safer, one that had brought him back to the window.

"Meredith, honey"—my father wiped my cheeks—"it's a game. Some you win, some you lose. You go on to the next one."

I was staring straight into his lying eyes. What a crock. He had also said that the whole point was to win. I managed to smile at him, and make him think we could go on now, on with our lovely day, but inside I was making a decision about who I would listen to in the future, and who I wouldn't, because I had something to celebrate even if no one knew it. I had a gift, the ability to look at a sheet of horses' names and get a feeling for the winner. It was about flashes of telepathy and moments of absolute knowledge that had nothing to do with odds and graphs, and I had it.

The only problem was, when I looked at the list of horses for race number two, nothing grabbed me. I'd think I was getting something, a spark, but then I'd get another one, and another, until it was clear I hadn't even had one real spark. I was trying way too hard, and with sparks that never worked. You couldn't will them, couldn't control them. You had to be in a certain frame of mind, and I was way too uptight. I had to win, and so I second-guessed every impulse until the whole business was pointless.

For the rest of the day, I tried different strategies to pick the winner. In race number two, I listened to my father. We both lost. In number three, I picked the name I liked best. Lost again. Then I closed my eyes and let my finger fall on the page. I even asked Peter for help. Total waste.

I learned to hate gambling. I hated losing money, hated knowing that they had it and I wasn't getting it back. Yet, the more I lost, the more I wanted to keep going, to play until I could regain my ten dollars and erase the entire experience. By the time we left I was a nervous, glum-faced wreck. In the car driving back, my father suggested stopping in Westwood for ice cream sundaes.

"I don't want one," I said. Of course Peter did. He was in such a good mood the car wasn't big enough. Between my father, who'd gotten bolder with his bets as the day wore on, and Peter, they had won almost ninety bucks.

"C'mon, Mere," Peter said, "snap out of it."

"Fine. Do what you want." My father was looking at me in the rearview mirror. I couldn't help it. I was still mad at him over Jet Trail, even though I knew, deep down, there was only one person to blame, one confused, greedy, overanxious, stupid stupid person.

"Mere?" my father said, still watching me. "Forget about it. You lost ten dollars, sweetheart. Ten stinkin' dollars."

Peter strutted from the curb to the ice cream store, showboating for all the world like a football hero in the end zone. "I'm in the money," he sang.

I slid into the booth facing away from the window, just in case. I didn't want to see anyone I knew. Peter got in on the opposite side, or tried to, but my father, who stood watching us, said, "Why don't you sit next to your sister."

"Why?"

"Humor me." It was such a strange thing for him to request that Peter and I exchanged looks.

"Okay." Peter switched sides with a shrug. The wall at the end of our table was mirrored glass. Sliding closer to it in order to accommodate Peter, I saw my chin sticking out the way it always did when I was unhappy. My mother would have been proud, because I tucked it in automatically.

The waitress brought water and asked if we were ready to order. "I know what I want," Peter said, rubbing his hands together. He ordered a banana split with three kinds of ice cream and three separate syrups, "and lots of whipped cream, pretty please."

"Nothing for me," I said.

"Get something," my father said. I told him I wasn't hungry. "She'll have a hot fudge sundae with coffee ice cream, and bring me a cup of coffee. I'll help you with it."

"Can we go again next week?" Peter begged. "Please? I want to try the Daily Double."

"We'll see," said my father.

"But we make such a great team. We're on a roll, my man. Don't let it die."

My father excused himself to call home. "I'm going to let your mother know where we are so she doesn't worry."

"The only reason you didn't win," Peter advised me, "was because you didn't listen to Dad. You have to go by the odds, and—"

I told him to shut up, but he was intent on helping me. "No, you have to listen. It really works."

I said, "All you did was copy Dad. You don't know anything about horse racing, so stop acting like you're Mr. Know-It-All."

"You're just like Mom," he said, giving up on me. I stared at the side of his stupid head and imagined pounding my fist into it. This made me feel remarkably better.

"Does Dad seem weird to you?" I changed the subject.

"No."

"Well, he does to me."

Peter considered the evidence. "Maybe. You may have something."

"Oh, thank you, Swami."

"Shut up."

My father came back to the table rubbing his face. The ice cream arrived shortly thereafter and we pushed our sundae back and forth until he finally gave in and took the first bite. "It's really good," he teased.

"What's Mom doing?" Peter said with his mouth full, then answered his own question. "She's probably meditating on a candle or something weird like that." He looked at my father for validation but was told instead not to be rude.

Peter resumed wolfing his banana split. My father wasn't eating. He'd only tried that first spoonful, so I pulled the goblet over to my side of the table and took a taste.

"Yum." I started shoveling it down.

"Go, Kirby," Peter said, but obliquely, so that only I picked up his reference to me as a vacuum cleaner.

"Keep it up," I hummed, sweetly, when my father was sipping his coffee, a threat of future action only Peter would understand. We enjoyed these sidelong digs at each other. They were a secret code between us, a language our parents knew nothing about.

"Want some more?" I shoved the half-eaten sundae in front of my father, who dipped the spoon but didn't lift it to his mouth. He twisted and twirled it without raising his head.

"So," he said, as if resuming a conversation in progress. "There's something I need to talk to you two about."

Just then, Jane Fonda appeared at the head of our booth, wearing a black cape and holding a clipboard. It was really her, and she was even more beautiful and radiant in person than on-screen. The three of us just stared, shocked beyond belief.

"Hello, have you heard about the fight against offshore drilling in southern California?" she said in that Jane Fonda voice. She explained she was talking to people in Westwood Village to get signatures for a petition. Peter slapped his forehead. He couldn't believe the day he was having. First the races, then Jane Fonda. He continued to stuff himself, excitedly, as she leaned over my father's shoulder to show him where to sign.

"I loved you in *Coming Home*," I said, after working up the nerve. I thought I was going to cry. She looked into my eyes and smiled, thanking me. She was so good, so beautiful on the inside, you could just see it. She didn't act like a movie star at all. She thanked my father and headed for a group of people just entering the store. Both Peter and I turned around to watch.

When we recovered, my father had his wallet out. Neither Peter nor I remembered a thing he'd said before Jane's appearance. "Mom's gonna be sorry she didn't come now," Peter said.

It was a short ride from Westwood Village back home. We'd driven it all our lives, past the sprawling grounds of the Veterans' Administration building, on to San Vicente Boulevard, then home. It was getting dark out, and cold. We couldn't wait to run inside and storm our mother with the celebrity news. It was all we talked about as our father silently chauffeured us home.

"What's wrong?" Peter said, when our father pulled to the curb about two blocks from our turn. He shut off the engine and twisted around so he could direct his words to Peter, who was in front, and me.

"Your mother's not at home," he began. "She's spending the night in

Newport Beach with her sister." Jane Fonda's face gave way in my mind to Aunt Eve's. Peter inhaled, about to speak, but my father beat him to it.

"Wait. I'm going to talk for a while now, and you're going to listen, and when I'm finished you can ask all the questions you want."

It was that time of day when vision requires the aid of memory and imagination, because we were fast becoming silhouettes in the disappearing light, which I now think of as merciful for protecting us from the sight of each other in that close, intimate space. Silence fell. Outside the car, traffic flowed west toward the ocean on a river of speed. "Your mother and I have decided to separate. We don't get along anymore, so we're going to try living apart for a while, see what that does." He sighed, heavily, as if to let us know what an emotional tangle the whole thing was for him. I couldn't tell how he really felt. He sounded angry to me.

I followed the outline of his nose with my eyes, nearly forgetting mine had once shared its distinctive contours. "Your mother's pretty angry at me. Maybe you are, too. I, uh, don't know what else to do."

I could hear Peter weeping. His fall was greater than mine, due to the frenzied peak he'd been whipped into as preparation. Why did they do us like that, play us for such fools? This was it, I found myself thinking. Something BIG, something BAD. And it wasn't happening to anyone else. It was all mine. I sat there trying to cry, to feel something approaching devastation. My father was saying how much he loved us. "We'll have lots more days like today," he promised. "I would never leave you kids."

Liar, I thought. Liar, liar, liar. My father wiped his eyes and sniffled, but it was Peter I bent forward to comfort. He was the one I yearned to hold. As my fingers sifted the soft layers of his hair, he began to vomit. I didn't pull away, even as wave after wave of the afternoon was expelled in excruciating abundance. I continued to stroke him and began crying myself. My father started the car, not knowing what else to do. We were suddenly, all of us, in a big hurry to get home.

The furnished apartment my father rented by the month looked like a display in a furniture store. Humans interrupted its icy perfection, its sleek gray and black surfaces. Clean because it included maid service, and impersonal because most of his stuff was still at our house, at least the apartment contained one item I enjoyed: a bouquet of spaghetti-thin silver wires bound together at the base and centered on the glass coffee table in lieu of something leafy. I liked to run my palm over the itchy bristles, make them sway like long hair underwater. I gathered and released them, blew on and otherwise provoked them until my father inevitably became annoyed.

"Well, I'm bored," I answered one Sunday, watching the strands dance.

"Only boring people get bored," he said, turning on the TV, then twisting the lid off a jar of peanuts.

"Hey, Dad? Is it all right if I call you Robert?"

"Not if you want me to answer." He was popping nuts in his mouth, his attention on the screen.

I continued playing with the wires. "Mom lets me call her Leigh." This was true. She tolerated it, but only because she was looking for a new identity, in general. In the six weeks they'd been apart she'd started training at the downtown clothing mart to be a buyer, traded her Mercedes for a secondhand Porsche with a license plate on order that would soon inform the world, FUN CAR, and gotten a new short hairstyle that made her look completely different.

"Is it just Robert you don't like? What if I called you Bob?"

"No."

"How come?" I had the wires moving in a beautiful counterclockwise wave, like tall grass in the wind.

"I like Dad. Call me that."

I studied my father across the room. What would it take to break the barrier that kept us from really knowing one another?

"Let me just try it." No response. "Hey, Bobby, pass the peanuts." He gave me a tired look. "You get to call me Meredith. I don't make you say Daughter."

"That's because I'm the father. The father gets to call the children anything he wants."

"You're just a human like me." We were keeping it playful but in truth I did want him to loosen up now that he was away from my mother. It was time he stopped pretending to be Mr. Authority, so I could assume my rightful place as equal, and all-around buddy. I envisioned it so clearly, my father and I having heart-to-hearts about the meaning of life and the hard knocks he'd endured as a child. Why not? There was so much time to fill now, time he used to spend with my mother, available for me and my brother. But Peter had his own fantasy. He wanted to bring our parents back together using a scheme he had yet to work out.

One afternoon, as we walked to the store, he shared a little song he had made up:

> Hold the pickles, hold the lettuce,
> Mom and Dad you sure upset us,
> get together—yeah!—and let us
> have it our way.

It was the Burger King jingle.

"Are you planning to sing that to them?"

"Maybe."

"I think not."

"What's wrong with it?"

I grimaced.

That same night my father came to the house to help me with my math homework. He let himself in, as usual, then fixed a bourbon and soda. When my mother eventually drifted in, she did this thing with her eyes, sized him up appreciatively in his dark suit and splashy tie. I noticed he made a point of looking extra good the days he came over.

"Guess who I heard from today?" she said.

He finished at the bar. "Who?"

"Callahan."

Peter said, "The gardener who made stew out of the Katzes' pet rabbit?"

"Yep. He called me up. He's on the wagon and wanted to know if we might consider taking him back."

"Terry," I grumbled. "He scared me."

"Sit down, Robert," my mother said. "You're making me nervous." He always stood now, as if poised to leave any minute. It was one of the few signs of their troubles. "You're not at a cocktail party, sweetheart. Relax." He sat down and almost managed to look at ease.

Peter said, "He used to get in his blue truck and drink from a little bottle in between doing our yard and the Katzes'."

"He was a good gardener," my father said.

"You're not going to hire him, are you?" I was practically pleading.

"Don't worry, Meredith." My father sipped his drink. "No one on this block is going to hire him."

"He did save our poplar tree." My mother stood up and walked past him into the adjoining room. "There's some mail I need you to look at."

"Did you see Carson last night, Leigh?"

"Of course." She stood at the antique secretary in the living room. "I almost called you it was so funny."

"A *great* bit with the tarantula," my father said.

Peter and I looked at each other hard. It seemed they were playing at being apart, using their separation to spice up their relationship. A half hour passed, then my father and I got cozy on the couch, sitting closer together than normal so we could both see the textbook propped in his lap. My mother stayed close by, reading a magazine.

"You know, the two of you look like newlyweds." She interrupted our discussion of algebra. "No, really. You look like sweethearts pouring over honeymoon brochures." It was her specialty. I don't think she had any idea how uncomfortable comments like that made me. She saw everything between the sexes—even between father and daughter—as sexual, so it was no wonder that instead of seriously considering the number of apples among Tom and Patty in the equation my father was explaining, I gave them faces and a neighborhood with trees and wondered why they were selling apples at all when they could have been doing something better, like kissing.

"You see how to work it?" my father said.

I felt my usual belligerence. "Why don't they just say how many apples there are instead of 'Patty has three times as many as Tom, who has half as many as Ernie'?" The whole point of algebra, as I saw it, was to trick you with so many twists and turns your brain *had* to wander. I had no idea how my father and I got through it each week, but somehow I consistently passed the tests.

"I'll just take a look at that garbage disposal," he said when we finished. He stood and stretched, looking to my mother. "You said it was giving you trouble before."

"Oh, would you, Robert?" She warmed, then, "No, you must be tired. I can call someone to fix it tomorrow."

It was getting to be a routine with them. First she mentioned a problem—the porch light, a fuse in her car—then insisted on taking care of it herself, only to gush thanks and tug his sleeve seductively when he finished the job.

"Anything else?" He lingered after fixing the disposal, ever hopeful he might be asked to stay over.

My mother began turning off lights and emptying her ashtrays. "I'm exhausted. Thanks so much for coming by."

"Okay then," he said, and back he went to the Comstock Arms, his towering apartment building on Wilshire Boulevard. I often thought of him there, alone in his cold shiny bedroom.

⋯⋯⋯⋯⋯

THE SUNDAY BEFORE CHRISTMAS, Peter and I were goofing with the wire sculpture when a smart-alecky knock hit the door. "Wuz happnin?" roared a graying, portly man who sounded remarkably like the Fonz.

"Hey, Burt. The kids are over. Come say hello."

"Oh hey, man." Burt raised his arms, a look of alarm crossing his face. "I can come back another . . . I mean, I don't want to intrude." He was stuck. I saw the fear in his eyes turn to embarrassment, then resignation as he came inside with a five-pound sausage in his hands. He nodded nervously as Peter and I approached. "Wow, so these are your kids. Hey kids, wuz hap-nin?"

"Hi," Peter said, staring at the sausage. My father told him our names.

"Cool," he nodded, up and down, up and down, as though he were listening to music. "Oh hey, check this out, Robert." His eyes darted in my direction every few seconds. "Remember that guy I told you I was friends with, you know, my brother-in-law's neighbor, Mike?"

"Yeah, I think so."

"The guy with the Italian deli on Doheny? You probably don't re-member. But hey, that's cool. Anyway, check this out." He licked his lips, which were on the pudgy side and seemed incapable of fully shutting. "Imported gen-u-ine Italian pepperoni, aged six months and extremely spicy. Care to join me in a little tasterooney?"

"You bet," my father said, stepping into the kitchen, which was right behind us. He opened the fridge. "How about a beer to go with it?"

Burt rallied with a satisfied chuckle and rubbed his hands together. "Your dad and me, we get together for some pretty good times around here. Isn't that right, Roberto?" he shouted, then turned back to us. "I live right next door." When we didn't say anything, he ditched us.

"I'll just slice this baby up," he told my father. The two of them were banging around in the kitchen. "So, uh, how's the reentry plan coming?"

"Hey-hey, not in front of them."

"Oh sure. Sorry. But I hope the atmosphere's improving."

"Could be."

"It's just a matter of time, my friend. I predict we'll both be going back home."

They came out of the kitchen with a platter of sliced pepperoni, some green olives, a couple of bottles of beer, two chilled glasses, and headed for the TV. We'd just eaten a big meal an hour earlier.

"These are neat," Peter said, examining one of the frosted glasses.

"That's a little trick I taught your father. Keeps the beer cold. And, of course, it looks cool. Gotta look cool in L.A." Burt guffawed.

I thought I recognized his essential unhappiness—or, rather, saw his gaiety for what it was, desperate and forced. He disturbed me in the way circus clowns always had, being grown men who behaved like buffoons, whose real faces were so plain they hid behind grotesquely painted smiles.

They switched on the football game and I wandered into the kitchen. The sausage was on the counter, a greasy cylinder the color of dried blood. The knife was smeared with fatty residue.

"What are you doing?" Peter came in.

"Standing here. What do you think of Burp?" I said, softly.

"He's cool." He took a glass from the cabinet and pressed a button on the refrigerator door, releasing a cascade of ice cubes. If the wire sculpture was my favorite doohickey in the apartment, this small breakthrough in home beverage convenience was Peter's.

Burt was suddenly back in the kitchen. For some reason, Peter and I made him nervous. As soon as he saw us he grew stiff. "Hey, kids!" His eyes pled for mercy while his wet lips hung loose in an idiot's smile. "Having fun at Dad's?"

What's my name, I was dying to ask him. I knew he wouldn't remember.

"Just came in for a couple of paper towels." He delicately maneuvered his way around Peter and me. I couldn't help looking at his midsection. I felt I was seeing the source of my father's burgeoning weight problem.

"He's a jerk," I said, once he was gone.

Peter shrugged. "Let's go watch the game."

I liked football. I liked the fact that no matter how well they planned it, the athletes never knew the outcome of a play until the ball was snapped and the green field opened into possibilities of its own. I liked the crazy struggle to get clear, to outsmart the opposition until you were free all the way to the end zone, the one who did the thing no one expected, whose body reversed direction, defied logic. I liked the overkill of four guys piled on top of one ball-carrying messenger. I liked when they played somewhere cold, where you could see the breath in front of their helmeted faces. I liked the contours of their bodies in the heavy padding. Bull men. Ant men. But I didn't like Burt.

Peter left to join the men. What I really wanted was to go home, by bus if necessary. All I had to do was go downstairs, wait for the RTD, and ride it all the way to Brentwood. I wouldn't even have to tell my father. I could say I was going for a walk, then call him once I got there. The football game would be another hour and a half at least. I went into the living area, where they were moaning and howling at the TV, and chomping pepperoni. On the screen, the black-and-white-striped referee made an L with his arms and blew a whistle. "I'm going for a walk," I said, slinging my purse over my shoulder. My father told me to be careful, without turning from the game.

-------------------

IF YOU CLOSE your eyes and really listen, the sound of passing automobiles is not unlike the roar of the ocean. The two are acoustically identical, or so I determined waiting for the number 86 bus. I waited a long time on one of the busiest stretches of Wilshire Boulevard, pathetic on my warped bench, my back against an advertisement for a funeral home. The traffic breeze played havoc with my clothes and hair while hundreds of instantly forgotten drivers had their look at me. Sound waves. Ocean waves. If you missed a bus in L.A. it could be another forty-five minutes till the next one. I felt my skin collecting microscopic particles of dirt. My nostrils were dry from the constant burn of exhaust. Thinking it would come only if I relaxed, I stopped looking in the direction of the expected bus. It didn't come. I closed my eyes and tried to will myself home, like Samantha Stephens on *Bewitched*. Amazing—when I opened my eyes I was still on Wilshire. I'd been sitting there forty minutes when the gleaming white Celica pulled up. I didn't recognize it, but, smiling and waving at me from the driver's seat as though we knew each other well was the luminous face of Kim Adamson.

"Meredith, you want a ride?"

In junior high we exchanged unacquainted smiles several times, but she had graduated a year before me and we never got to know each other. I got in the car.

"I noticed you at school in September." She was looking at traffic as she pulled away from the curb, transporting me into the flow of cars I'd sat outside of for so long. "Do you remember me?" she said, sucking a piece of candy and rapping the steering wheel lightly to "I Will Survive," which throbbed from the radio.

"Of course. I worshiped you in eighth grade." Kim Adamson had it all—the clothes, the friends, the looks. She laughed as though I'd told a funny joke.

"You're sweet."

I liked it. Yeah, somewhere deep and kept away, I was terribly, remarkably sweet.

I noticed Kim's professionally manicured nails and the expensive little rings adorning several of her suntanned fingers. The car smelled of delicious rose perfume.

"You look great," she said. I felt like Miss Dirty Hair, Miss Slob. "Did you change your hair?"

"Try again." I pointed to my nose.

"You're kidding!" We talked about the surgery, then I told her where I lived and how I'd ended up at the bus stop.

"My parents are divorced, too," she said.

"Mine aren't divorced, just separated. They'll probably get back together. I know my dad wants to. I think they're just going through a phase." I hated seeing my block. I wanted to drive around with Kim forever.

"We should do something together," she said. "Give me your phone number and I'll give you mine."

The bliss ended abruptly when I got inside and discovered my mother dancing barefoot in our living room. She didn't hear me come in, on account of the drums and Arabic wailing blasting from the stereo, so I secretly watched her swing her head round and round, and paddle her arms through the air, her entire body undulating to the Middle Eastern rhythms. She looked ridiculous, like somebody *trying* to lose herself, to flow. She lifted her skirt above her knees and began twirling, which sent the strap of her camisole flying.

"Don't stop, my darling, you are glowing!"

I inched my startled head around the corner, and there, in the yellow armchair against the wall, was a strange man with dark skin and hair, nodding at the spectacle before him. His foot began to stomp.

"Careful, my beauty." He laughed as my dizzy mother stumbled into the étagère. His thickly accented voice commanded the room. "I don't want bruises on that fantastic body." She regained her balance and began a slithering path toward him, her eyes never leaving his face.

He growled. "What are you doing to me, Leigh? You are like the moon calling the waves." Then he rose and put his hands on her, and began doing something with her ear I assumed, at first, was nibbling. As the music faded it became clear he was speaking to her, rapidly murmuring endearments in a language I would later learn was Farsi. To me the words sounded infantile—all *oocha-koocha-kaaba-reemi*. Then I caught a glimpse of my mother's softly lidded eyes, and her lips, parted in a quivering half-smile. To her his sexy gobbledygook was nothing short of manna.

"I have a lover!" she told Judith over the phone. Not boyfriend, not suitor, but *lover* she had to call him, as though her life had suddenly become better than everyone else's. I hated the word. It sounded so simmering and breathless, describing someone whose sole purpose was to make passionate love then disappear until the job needed doing again. *Lover* made me think of frantic tongue work and tight clothes being torn away.

Judith must have said something about Muslims, because my mother came back with, "So we're told, but if this is oppression, bring on the shackles. I'm telling you, he makes me feel freer than I've ever felt in my life. He's so intuitive. You should see the furniture he makes. I think I've found my Alan Bates!"

My mother's lover was named Kamran. He wasn't much like the painter in *An Unmarried Woman,* but then my mother wasn't any Jill Clayburgh, either. He was sexy and artistic like Alan Bates's character, but not warm or cuddly or the least bit interested in getting to know Peter and me. I found him in our kitchen one night, leaning against the counter in his silk boxers, calmly eating a peach in the dark. I assumed he was taking a break from his lover duties before going back upstairs for round two. I almost didn't go in, but then I figured, This is my house. Let him leave the room if he doesn't like it.

"Hello," I said, testy as I turned on the light. I had to make my lunch for school the next day.

"Uh," he grunted. He was really enjoying his peach, slurping up the juice, licking his fingers noisily. I opened the fridge and started pulling out what I needed. When I turned around, he was right behind me, looking over my shoulder at the brightly lit contents. His tautly muscled body, sharp-smelling and dark-skinned, was repellent to me. When I was out of his way, he removed half a cantaloupe and came back to the counter to start on that. It was strange to see a man choose fruit. My father and Peter acted as though eating raw produce were a form of punishment. The wet sounds of Kamran's eating annoyed me.

"Hungry, huh?" I said.

"Not really." His mouth was full. Then he swallowed, and continued, "We don't eat fruit to fill our stomachs. We eat fruit to satisfy our senses."

I stopped what I was doing to savor that. "Good point." I tried to match his detachment. "My mom said you're from Teheran." No response. "How do you like L.A.?"

He was working his tongue between his yellowing teeth. After a moment he shrugged, and with a vaguely disgusted look, said, "Oh, well, I love it." I had to wonder if he understood the meaning of the word. It seemed he'd gotten love confused with some other term, like loathe, but then he added, with the same dreary ennui, "And of course I hate it. How is it possible to love something without also hating it?"

I began wondering if all Iranian men were like this, fiery and mysterious, prone to saying wise, obvious things we TV-trained Americans could only gawk at?

Kamran slapped his belly a couple of times, muffled a belch, and left the room, unaware he'd transformed himself into the unlikeliest entrant in my never-ending pageant of fantasy guys. My favorite scenario had him coming to my room right after making love to my mother. He'd say he was going to the bathroom, then find me doing my homework. As his strong brown hand, which smelled of sex, covered my mouth, he'd tell me not to make a sound. Then he'd murmur that sexy foreign stuff in my ear while his hands traveled under my clothing. "Someday I'm going to teach you everything," he'd promise, fondling me expertly while down the hall my mother began calling for him.

---

IN MY MOTHER'S favorite movie, *An Unmarried Woman*, Erica (Jill Clayburgh) is sad and angry because her husband has left her for another woman. She goes through a period of wanting nothing to do with men. Then, at the gentle urging of her shrink, she decides it's time to "get back in the stream of life." She wants to see what it's like to have sex with men she's not in love with. Enter Saul Kaplan (Alan Bates), a classy British painter, very successful, whom she uses for sex, or means to, but Saul is curious about her. He charms his way into her life, and little by little they fall in love. Saul begs her to spend the summer with him and his kids in the country, but she clings to her new independence and resists the urge to couple. He doesn't seem to mind, saying only, and affectionately, that she is a willful woman. The movie ends with him going off to Vermont, leaving Erica dragging a gigantic canvas of his through the streets of New York City. She must balance her own self with her unwieldy love for this man, who tempts her away from her center.

Where was my mother's center? When had she ever taken time to cultivate one? The answer was that she hadn't, of course, yet she genuinely believed she was living the dream at last, that Kamran's attentions would turn her into a real-life Erica.

1979

"How's your mom?" My father paused over a dripping Reuben sandwich. He was becoming more and more bloated.

"She's fine." I stuffed my own face with bagel, lox, and cream cheese. What was I supposed to say, that she was having the time of her life with a Persian dreamboat?

The three of us—Peter, my dad, and I—were at our usual spot for Sunday brunch, Junior's Deli on south Westwood Boulevard, where each table sported a complimentary mini-barrel of kosher pickles. I looked away from my father's food-filled cheeks, because I minded the sight of the overweight shoveling in more food.

"She still seeing that guy?" He tried to keep it casual, conversational, in case we didn't know as much as he hoped, or didn't feel like divulging our mother's secrets.

"He's still around," Peter confirmed.

My father knew about Kamran, but he couldn't have guessed how brazenly our mother's affair was paraded before us.

That morning, when he came to pick us up, one of Kamran's boxy, bright blue chairs had greeted him in the foyer. "I haven't decided where to put it," my mother said. Her entire demeanor was energetic, full of optimism. My father stared at the whimsical piece of furniture as if it were Kamran himself blocking the way.

As I watched him dunk a french fry into his grease-splattered ketchup, I wondered if I'd have the nerve, after breakfast, to mention the knee-length red cardigan I wanted. He was bound to ask, as he always did, if there was anything Peter and I needed. It was that word, *need*, that stopped me cold every time, that kept me from obtaining the thing, while Peter, with clear conscience, had recently scored a Mickey Mouse watch, a tennis racket, and a pair of Wallabies.

"It beats sitting around his apartment all afternoon," Peter said. "Just don't think about it. He likes buying us stuff. It gives him something to do."

Silently, I rehearsed my part. "I could use a sweater," I would say, as if only just thinking of it. Or, "There's a sweater I saw at Bullock's. You could buy it for me." But no matter how I prepared for the inevitable moment on the sidewalk outside Junior's, when he would ask if we needed anything, the thought of leading my father in his sad state to a department store silenced me.

He motioned to the waitress for our check. "So, is she serious about this guy?"

Peter shrugged. "All I know is he's weird. The guy sits in the shower. He doesn't take a bath, where you're supposed to sit down. He sits in the shower, where you're supposed to stand."

My father pulled a twenty from what appeared to be dozens inside his wallet. I fortified myself at the sight. There was no reason to hesitate about the cardigan.

Peter went on, stressing every word to show my father the gravity of the situation. "He—puts—a—plastic—chair—in—the—tub, turns—on—the—shower—and—just—sits—there—without—moving."

My father stared. "I don't understand. You've seen this guy in the shower, Peter?"

"God, no. Mom told me, plus I've seen the chair in there. And he doesn't use shaving cream, either. He sits on the chair awhile, then rakes his face with a bare razor. Pretty strange, huh? And he never ever cuts himself."

Hearing the finer points of Kamran's personal hygiene regimen wasn't what my father had in mind. It sounded as if Kamran lived at our house, when in fact he was rarely there, at least when we were around. In an attempt to salvage things, I said, "She usually goes to his place." My father winced. "I mean, I'm not sure he's serious about her."

"Are you kidding?" Peter disagreed. "He likes her a lot."

"How do *you* know?" I demanded.

My father said that was enough. He sighed and spread his arms across the top of our booth. "Poor Leigh." He chuckled, shaking his head. Yeah, right, Dad, I was tempted to say—poor *Mom*. Have another plate of deep-fried food, why don't you.

I had always hated Sundays, only instead of grumbling my way through their slow, migraine-inducing, Monday-dreading haze, I was now expected to cheer up MY FATHER, who had previously been, simply, my father. He was equally lost in his new role, which required him to demonstrate an interest beyond his means in the lives of Peter and me. No wonder our days together sagged the moment we left Junior's only to realize there were several more hours to fill.

"I had an idea for today," my father said, twirling a toothpick in his mouth. "I thought we might go miniature golfing."

Was there any way, I wondered, to work the sentence "I could use a new sweater" into that equation?

-------------------

I NO LONGER RODE the school bus. Kim Adamson added me to her carpool, and just like that I was sitting in splendor among the likes of Beth Conrad, Susie Pittman, and Jessica Fargas, whose father was a well-known TV producer. I felt like an eavesdropper as they talked about jazz dance class and a party they'd gone to at the home of ultra-fox Jeff Karlin. No one questioned what I was doing in the car. They were exceedingly nice to Kim's new tenth-grade friend. They were curious, welcoming, and I soon found my place as "the funny one."

It wasn't intentional, at least not at first. I was just naïve about certain things. My questions on dating, drunken behavior, and making out could be so direct and so basic, the fact I wasn't embarrassed to ask them made people laugh.

"You are so funny," Kim said one Saturday at McDonald's. "I can be myself with you. I don't have to pretend."

"That's me." I smiled. "I pretend so others don't have to."

"Huh?"

Once in a while, a bit of unintentional sharpness got tossed in with my comments. It happened when I strained for that almighty validation of another person's laughter. "Just kidding," I quickly said.

I took a big bite of my Quarter Pounder. Kim drank Tab through a straw. I noticed she had a dainty way of doing just about everything. As she sucked the diet soda, she held the top of the straw with the tips of her manicured fingers, like a little squirrel.

"You going to eat that?" I said. We'd been sitting twenty minutes and she hadn't touched her hamburger or fries, though I'd watched her carefully drizzle ketchup on both.

She stopped hydrating herself and grinned, as though I'd said the funniest thing. "See, that's what I'm talking about. You don't BS. I love that. I don't want to be bloated for class." Her fashion-modeling course was in thirty minutes in a building around the corner, just one more extra in a life that included all the things I secretly wanted. Kim *lived*, while I seemed merely to exist. She wore unique, daring clothes, was always going to parties, knew how to dance and sing well enough to be in the school musicals, had a taste for adventure, mischief.

"I have a secret," she said, "but you have to swear you won't tell another soul."

I swore.

"Because, if anyone found out about this I couldn't handle it. I'd be in so much trouble." She'd gone very serious, her eyes locked on me, broken only by glances around the restaurant to make sure no one was listening. The story that emerged was like a little movie, about a casting agency down the hall from the suite where she took her modeling class. She often passed actors preparing to audition for commercials and TV shows. They lined the corridors and were given to spontaneous shouting, intricate miming, whatever the part required. "You should see some of these guys," Kim said. "They're already professional models. I mean, it's Babe Central in there."

The front of the agency was glass. Kim could look in and see all the action, which was how she met Brick. He was behind the front desk, directing traffic a couple of Saturdays earlier. According to her, the attraction was so strong, he chased after her and introduced himself.

"He's, like, six-six, and built! Anyway, one thing led to another. The guy is hot to trot, Meredith, and I'm thinking of going for it. He's been in a few movies and on TV. He got in some kind of trouble—I'm not really sure about that part. Anyway, a friend of his runs the agency, so he helps out while he's trying to get his career going again. You'd probably recognize him if you saw him. There's just one little problem."

Kim looked away, then back. Then she shut her eyes so tight her whole face wrinkled up. "He's married. With two kids." She relaxed her face. "But he's so nice to me, and really, if you think about it, he's the perfect person to lose my virginity with, because there's no strings. It's only sex. He said he thinks about me all the time."

For once I had no witty comeback. I was way out of my league. Instead of saying the wrong thing, I found myself studying the sharp curl of Kim's dark lashes, the creamy smoothness of her skin. A married man, with children, yet Kim's eyes and teeth sparkled. Probably twenty years her senior, nearly three times her size, and the thought made her ecstatic? I imagined his penis would be gargantuan and painful to experience. She was so thin and delicate, so exquisitely sensual-looking. The gold S-chain around her neck fell like a trickle of water over her pronounced collarbone.

"What are you thinking?" she said.

Condemning them would have been too predictable, too easy. And who was I to judge? Kim's mind was clearly made up. I could be a friend and support her or I could tell her how creepy it sounded, knowing full well she would do it anyway.

"Go for it."

"You're so great, Meredith. You really think I should?" The tip of the straw grazed her bottom lip as she waited for my permission.

"Why not?" I leaned back, away from her probing gaze. "I can't believe you didn't eat one bite."

"There's one more thing I need to tell you." She smiled a little, then began blowing bubbles into her drink. "I don't really eat. I hate being hassled about it. Food makes me sick, so if we're going to keep being friends you shouldn't make a big deal out of it."

She could see I didn't understand. "It's called anorexia nervosa. I feel fat when I eat."

I'd noticed she was extremely thin—it was impossible not to—but I liked that look, envied it, in fact.

"How do you stay alive, if you don't mind my asking."

"Ice cream. It's the only thing I can keep down."

"And your parents don't mind?"

"I fake it when I'm with my dad. I eat a little and put the rest in my napkin to throw away later. My mom is just glad I eat the ice cream. My stepfather's never around."

"Well, I think you look fantastic, and so does—what's his name? Brick?" Kim reached across and squeezed my hand. Then she started singing "Brick House." We both sang.

Outside McDonald's, she demonstrated the proper way to walk a modeling ramp. Leaning back, she put her hands on her hips, like a cowboy bracing his holster, then sucked in her cheeks and fixed her eyes in front of her, face deadly serious. After five steps forward she pivoted sharply and returned, remaining in character until she was back in front of me, at which point she burst out laughing. I'd never heard her laugh like that, as though her body were tumbling upward through the sky. It was beautiful and contagious, and with it a chaotic devotion spread through me.

---

JESSICA FARGAS GESTICULATED wildly as she told us all a hilarious story about being an extra on her father's TV show. Feeling something on my sleeve, I turned and there was Leslie, smiling awkwardly at me. "Can I talk to you?" She looked so little, and young, compared to Kim's circle of friends, now my circle, too.

"Sure." My tone was overly cheerful, as if I didn't recognize the trouble in her eyes, the obvious sadness aimed right at me. I stepped away with her.

She looked a little embarrassed at first. "I miss you." I thought she was going to cry. "You never call me anymore. We hardly talk."

"That's not true." My smile held. I was going to deflect her by acting unaware of the problem.

"We used to be best friends, Meredith. Now you only have time for Kim. It's like you're in love with her."

Suddenly I felt cruel. "Maybe I just got tired of hearing about you and Lars all the time, and the weird things you try from *The Joy of Sex*."

"I thought you wanted to hear about it. Half the fun is telling you what we do."

"Fun for you." I couldn't imagine actually telling her I found something larval about the two of them, something teeming and glistening and better left unexposed.

Her chin began to tremble and her eyes got red and watery. "We used to have such great times."

"Leslie, don't cling to me right now. We're still friends. We'll always be friends. Sometimes friends grow apart, you know."

Her mouth hung open. She looked at me as though I'd said the unthinkable, as though I were someone she never imagined. Then she walked away and I went right back to listening to Jessica Fargas's crazy story.

--------------------

"NEXT FRIDAY'S the big night," Kim yelled. We were driving east on Sunset Boulevard with the windows down. "Brick's wife is going out of town with the kids."

I'd seen Brick Tyler on *Fantasy Island* the week before, playing an aging leading man who was constantly being passed over for serious roles. "I can act, Mr. Roarke," he whined, unconvincingly. In other words, he played himself. My problem with him was simple: he was too much of a Man, not enough of a Guy. The distinction was subtle, but to me very important. Men treated women with reverence, called them "ladies." Guys approached the opposite sex with caution, and rarely called. Men knew what they wanted, or at least pretended to. Guys drifted, were lost children who knew largely their own pain. Men bore their problems stoically. Guys turned their lives into chaos. It wasn't as clear as that, but Burt

Reynolds was a man, Warren Beatty was a guy. James Garner, Michael Landon, Lee Majors: all men. John Travolta, Al Pacino, Martin Sheen: guys. Kim liked men, I liked guys, and that, I believe, explained why, whenever she talked about letting Brick deflower her, I couldn't help thinking he'd be my last choice for the job.

At Foothill we turned left and climbed until we turned left again, passing ever northward through the grand stone arch into Trousdale Estates. It was my first time going under. After just moments on the pretty twisting road we turned off sharply, stopping head-to-head with a classic white Rolls and a bright red Lamborghini. We were barely out of the car when two small white dogs came running and barking into the driveway. "Wait for Mommy," a voice followed from the house. Natalie, Kim's stepmom, actually looked the part, all in white, her dyed hair more alabaster than blond.

"Hello, babies! Hello, Tikki and Dede." Kim greeted the panting doggies. Natalie and I exchanged friendly smiles.

"Hi," she said to me, extending a limp wave before draping her strengthless arms around Kim. I caught sight of her impossibly long fingernails, each painted marshmallow white and carefully appliquéd with a yellow flower. They curled, fanglike, against Kim's back.

Natalie stepped toward me and touched my arm. "I've heard so much about you." I graced her with my best smile. I offered a reciprocal pat. There was no question but that the two of us would get along. It was a foregone conclusion, based upon the importance to me of Kim's friendship. But privately—meaning behind my smiling face—I found her unsettling. She had dark brown eyes, for one thing. She was a brown-eyed brunette, and all the chemicals in the world couldn't change that. I would also have bet there was a strong, clear voice underneath the breathless half-whisper she favored. It didn't matter, of course. She was nice enough, but her fragility seemed as imported as the water she drank.

Luckily, Natalie neither wanted nor expected us to visit with her. After the three of us came inside she suggested Kim and I take our things up to the guest room. Halfway up the stairs, we met Kim's father.

"You didn't tell me she was such a beauty," he said, extending his hand to me. "It's a pleasure to meet you, Meredith." He had a high, nasal voice and hair like an old Brillo pad, but there was a self-assured sexiness in his eyes. "You can call me Art, but only if you promise to dance with me later." They were throwing a big party that night.

"You got it, Art." Flirting with him was effortless, as though we'd been doing it, unharmed, for years.

"I'm on my way down to give Nat a hand. I'll see you girls in a while."

"Wait till you see the guest room," Kim murmured before entering the first room at the top of the stairs.

It was a deep purple fantasy, done up like an Arabian tent. I don't know how, but the satin walls were convex, covered with pleated fabric that gathered under large central "buttons," like throw pillows. The ceiling was the same, resembling the underside of a hot-air balloon, only its billowing folds converged at a huge golden tassel suspended low enough over the bed to be menacing. Would I actually be able to sleep beside Kim in that room?

"I feel like I'm inside Barbara Eden's bottle on *I Dream of Jeannie*."

She gave me a look, her left eyebrow rising. "Just don't make any jokes about it around Natalie."

The house was small, nothing special, but when we took a long trail of steps from one of the living areas down to the poolhouse, the magnificence of the location became clear. We were high on a mountainside overlooking the vast hills and far reaches of east Los Angeles. Kim pointed out the Hollywood sign directly across from us many canyons away, though it was virtually unrecognizable from our oblique angle.

I checked out the poolhouse, which contained a bathroom, a wet bar, and a pool table. It smelled of cigars, and, from the photos of Art and his associates on the walls, was clearly his domain. Walking through it made me feel slightly intoxicated, as though I'd arrived at a ritzy resort for the weekend where anything could happen. Even the swimming pool was lavish. It wasn't your standard rectangle or kidney bean, plastered white and filled with water. It was a tropical cove complete with islands of pretty plants and flowers, and two small wooden bridges crisscrossing its stepped progress. Lucky Kim, I kept thinking. What a life.

As we lay in the sun, our bodies greasy with Bain de Soleil, I tried to imagine how Natalie did simple things with those nails of hers. How did she peel an orange, dial a phone, masturbate? Soon, the baking heat and random sounds of afternoon lulled me into a fantasy of being alone there with Kamran in the full brightness of day, me in my bikini, my head thrown back toward the beating sun, him staring at the tightly clad areas of my body with an uncontrollable urge to get underneath the fabric.

"What do you call a guy with no arms and no legs?" The voice came from directly in front of us. Both Kim and I shaded our eyes to squint at the tall, good-looking guy looming in swim trunks. He was eyeing me.

"Mat," Kim said.

"Oh, you already heard it."

"In second grade, Scott. Say hi to my friend, Meredith." He was Kim's older brother, a student at UCLA, and he kept checking me out.

For months I'd been pressing my hands together in front of my chest several times a day, exerting all the force I could, with no place for it to go but my bust. It was called isometrics and it worked. I had developed shapely little breasts, though my mother claimed they would have come anyway. Brought together in a bikini top they almost created cleavage.

"She looks like Linda, don't you think?" Scott said.

"You're so full of it." Kim put her head back down and closed her eyes.

"I'm not. She really does."

"Who's Linda?" I said.

"My ex-girlfriend." I couldn't believe how much male attention I was getting that afternoon, first from Art, then from his son. And later, at the party, I flirted with three guys from UCLA. Art, whom I danced with a couple of times, made very sure I understood I was on my way to becoming irresistible. "In another year or two, forget it!" he hollered, twisting tastefully to "Disco Inferno."

The party was unusual for its mix of generations. There were Art's friends and associates. He was forty-six. Natalie's friends. She was twenty-nine. Scott and his friends. He was twenty. And Kim and me, the only high-schoolers, or so I thought. I was trying out the sushi, which had been ordered in abundance because it was Natalie's new favorite food, when I saw her outside with an interesting-looking guy. Not one of Scott's friends, judging from his zebra-striped blazer and wild brown curls. He was younger than Scott's group, or rather, less interested in appearing adult. She was speaking and he was clearly listening but also taking in the sights and sounds around them. I popped another piece of California roll in my mouth and decided it was the air of alertness that I liked about the guy, the bemused curiosity just behind his sharp, intelligent features. When his roaming eyes discovered mine watching him, he raised his hand and calmly waved. Curious, Natalie turned, then summoned me.

It was a classic handoff. She introduced us, then excused herself to take care of something. Not that Chester or I noticed her departure. "That's really your name?" I said. "The one your parents gave you?"

"What kind of question is that? Where did you learn to mingle, in juvenile detention?"

I laughed, touching the fringe on the scarf around his neck. "Nice. Makes you look very sophisticated. What are you, an artist or something?"

He lifted the scarf and tickled the tip of my nose with it. "You're adorable, you know that? Sharp as a wooden spoon, but a cutie." Again,

Chester made me laugh, which seemed to make him more confident. He had large light-green eyes, and small lips that twitched on the verge of laughing or speaking. Thinking lips. Busy lips. Sensual and pink and bud-like. In no time we were wandering off to the poolhouse to smoke the doobie in his pocket. I hadn't heard that term before, except in conjunction with the band, the Doobie Brothers.

"Please," Chester said. "I see I'm going to have to teach you about music. That makes music and mingling so far, right?" We were both jiggling pretty hard with laughter.

"Did I say I liked them?"

"You called them a band. That's bad enough."

The poolhouse was full of people, so we ended up off by ourselves on the diving board, right over the water, facing the sprawling lights of L.A. I'd smoked pot three times, and only felt it the third, after learning to inhale and hold the smoke down. Chester handled the doobie expertly, smoking it as casually as a cigarette. There was a caring, almost paternal quality about the way he watched me smoke his pot. His approving eyes made me feel our connection stretched further back than twenty minutes and further forward than I was ready to think about.

I took one hit to his three or four, and soon the doobie was gone. All the same, I was the one who got queasy, who panicked as soon as the cannabis took hold in my bloodstream.

"Go with it," Chester said. "Don't fight it."

I closed my eyes and immediately the blackness began racing around me. I thought I was going to throw up or fall off the diving board, but just when I couldn't take it anymore, stasis. The spinning completely ceased and I entered what turned out to be a very good and long-lasting high.

"I know Natalie." Chester was explaining how he had come to be at the party. "I work at the Beverly Hills library and she comes in a lot."

"*Natalie* does?"

He nodded.

"You're a *librarian*?" Everything coming out of my mouth sounded unbelieving and hysterical. I felt big-faced, a jack-o'-lantern. I told myself to calm down, act cool, get a grip. I wondered why he didn't seem stoned.

"I'm only seventeen, Meredith. I'm a clerk after school."

"Oh." I started to ask him another question but couldn't remember it and ended up giggling.

"Look at the whirlybird. She's flying. She's transcontinental. No more weed for you."

"Stop it. Wait. I had a question."

"I had a quest on, too, but then I met you and all my quests were canceled." He talked fast, as though he were singing, turning language into song-thoughts. I stared at his face in amazement and found myself thinking, I'm falling in love with this weirdo. Then I got up, restless. "I think I need to move a little."

"Want to take a tour of the house?" Chester peered deeply into my eyes. I had no idea where Kim was at that moment. When last I'd seen her she was dancing with a handsome, conservatively dressed friend of her brother's who had all but attached himself to her. He wasn't my type, of course. Too straight, stiff.

I showed Chester the guest room, then we headed for what could only be the master bedroom. Without hesitation, he opened the fully shut door at the end of the hallway and drew me in, closing it behind us. "What are you doing?" I whispered, thrilled. It was like playing Sanchez with Peter.

The lights were on, even in the closets, but it was just a regular-looking bedroom, no theme, no garish colors.

Chester disappeared into the bathroom. "Get your heinie in here, Miss Herman," he called. "You've got to see this."

I found him in a huge heart-shaped bathtub as red and shiny as Art's Lamborghini. His arms were stretched along the sunken rim. "Care to join me?" Chester patted the seat beside him. I stepped forward.

"Is it dry?"

"As the Sahara."

Our eyes were at floor level, our shoulders and thighs cozy against each other in the tub. "Very romantic," I joked.

"It is." His face turned ardent as he shifted his body toward mine. "I'm dying to kiss you."

It was the first real kiss of my life, perfectly soft and gentle. Then, without warning, Chester's tongue dived inside my mouth like a warm animal squirming away from the sun.

"What?" He drew back.

My eyes had popped open with disgust.

"It's so wet."

He looked wounded at first, then his face turned inquisitive.

"Haven't you ever been kissed?"

"Not like that."

Starting over, he slowed way down, worked in short, dry intervals that ended with the tip of his tongue venturing a little farther into my mouth, each time remaining longer. He fed me kisses like a bird tending its young and I strained my head to meet his winding tongue. Soon, I was floating out through space.

"You're a good kisser." He looked at me adoringly.

The outer door opened and someone entered the bedroom, so we hurriedly resumed our side by side positions, looking perfectly respectable except for being in that tub. Kim appeared and just stared. Before I could think what to say, Chester patted the empty seat on his other side. "C'mon down. We're discussing OPEC in here, and the whole Egypt-Israel peace thing. What's your opinion?"

She glared. Chester pretended not to notice. "Or we could talk about *Close Encounters of the Third Kind*. I'm easy."

He seemed like a big jerk from Kim's point of view, and I could see how she would get that idea. He was trying way too hard.

"Sorry." I stood up. "We were just goofing around. We've only been in here a couple minutes. I'm kind of stoned. Is everything okay?"

"I spent the last twenty-five minutes looking for you."

"Stagflation!" Chester yelled. "Now there's a good topic."

"Your friend's a real riot," she added.

I didn't know what to say. She had suddenly drawn a line I wasn't ready to cross. Sensing this, she shook her head—"Sorry I bothered"— and left.

I sat back down, moaning. "I think we should get out of here."

Chester didn't budge. "Who was that?"

"This is her father's house and I'm her guest."

"Where's her proctologist? There's something up her butt that needs removing."

"I'm leaving." I said it but didn't get up. "I need to go talk to her."

"Don't leave me."

"Why shouldn't I? You're bugging me, you know. I want to go outside."

He stood up and stuck out his hand. "C'mon."

I didn't move. "Where?"

"Wherever you want." It occurred to me I wanted to go anyplace that didn't include him, wanted to shake him off, make him disappear. "You're really mad. I didn't mean to make you mad, mad Meredith."

I took his hand and got up. He was bummed out, and so, of course I began wanting to cheer him up. Our faces took a meeting which ended in a kiss, then another and another. I whispered in his ear, "Kim has anorexia."

That night I learned to play eight ball, to rack the balls good and tight and explode them with one focused jolt from my biceps. I learned that what Art and Chester called "slop"—a ball going in by chance rather than design—I considered the inevitable random magic of the universe. I wasn't bad for a novice. Art complimented my smooth stroke and Chester said I had a natural feel for the physics. What pleased me most was the gliding motion of the balls, which seemed to rumble over the soft green felt, knocking each other with a sexy little clack. The colors and numbers gave them each personalities, and I admit I felt pretty powerful turning the corners of that table, cue stick in hand, looking for my next shot while Art and Chester watched.

At one in the morning Art went back to the house. Almost immediately thereafter, Chester produced another doobie, which he lit and quickly toked as casually as scratching his head.

I declined any more. "How often do you smoke it?"

"Three or four times a day." His eyes spiked wide as he waited for my reaction.

"So, you're always high?"

"To me it just feels normal."

He snuffed out the joint and put it away. Watching Chester, I began to think he was some sort of genius. He was so smart and quick, so creative and well-informed and unique. His attachment to pot concerned me, but I was damned impressed he functioned so well under its influence.

"So, that was Arthur," he said. "I've been curious about him for a while." The relationship between Natalie, the twenty-nine-year-old powdered doughnut from Trousdale Estates, and Chester, the seventeen-year-old smart kid from the library, baffled me.

"She's a lonely lady, Natalie. She doesn't have anyone she can talk to, so she talks to me."

"What does she talk about?"

"It's what she doesn't talk about, angel face. She talks about Art and her dogs, and wanting to learn Spanish, and blabity blah. She talks about the way she used to be when she was my age. She has a special laugh. I can make her laugh. We bring each other little gifts, clippings from the paper, funny cartoons, stories."

I didn't want to hear about Natalie anymore, so I asked about his college plans. "What plans? I'm going to Europe, my dear, to fart around awhile. How do you like them plantains?"

Europe was meant for someone like him. Suddenly I felt a sad, inexplicable longing. "What about a career? Have you thought about what you want to be when you grow up?" He studied me, suspiciously, then poked my belly.

"Yes. In fact, I plan to be a psychologist . . . and a jazz piano player. And what about you?"

I drew a blank. All I could imagine at that moment was living in a beautiful house with my psychologist/musician husband. When I didn't answer, Chester kissed me some more, then said it was time for him to go. He wrote down my phone number and talked of going on a picnic where he would feed me grapes and serenade me on his harmonica. I stayed alone in the poolhouse after he left, my eyes closed, a smile stretching my face.

"There you are!" Kim welcomed me back to the party with a hug. "I'm sorry for being a bitch. You know I love you." We held each other tightly, then said our good-nights to Art and Natalie before retreating to the guest room.

"I thought Chester was a party crasher," she said, lying beside me in the darkness of our padded harem, our bodies sucked centerward by the all-consuming featherbed. "That's why I was so rude." I told her to forget about it.

"I mean, he's not your average guy, and you were getting pretty cozy with him, so I was a little worried."

"He's definitely different." My glee was blessedly concealed by the dark.

"Anyway, I finally found out Natalie invited him, and she told me his story."

"According to Chester, they're pretty good friends," I said.

"Well, according to Natalie, he needs all the friends he can get." Kim rolled onto her back and I had to struggle to keep from tumbling into her. "She said he's sweet and super-smart, but kind of an outcast. People don't like him because he thinks he's above it all."

Natalie had said this? I went rigid, was suddenly wide awake with adrenaline. "How come she invited him?"

"She likes him. She also feels sorry for him. She said he just needs to grow up."

The idea that I'd just spent most of my evening with—kissed!—the one guy no one liked was suddenly excruciating. My chest tightened as I began to see what I'd perhaps missed earlier: that Chester was an arrogant, flashily clad jerk passing himself off as Mr. Cool.

"I hope I'm not spoiling anything. Do you really like him, Meredith?"

I recalled him breezily talking about Art and Natalie as if they were his research subjects. And how he had trashed the Doobie Brothers, whom I kind of liked. I began to realize I'd been duped, taken in by a verbose, clever little creep.

"I don't know," I said. "He was fun to hang out with, but maybe that's because I was stoned."

"Did you guys kiss?"

"God, no! I'm not that crazy." It was a nightmare. I'd gotten myself tangled up with the exact wrong person at the party, had let everyone see me with him. It was humiliating, and I couldn't sleep for having let myself be such an idiot. Over and over, I privately vowed never to see or talk to Chester again, no matter what that happy girl back at the poolhouse thought she wanted.

———

MY FATHER STARTED a beard. Like the hairs on his head, the ones on his face came in dark and thick. "It's sexy," my mother said, studying him while the two of us struggled through my algebra. The telephone rang and she left the room, even though there was a phone right behind us. "I don't want to disturb you," she called back, sweetly, but we could hear her bright voice almost as easily in the kitchen.

"What time is the terrorist coming over?" my father said when she returned.

"Very funny. As a matter of fact, 'the terrorist' is busy tonight."

"That's right, I think there's a flag burning down at the Federal Building."

"You're terrible." She giggled.

That was the night our father asked to come back home. Peter and I, posted in our usual spot at the top of the stairs, heard everything.

"Robert," my mother whined, as though he were trying to get around an unwritten rule. "I don't know, I don't know."

"You're not serious about Kamran, are you?"

Peter and I looked at each other. She was gaga about the guy.

"I've only known him a month."

"I really think we made a mistake, Leigh. I miss you, babe."

They kissed, then my mother said, "Let's think about it, okay? And talk some more. It's a confusing time for me."

"Well, don't take too long."

"What's that supposed to mean?"

"I don't know. I honestly don't."

"Think they'll get back together?" Peter said, once our father had left and our mother went into the kitchen to use the phone. At that particular moment I didn't much care. I was used to them being apart, to the limbo. I felt sorry for my father but my life was growing easier, happier with them separated, because my mother was simply too busy, or love-struck, or both, to be on my case.

"Judith?" She was loud and clear from the kitchen phone. "Help. Robert's being wonderful, but he wants to come back home. Sure, it's great, he's great, as long as there's another man in the picture." And just like that the conversation shifted to their favorite subject. "God, Judith, he's pure poetry." She lowered her voice, and we heard lascivious snickering. Then she shared a story Kamran had told her about peacocks, how the male singles out a female, arraying his full plumage before advancing on her with all he's got.

"What am I supposed to do with that?" My mother sighed. "He apparently learned a great deal from watching birds."

amran lived in the back of Obla Dada, his own gallery in Venice Beach. The public part was full of sunlight and paintings, gorgeous Persian rugs and Kamran's dazzling creations, but the back was nothing—a room with a concrete floor, makeshift kitchen, and cramped, industrial-quality bathroom. Kamran had added one or two nice touches, namely a magnificent four-poster bed that floated in the center of the room like an antique ship. Still, the floor was gritty with dirt, the walls bare. Across an alley, in back, was the studio. That's where my mother and I were standing, arms folded, looking down at Kamran and his blowtorch on the floor. He was turning a rod of metal into a gnarled vine that would one day be a floor lamp.

"I miss you," my mother said, as a cascade of red-hot sprinkles shot like water from the torch. I watched them bounce on the ground and go out. The metal, where he worked, became silver and shiny, looked hammered, textured.

"You want to try it?" Kamran held the blowtorch out to me. "I will show you what to do."

"No, she doesn't want to try it," my mother snapped. Kamran studied her.

"A sense of humor is so important, Leigh." That's when she told me to wait inside the gallery.

"Why haven't you called?" I heard on my way out, followed by a dismissive puff of air from Kamran.

"I've been busy. It's crazy, Leigh. Every day I'm getting more orders. It's great, but then I have six lamps to make."

I wandered around the gallery while a friend of Kamran's jabbered away on the telephone in Farsi. He wasn't sexy like Kamran. He had wild gray hair and a big round face that smiled at me when I entered. I found myself drawn to a table lamp fashioned after a purple-red flower. The base had been intricately welded into a meandering stem that, in Kamran's hands, had become so tortured and delicately expressive it made me hurt a little.

"You like that lamp," the man, interrupting his phone call, yelled across the room. It wasn't a question. I met his eyes, his open, friendly face. "I saw you looking."

"It's nice."

He laughed, as though he could see right through my phony reserve. "Kamran's pretty good, uh?"

Just then, my mother and Kamran came into the gallery arm-in-arm. She was happy again—big surprise. He'd probably kissed her or patted her bottom, or said something mysterious and stirring. He knew how to bring things to life. The man got off the phone.

"Have you met Miss Meredith?" Kamran addressed his friend. Then, to me, "Meredith Herman, meet Moh. Moh is my business manager." The two of them laughed, an inside joke, apparently. "Moh keeps me from going broke." More laughs. Kamran led my mother to the front door and, fixing her with his lady-killing stare, said, "I will call you later." Then he turned her wrist to his lips and placed a row of kisses inside her arm, all the way to the eye of her elbow. "I hope to see you tonight."

In the car I was still thinking about that flower lamp, wondering how I could get my mother to make Kamran give it to her. "I like that place," I said. "His store is really nice. I saw about ten things I wouldn't mind owning."

"Hush, will you? I can't hear myself think."

At the market, where we went next, she bought a lot of fancy fruit—pineapple, melon, berries, and Kamran's favorite, mangoes. She bought some cheese and flatbread, and as soon as we got home, arranged a big platter that sat in the refrigerator with a sign: DO NOT TOUCH! Never mind the roses that were waiting for her when we got home, two dozen long-stemmed beauties. "Shit," was all she had to say when she read the card from my father.

"I want the two of you to keep out of sight when Kamran gets here, all right?" Peter and I had just finished our dinner. "You can watch TV upstairs or do your homework, just please give us some privacy."

"What's with the fruit tray?" Peter said. "Is it his birthday or something?"

"And stay off the telephone, too, until I hear from him."

"Do they celebrate birthdays in Iran? I mean, like we do?" Peter continued.

"It's not Eye-ran, it's Ee-rrahn," I said.

"It's not his birthday," my mother said. "I just want to make it special." Then she lifted her hands up high and snapped as though she were holding castanets. "A little romance, you know what I mean?"

The thing my mother failed to grasp was that Peter and I had no interest in knowing her this way. We didn't want to think about her boyfriend, or have to see her lips curl into a simper at the thought of him.

Be a mother, we wanted to protest. Have some dignity. If nothing else, please shut up.

The phone rang and she sprang from the table, all brightness and delusion. It took her several moments to understand it was her husband calling, not her lover, and that he wanted to know how she liked her roses.

"I was just about to call you," she lied, seamlessly switching into warm receptivity. "So beautiful, Robert. So thoughtful of you, sweetheart."

Peter and I watched her spoon-feed him hope, even though he was tying up the phone and keeping her from loverman. "I know," she listened, her face taut with impatience, her voice calm and reassuring. "Yes, I think I'm starting to feel that way too." She closed her eyes. "Well, we'll just have to see about that." Then a tinge of rebuke entered her tone. "Just what I said. Let's wait a bit longer, okay? Don't pressure me about Valentine's Day, Robert. Look, I have to get off. I'm expecting a phone call. I will think about it, yes."

My mother took a bubble bath, got all dressed up, and burned incense in her bedroom. She positioned the roses where Kamran would be certain to notice them. She put on her Middle Eastern record and switched back into blue jeans. Her hair kept changing looks.

"Now she's playing Phoebe Snow," I said, coming into Peter's room and closing the door behind me. He was watching *The Waltons*. I climbed on his bed and quickly lost interest in the drama taking place inside our house. John and Olivia Walton were the only parents I wanted to deal with. A half hour later, as the members of the Waltons called good-night to each other in the country darkness and calm, my mother knocked at, then opened, Peter's door. She had changed into her red jumpsuit and heels.

"Who wants to make an easy dollar?"

"I do!" Peter and I both cried out.

"One of you has to call up Kamran's studio. If he answers, just say, 'Sorry, wrong number.' "

"That's it?" I said. "Why can't you do that?"

"I'll do it!" Peter jumped up, and just like that I was out of the running.

The three of us went into my mother's bedroom. They ran through what he was supposed to say, and the kind of voice he should use not to sound like a kid. "But I doubt he's there," she said. "If he were there he would have called by now, unless he's working and lost track of the time—the bastard. Ready, sweetie?"

Peter dialed and cleared his throat. My mother and I held our breath. "Sorry, wrong number," he said, using a gruff, theatrical voice.

"You're sure it was him? It couldn't have been anyone else?" she fretted.

Peter was sure.

"Well, that's it. It's over." She slumped. Her eyes lost their joy.

I have a memory from that night, though I'm not sure if it really happened or I dreamed it. I believe I awoke to the sound of voices in the house. And movements, like wrestling, on the stairs. I heard my mother's laugh, then a man shush her. They struggled. She said no in a muted voice. I got out of bed and tiptoed to the door. On the other side I heard Kamran's rich voice say, "At first it hurts, yes, but after that I guarantee you will like it. Let me try." She murmured no again, and then more wrestling up the stairs. I could hear their bodies brushing the walls, their elbows knocking the metal banister, then they fell hard onto the carpet. There was more laughter. "Relax," he told her. "Relax, and it will be beautiful." She made a choking sound, followed by a whimpering that filled me with fear. There was no more banging around after that, just low moaning and then silence. I'm unclear about the veracity of this memory, because the next morning, when I asked where Kamran was, she said, rather convincingly, "Kamran?" I said I thought he'd been over. "Nope," she swallowed.

----------

THE FRIDAY BEFORE Valentine's Day, Kim kept to her word. She entered Brick Tyler's house a virgin and when she left she took a small piece of him with her. At least that's how I saw it. If she'd been pure before— unmingled and blank—she now had a bit of color, a touch of other added in. The night she told me all about it I watched her eat for the very first time, saw her consume an entire quart of extra-rich Pistachio Swirl.

"I never should have told him I was a virgin." She wrapped her tongue around the frosty, pliant confection. She ate as she did everything: with sexy enjoyment. "Once he knew, he freaked. He was so worried about getting in trouble." She groaned. "Plus, I wanted it hard, you know? He was so gentle and careful, it was kind of a bummer."

About his penis she said, in answer to my questions, "Well, obviously it felt big, but what do I know? It was my first one." She stopped eating suddenly. "Get this. After we did it he says, 'How come you lied about being a virgin?' I didn't know what he was talking about. 'Your hymen was broken,' he says. Uh, duh, I use tampons, idiot."

Kim rolled her eyes, then laughed, wickedly. "The second time we did it was better. He was more relaxed, and I was starting to get the hang of it. I guess it was pretty good. Anyway, I got devirginized."

That was the important thing, her entry into the ranks of those in-the-know. I felt it separate us. She'd done this major thing, sexual intercourse, and would probably do it again soon with someone else.

"Maybe I should try it," I said. It had changed Kim so little, wasn't at all the big deal everyone made it out to be.

"Nah, wait till you're sixteen. It's the perfect age. Then you can drive."

---------------------

TWO DAYS BEFORE Valentine's, my mother hadn't heard a word from Kamran. A week had passed without contact, the longest they'd gone since meeting the month before. She was running on empty, scared her joyride would soon be over for good.

"Looks like I'll be spending Valentine's Day with your father," she told Peter and me Tuesday night at dinner. It was as if she were trying out the idea, seeing if uttering the dreaded words might hasten an intervention by the gods of romance and send Kamran to the telephone. There was only silence. With a fresh face and upbeat sigh, she said, "Now, I want to hear all about you two. Tell me what's new at school." She folded her forearms on the table and waited, a tense smile on her face.

Peter started telling her about Mr. Waliff, his science teacher, who paused during his sentences so many times you couldn't remember what he was talking about.

"Sometimes he just goes, 'Uhhhhh,' for like, I don't know how long. It's hard to stay awake."

My attention shifted from Peter, who knew how to tell a story and did great impersonations, to my mother, who, no matter how hard she tried to focus on others, always looked a bit vacant. Peter and I were used to talking for each other's entertainment while our mother observed as if from a distance. It wasn't her fault her children didn't particularly interest her. She was different from other moms in that way. You almost felt sorry for her for being so bad at it.

"It'll be nice going out with your father on a date," she said when Peter finished. "Don't you think?"

"Yep." He tried not to mind that she hadn't heard a word of his story, but he minded anyway.

"And Meredith?" She turned her attention to me. "What's new in your busy world?" I was about to talk when she added, "And, please, go slowly and enunciate. There's no need to hurry."

This annoyed me, since my mother's limited attention span was the specific cause of my tendency to race through stories. "I might get to work on the yearbook," I said. "There was a meeting today—"

"That's terrific." She cut me off, standing up to clear the table. I stood up, too, to help. "It's really hard if you're a freshman, but Mr. Dorion said everyone should try. He's the photography teacher. He said it just depends on how good your stuff is."

She began energetically wiping down the table. "I figure I'll bring my camera to school from now on. You never know when something spontaneous will happen."

"Good," she said, leaving the sponge in the center of the table and crossing to the phone on the wall, pressing the buttons with well-practiced fingers. That *Twilight Zone* feeling came over me as I entertained the possibility that I wasn't really there with her, that this was the reason my mother couldn't see or hear me.

"Guess who?" she said. With Kamran she had to be careful about her tone, delicate with her demands. He was an altogether different sort of man from my father, which was how you could easily tell which one she was talking to.

*Mama, it's me,* I imagined my spirit-world self pleading, to no avail. *Me, can't you see me, Mama? It's Meredith. I'm back.*

In the *Twilight Zone* version, of course, she wouldn't be talking to Kamran. She'd be making funeral arrangements as a result of the recent tragic death of her only daughter, Meredith.

"What if I come to you? I could come later, when you're done working. I don't care how late it is. You didn't used to be too tired for me."

It was time for her to give up if she wanted to preserve the illusion she'd created of herself as an on-the-go, liberated lady. But she couldn't help herself. "Look, Kamran, there's someone else, isn't there? No, you don't. You don't care what I need." He was finally seeing the woman my father knew so well. She could be a dance or a beating, my mother. It was only a matter of time before one side met the other. "You know what? Don't strain yourself," she peaked, before hanging up on him. For a strange, suspended moment we stared at each other.

"I'm sorry, sweetheart. What were you saying?" I told her never mind and left the room.

Kamran refused to be extinguished like one of her cigarettes and called right back. I have no idea what sort of speech he delivered, only that it lasted at least two minutes, and every time she tried to get a word in she was instantly stifled. Finally, she was allowed to beg his forgiveness, which, though a long time in coming, was eventually hers. "I didn't mean it. I'm a little crazy tonight. You're not mad? Forget I said it, darling. I don't know why you put up with me. Promise you forgive me. Will you call tomorrow? You know, Thursday is Valentine's Day. Oh . . . how long will you be away? Okay, tomorrow is fine. Yes, I will. Talk to you tomorrow. Bye-bye." Sometime later that night she called my father and accepted his dinner invitation for Thursday.

It wasn't any surprise Kamran never called again. The real surprise was my mother's reaction. Instead of letting it get her down, she clung to a prideful new perkiness. She played Nina Simone's "I Hold No Grudge" over and over on the record player, and by the time my father showed up Thursday night bearing a fresh supply of red roses, she had gained a new appreciation for his unwavering loyalty.

"How much do you want to bet he spends the night?" Peter said, as soon as they left the house. We were standing around the roses.

"This is it," I agreed. "I say he spends the night and moves back in this weekend."

We celebrated in advance with ginger ale, which we pretended was champagne, and guacamole and chips. We enacted several versions of their grand reconciliation, Peter in the role of my father and me doing my mother.

"But what about Kamran?" my brother/father said.

"Oh, him. His dental hygiene left a lot to be desired," my mother/self replied. "And you, Robert? How come you never dated?"

"There's no one as beautiful and sexy as you, Leigh-Leigh, baby."

"Tell it like it is, Tiger."

We put on a Frank Sinatra record and danced cheek-to-cheek as our parents back in love. I was feeling pretty good because earlier that day I'd received a Valentine from Chester. He painted the envelope a wash of colors and taped a picture of Frankenstein to it. The word balloon coming from Frankenstein's mouth said, "Meredith—Good." Inside, he wrote:

```
Roses are flowers,
Violets are, too
I've had 20 showers,
Since the heart tub with you.
        XXX, Chester
```

We'd spoken on the phone since the party, and though I'd avoided making a date, I definitely liked him. The Valentine clinched it. When Peter and I finished goofing around I called Chester and agreed to our first date, a picnic that Saturday.

We didn't see our parents again that night. At eleven or so, the phone rang. They had decided to stay at his place. Peter and I slapped our palms together, then went, as ourselves, to our separate bedrooms.

I was too excited to sleep, so I lay in bed listening to the eerie, siren-like wind outside. A tree branch snapped off and scraped against the house. I attempted to conjure Chester and turn him into my new fantasy guy, but my pillow had only one face: Kamran's. "Listen to the trees," he murmured between kisses, the whites of his eyes opalescent in the dark. "You are beautiful, Meredith. All along it was you I wanted." He pushed apart my legs and quickly entered me. What a feeling it was, so fulfilling and complete. I moved my hips in rhythm with his thrusts. Then he pinned my arms above my head and rocked harder, looking at me with unbelievable fire.

I eventually drifted into a dream of sorts, in which I was on my bicycle, cresting a great hill, about to begin racing down the other side, but as I began to whip along, a rock got caught under my wheel, downing my bike and sending me soaring through the air. I awoke with such a violent convulsion it left me panting.

In the morning they were waiting for us in the kitchen, their arms draped around each other. "We have some news," my mother started. "You tell them, Robert."

"Your mother and I have decided—"

"No! Do the voice."

Hesitant at first, but smiling, my father embarked on a Cockney accent that in all my life I'd never heard from him. "Roht," he began. "Now, then, let's see." He scratched his beard. "What your mum and I are trying to get at is this. We've decided to give it—the mairge an' all that rubbish—another go round, another look-see, if you get m'meaning."

My mother's eyes danced with delight as he spoke.

"You see, if I'd only known your mum 'ad this weakness for foreign blokes-like, well, none a this mess would 'av ever 'appened."

I don't know what Peter made of the performance, but I was dumbstruck. Not only was his voice different, but the accent unlocked in my father a whole new world of facial expressions and arm gestures, until it occurred to me how very much, thanks to his beard, he had come to resemble the indestructible Brit himself, Alan Bates.

"Don't thinka me as your ol' dad, with his stodgy ol' ways. Thinka me as Clive, your new, wildly alive dad."

"All right!" My mother patted his arm. "Enough, enough." And just like that he was Robert Herman again, asking where we wanted to go later for a celebration dinner.

We ended up at Gulliver's in Marina del Rey, where the waitress introduced herself and added, "I'll be your serving wench this evening." Her low-cut, square neckline bared her to us from throat to upthrusting breasts, which appeared to be bursting from her tightly laced bodice. I pretended to study my menu, secretly stimulated by the words "serving wench" and the revealing outfit. When the bottle of red wine came, and my parents both had full glasses in front of them, my father raised his. "Here's to the end of my beautiful wife's midlife crisis. Leigh, honey, you had me scared there. I thought you were never going to snap out of it, sweetheart."

We offered wide, congratulatory smiles and pressed our goblets together until they touched. Then we proceeded to consume juicy red roast beef, creamed corn, and Yorkshire pudding. We got to know our serving wench, who turned out to be a grad student at USC. We had dessert, after which my father poured the last of the wine and made a final toast. "Let's drink to the future." We brought our glasses together again. He looked at my mother. "Here's to Ali Baba finally being out of the picture." They clinked their glasses and smiled at each other. "Just the thought of the guy gave me the creeps, babe. Can I say that now?" My father shook his head, distastefully.

"Kamran," she corrected, watching him.

"Whatever."

My mother looked to me and my brother to see if we shared our father's sentiments. We were already watching her for the same reason. At that moment, Kamran's absence had a strong presence of its own, an echo made by my father's careless words. I recalled the time my mother told Judith she could spend the rest of her life with a man like Kamran.

After dinner we drove back home, pulled out the carousel of red, white, and blue poker chips, and played blackjack and five-card draw for a couple of hours. It felt remarkably normal, as though my father had been back awhile. Before going to bed, Peter and I hugged them both good-night. "You two going to help me move boxes tomorrow?" my father said. I had my picnic with Chester, but Peter happily volunteered to help move my father back in.

----------

ALL THE WINDOWS in my bedroom looked down on our swimming pool. When I awoke the next morning to the sight of Peter carefully trying to open one, he held his finger to his lips and implored me with his large brown eyes to keep quiet. The same finger then pointed to the pool. My bed was directly under the windows, so I only had to sit up to see my mother and father at the water's edge, their backs to us. "Something's up," Peter whispered.

The surveillance of these people, our parents, had become so habitual we didn't even question our right to conduct it. Peter squatted below the open window and, raising the binoculars hanging from his neck, trained them on the figures by the pool, a man and woman under the mistaken impression their conversation was private.

The transmissions began in progress, Peter becoming a human conduit for the near simultaneous broadcast of our parents' conversation. Anything he could overhear or lip-read he delivered verbatim in a hushed monotone. I lay back, closed my eyes, and listened.

—What more can I say? I got carried away.

—This isn't about last night, Robert.

—Well, then, help me out here. I'm lost.

— . . . mistake. I realize that now. I just can't do this.

—Can't do what?

—Any of it. I don't know what kind of life I want but I know this

isn't . . . don't want to . . . can't . . . being laughed at by my husband . . .
understanding, or patient, or bitchy, do you understand?

—Anything you want, babe. We can make it happen together.

—No, we can't, Robert. I don't want to be called babe . . . I . . . I
don't think I love you anymore . . . not sure . . . confused. I think we
should stay separated for now.

—That's bullshit, that's what that is.

—You see, Robert? That's the problem. You call my feelings bullshit.

—No . . . apart is bullshit . . . work it out together. If I leave again,
Leigh, if you make me, I won't be coming back . . . don't do this, please.

Peter said, "I can't hear them anymore. They're practically whispering."

I looked at my brother, his eyes slaves to the binoculars, his attention
galvanized, and realized I didn't want to do this anymore. It wasn't
thrilling, it was perverted. I didn't want to know how bad my parents
were being to each other, and I truly saw that what we were doing was
bad for us in every way. If our parents were fucked up, we were even
worse. Peter resumed broadcasting.

— . . . you're killing me here, you know that?

— . . . grow up, Robert.

—Just tell me, I really want to know when you changed. When did
you become so cold and angry?

"Peter, stop. I don't want to hear it anymore," I said.

"She's turning around," he announced. "She's walking away."

We both heard my father yell, "Beautiful! Just beautiful, Leigh!"
Then my mother came in the back door and went out again through the
front. I sat up. My father's head was lowered, his hulking back strangely
blank, as my mother's Porsche, sounding more like a rocket than a car,
blasted its engine. The car was nothing if not an emblem of my father's

lost power. Alone by the swimming pool, he had to be painfully aware of that. What else could have possessed him to drag, by the tip of his shoe, each and every piece of our blue-and-white patio furniture to the edge of the placid, waiting water? With a final shove, they floated at first, the royal blue canvas turning a wet, velvety black before sinking silently to the bottom.

We turned on the TV in my bedroom as he came inside, and arranged ourselves appropriately so as to appear utterly engrossed in Saturday-morning cartoons. Our father passed right by us on his way to the bedroom. Forty minutes later, he came out and stood at the door. "Look, you two. Your mother and I had a fight. I guess I'm leaving again for a while. When she gets back, tell her . . ." He looked disgusted, but sadly resigned. "Nah, forget it."

We went out to the pool after he left, to see the sunken furniture. "It's kind of cool," I said. It looked ghostly and distorted. If I'd owned an underwater camera, I would have donned my bathing suit and shot a roll.

"Quite dramatic," my mother concluded later that day. Then she went back inside and closed the door, amazingly calm.

"I hate her," Peter said.

A week later, when she was served with divorce papers she said it again. "Quite dramatic." Then she called my father to calm him down.

"Is this really necessary, Robert? You're just angry." He told her he was about to leave the country and preferred not to see any of us for a while. The day he left she called a lawyer of her own. After that she called a math tutor.

Chester approached me with a print dress from the 1950s. "Look what I found for you." He tried to make it sound enticing, though I'd already told him I wasn't buying anything in that smelly place, Muskrat, where he found many of his clothes.

"No thanks."

"It's in perfect condition, only five bucks." He made it dance for me.

The dress was pretty, and probably my size, but I couldn't get into some stranger's old clothes that had been collecting dirt for twenty years.

"Just try it on. I want to see how you look."

"I don't think it's been cleaned."

He held the dress to my body. "This would look so good on you." I said I thought we'd come to get a vest and skinny tie for him to wear that night. The Chester Geller Trio was making its debut at Beverly High's Ice Cream Social.

"Please? I'll buy it for you."

Secretly, I liked having someone in my life to whom it actually mattered what I did, how I looked, where I went. Chester didn't act cool toward me, or detached. I took the hanger, received my peck on the nose, then wandered off to find a dressing room. It was our third date, fourth counting the party at Art and Natalie's, and Chester was still crazy about me. I was clearly *his* fantasy girl, the one he dreamed about at night. He got a look in his eyes when we were together. I knew what it meant, and it made me happy, but I missed the exquisite torture of my own longing, which, it seemed, I could feel only for guys I hardly knew. When I tried to create romantic fantasies around Chester, nothing happened. He was right there, calling me up, eager to see me. It was like wishing for something you already had.

We put my dress and Chester's new clothes in our apartment, AKA Chester's ugly yellow Datsun. It was our favorite place to eat, listen to music, make out, get high. As we drove away from Santa Monica, I had to yell to be heard over the frenzied saxophone music on the stereo. "I feel a little weird just dropping in on your friend."

I pretended to like the worst of his music: cacophonous, antimelodic, improvisational jazz. He said it was an acquired taste, so I tried to understand it, but only grew stronger in my feeling that the "brilliance" Chester spoke of had to do with the uncanny ability of these people to reproduce, musically, the exact experience of a bad headache. "Shouldn't we call ahead?"

"That's how you visit Ross. You just show up. Half the time there's two or three other people already there."

I was excited about meeting Chester's pal, who had recently received a scholarship to a big-deal music school in Boston. Even his name, Ross Cavinaugh, seemed to ring of future stardom. As we parked in front of the house, I imagined album covers bearing his highly respected name.

"Hey, man." Ross opened the door. He had dark wavy hair flowing all the way to his waist, and his gentle, understated style, I quickly decided, was no doubt characteristic of the super-talented.

"This is Meredith, my girlfriend." The word surprised me, as though it had been invented to keep Ross and me apart.

The three of us went into the living room, then struggled to make conversation. That's how it felt to me, but then, I wasn't good at being "low-key" in new situations. Chester pulled out his Baggie of weed and his pipe. Ross picked up his guitar and started fooling around with a jazzy tune. I had no idea what I was supposed to do. The two of them talked about Ross's father, who was in poor health, then they got going about a musician I'd never heard of, which led to a record being put on, then focused silence as they listened to a particular cut. No one looked at me, or spoke to me, and, feeling irrelevant, I began minding the way Chester had dragged me along, an appendage he could place on the couch and ignore. *His* girlfriend. I didn't feel like his anything. When Ross finally looked up, I flashed him my best smile. All my frustration went into it, all my desperate, hungry charms. Ross's confused face was my reward. I held him, spellbound, for a few agitated seconds before he went back to staring at the carpet. Chester, who hadn't noticed any of it, picked up the record jacket and leaned over to explain what we were hearing and why it was worth paying attention to. I pretended to listen, but was ashamed. Poor Chester couldn't have guessed the disloyalty going through my mind. I imagined dumping him for a scrap of his friend's attention. It was a game, of course, something to keep me occupied until we left. It wasn't a game. I thought Ross was cute, and, given his bright future, wanted to make myself memorable.

We stayed less than an hour. Ross and Chester discussed what they would play that night, finalized the time and place to meet Tony, their bass player, then we said good-bye.

"I'm sorry," Chester said as we drove off. "You were bored." He hadn't noticed the sugar in my voice when I said "See you later" to Ross.

That's what knowing Chester was like. He thought the best of himself and his friends.

"Don't." I squirmed when he squeezed my leg. I was angry at him for imagining I was somebody else, somebody better, kinder. He lived in a cloud of marijuana smoke that enabled him to go forward full of self-confidence, unhindered by silly doubts. He threw himself into things and enjoyed life immensely, and all I could do was resent him for it.

"Want to paint?" he said, setting up the watercolors in his bedroom. When I said I didn't know how, he kissed me on the cheek. "Oh goody. Even better." We only had an hour, but in that short time I came to regret every mean thought I'd had about Chester that day. First, he put the Keith Jarrett record I loved on the stereo. Then he sat beside me at his desk and, without much talking, the two of us proceeded to get lost in color. We watched as the paints ran and bled, burst and blended. We moved our brushes into and around each other. We laughed and we hummed and in the process enormous happiness rose within me.

"You're amazing," I said. He'd made me feel safe, a kid at play.

"And you"—he leaned over and kissed me—"are a humdinger." I wanted more kisses, but he wisely denied me, not because he knew it would make me like him more, but because it was time for us to put on our secondhand clothes and get going.

··················

THE PROBLEM, as I understood it, had to do with the name, the Chester Geller Trio, which reflected Chester's efforts to recruit and organize its other two members. And it was a fine name, if your name happened to be Chester Geller. If your name was Ross Cavinaugh or Tony Mann, it was outrageous, conceited beyond belief. That's what they insisted after the concert, which had gone beautifully. Like true pros, Ross and Tony steamed silently until the end. Now the three of them were standing outside the auditorium, shouting.

"The fact you didn't tell either one of us beforehand proves it," Tony said. "You knew it was the wrong thing to do."

"Bullshit," Chester said. "I didn't think you guys cared *what* we were called. It was a one-night gig. Jesus. If we play again we can call ourselves anything you want."

"It's the principle, man," Ross said. Chester rolled his eyes. "No, man, it was arrogant."

Tony added, "You're an egomaniac, Geller."

Chester threw up his arms and walked away, prompting the other two-thirds of the Chester Geller Trio to go home.

"Let's drive to the beach," I said. Poor Chester was practically in tears. He'd played wonderfully and received many compliments, but that only accentuated the sad turn of events.

"I still can't understand why they got so mad at me, you know? What did I do that was so wrong?"

We got in the car. Earlier, I'd sat in the audience, proud of my boyfriend and his trio. Now I was staring out the window at the deserted campus, wondering how I ended up with the fathead who caused all the trouble. I could see their side of it—why couldn't he? He'd been so thrilled to name the group after himself. Why was he denying it? Kim's words came back to me, about him not having friends because he acted above it all. Why hadn't he simply acknowledged their feelings and apologized?

I sighed, and reached across to massage the back of his neck. This sent him into full-blown tears.

"Chester, stop," I heard myself say, removing my hand. My voice wasn't the least bit tender. He continued crying as though he hadn't heard me, and he probably hadn't. He was lost in self-pity. "Look, I'm not having fun, and I think you're being a big baby."

His head snapped up, his wet, incredulous eyes glaring. Then he started the car. After a moment I said, "What are we doing?"

He didn't answer.

"Are you taking me home?"

"You said you weren't having any fun. We can't have that, can we?"

I should have been relieved, but the closer we got to my neighborhood, the more I feared I was just like my mother: monstrous, cruel, unfeminine. I looked at my lap and the pretty dress Chester had bought for me. All evening, I'd felt special wearing it.

"I feel terrible," I blurted, a few miles from home.

He pulled onto a quiet residential street and parked.

"I'm so sorry," I began.

"I'm the one who should apologize. You were right. I am being a baby. I'm often guilty of that." I stared at him. "What?" he said.

"Wow. I didn't expect that."

Chester laughed. I tried to apologize again, but he got a sexy look in his eyes and suggested we retire to the bedroom, meaning the backseat.

It wasn't that I *didn't* want to make out, I just didn't *want* to, especially. The very suggestion surprised me more than it should have—alarmed me, in fact, because I saw there was no getting out of it without upsetting Chester all over again. He was depending on me and this time I didn't want to let him down. I flashed him an equally game smile, then we got out of the car, popped the front seats forward, and climbed in back.

"Can I have some pot?" I said. It was cozy next to Chester, but kind of disconcerting to be parked on that strange street.

"You?" Then he addressed his ever-present invisible audience. "You heard her, folks, she asked for weed, right? I didn't imagine it. You were right here."

"Just because I don't smoke it every couple of hours . . ." I appealed to our faceless fans. Chester prepared a hit for me, then lit the pipe. I sucked in the pungent smoke, looked at him looking at me as I held it down, then relaxed into the seat as I exhaled. Chester's face appeared large before my own.

"She's one in a million, folks." His lips joined mine, delicate and sweet-tasting, then his tongue began a feverish dance in my mouth. He was a great kisser, usually, but that night his tongue felt overlarge and relentless. It seemed tireless in its travels. Still, I very much wanted to make Chester feel good, give him the reassurance he craved, so I resolved to go with it. I listened as he groaned with pleasure. I felt his hot breath on my neck. His hands were like his tongue, restless, determined to arouse. But I remained Little Miss Halfway. Half into it, half out. My body turned on, my mind concerned with who might be lurking outside.

Eons passed. We were both fully clothed. He was grinding hard into my pelvis when a voice in my head announced, This has to stop, he's suffocating you. You're losing it. You're being eaten alive. I became claustrophobic, needed to feel my own body in space, its outline and the air around it. "Stop," I finally said, forcing him off.

"What's wrong?" It was as if he'd been asleep. He seemed groggy and far away.

"I don't know. I feel sick." He stroked my arm until I yanked it away. I imagined hitting him, or throwing a wild, wall-banging tantrum if he touched me again.

"What can I do?" Chester said. I assumed he meant what could he do to fix me so he could get back to consuming my body. I'd lost the ability to see him as anything other than a parasite.

"Just take me home. Please."

He was starting to wake up. "Did I do something wrong, Meredith?"

"I just need to go home now. I need to be alone." Of course it couldn't be that simple, not with the Chester Geller ego. He kept asking me questions, trying to learn what had gone wrong, why I'd turned off. I said it was my problem, and it was, but he insisted on making it worse by trying to fix it and absolve himself there and then. I had no idea how close to the edge I was until I started screaming, hysterically, that I wanted to go home. "Just leave me alone!" I shrieked when he tried to hold me. "Get away from me!"

I was at the front door of my house within five minutes, watching Chester's car disappear down my street. I was glad to see him go, or so I thought, until it dawned on me, weeks later, that he was never coming back.

---

KIM STRETCHED ACROSS her bed like a languid pussycat. "Want to hear a secret about my mother?" She gave me the "prepare yourself" look, then made me wait.

"What is it?"

"She's never had an orgasm."

"That isn't possible." I thought of Diana Adamson's painted lips and sultry voice, her clothes, her style, her tan. It had to be a misunderstanding about the word and its correct meaning. The woman reeked sophistication. "I'm sure she's had at least one," I said.

Kim smiled at my disbelief. "Nope. She told me she's frigid."

I'd read in "Dear Abby" that there were no frigid women, only incompetent men. "What about masturbation?"

"She's tried."

I didn't know what else to say. My mind was undergoing a revolution, making room for the possibility that my understanding of the world wasn't the definitive one. I said, "I guess if you never had one, you wouldn't know what you were missing."

"She says it's why my father left her. She fakes it now, with Ted."

"Wow." I yawned, suddenly sleepy.

So often, we were the only ones in that split-level house of hers. After a night of strutting around Westwood, telling guys our names were Jacqueline and Sophia, we'd land on Kim's twin beds, propped on our elbows in the glow of her pink-shaded lamps, and talk until we couldn't stay awake any longer.

"Oh," Kim remembered, getting up from the bed, "I have something for you." She searched her cluttered jewelry box and came back holding out a silver ring with a pair of clasped hands on it. "Pull them apart."

It was really three rings that moved together and apart, with a single heart at the center. I slipped it on my finger. "This is beautiful."

"I got one, too. The only thing is they're kind of big, but the lady at the store said we could put tape around them. They're friendship rings."

I stared at the loving gift. What was it about jewelry that could make you feel instantly better? You put it on and felt more substantial, less alone in the world, at least for a couple of hours. Kim's ring made me feel more than that, made me feel exalted, doubled.

The next morning, when she dropped me at the curb in front of our house, I encountered Peter coming from the store with several empty cartons. "What are you doing?" I said.

"Getting ready." When I asked what for, he squinted at me. "You'll find out soon enough."

I followed him inside and up the stairs, but when we reached his bedroom he said, "From now on, my room is off-limits. If you want to come in, you'll need a passport."

"What the hell are you talking about?"

"I'm going to make them. Show it at the door and I'll sign you in, if I feel like it."

He was still on the topic at dinner, telling my mother and me that his bedroom was now booby-trapped. "So I'll know if either of you try to violate the perimeter."

"Eat your lima beans," she told him.

"I'm serious. You could get hurt if you come in my room."

"What's your problem?" I barked. "No one wants to go in your stupid room."

My mother changed the subject, said she was going to a restaurant in Beverly Hills after dinner to have a drink with a friend.

"A singles bar," Peter sneered.

"Don't be rude," she warned him. "And finish your lima beans."

My father had been out of the country three weeks. A single postcard had made its way to us from Rome. Addressed to Peter and me, it pictured a fountain with naked, godlike men reclining at every corner beside charging horses, all carved in white stone. "Greetings from Roma," it read, "Love, Pop." Peter claimed it as his personal property and I didn't see it again.

"Can I be excused?" I said when the phone rang. My mother got up to answer it. It was Aunt Eve.

She covered the mouthpiece with her hand. "Your brother's still eating."

"No I'm not." Peter pushed away from the table and stood by his chair, the lima beans glistening in front of him. "I'm done."

"It's called the Ginger Man," she told her sister, commanding Peter with stern finger and bulging eyes to sit back down and do as he was told. "Supposed to be a very posh place. Maybe I'll meet someone."

Peter defiantly left the room.

The next afternoon, my brother handed me a card made of posterboard and said, "Here's your passport." It had my name and a bunch of little squares he'd painstakingly drawn in neat rows. "Every time you visit my room, I'll punch a hole through one of these squares."

I studied the card. "What is the point of this? I've already been in your room three times today."

Peter never learned. He could be played with like an insect. "That room is booby-trapped," he argued. "I would have known if you snuck in."

I tortured him with a smug little laugh. "That's what you think. I know what you're up to in there." His eyes flashed wildly.

"Liar. You're full of it."

I smiled, though I sensed I was losing my edge. There was nothing else to do. I ripped up my passport and salted his head with the bits.

In mid-March another postcard came, this time from Lisbon. "Back in a couple weeks—Pop." Peter showed it to Uncle Pinky the Sunday morning he and Aunt Eve came by with a feast. While Pinky studied the photo of the Portuguese castle, Peter whispered in his ear.

"Well, I'd do the same thing myself," Pinky replied. Then he winked at me.

They were glamorous people, my aunt and uncle, not just because they had more money than we did, or traveled, or gave a lot of parties. They were glamorous because they knew how to enjoy these things. "Some people are too stupid to be depressed," my mother had said after one of their visits, years ago. "It's easy to be happy when you don't think about anything." To which my father had said nothing, as usual.

Eve and I organized the spread on the dining room table. They brought roast beef and turkey, Swiss cheese, bagels, coffee cake, and potato salad. "Look at you," she said, "look at that gorgeous young skin. I hate you, you know." Our love affair was long-standing. I treasured her sunny nature and kind words, and most especially the arms she wrapped around me without fail every time we saw each other, though I'm not sure what she loved about me, other than the fact that I was her sister's child.

"Elliot will be home for spring break next week," Pinky said once we'd all sat down to eat. "What about a family exodus to Disneyland next Sunday. Leigh, are you up for it?"

"Oh yes, say yes, please yes," chanted Peter, begging.

"Our treat, of course," Eve added. "The kids can invite a friend."

"Yes, don't say no, say yes, please, please," Peter continued. "Pretty please, peas and carrots, please and thank you—"

"Stop it, Peter!" my mother snapped. "You're acting like a moron."

"Can we, huh? Can we go? Can we go? Huh? Huh?" He held his hands up like doggie paws, and started panting, his tongue hanging out. The rest of us laughed.

"I think he wants to go," Pinky said. Peter began whimpering in agreement.

"I'm warning you," my mother said.

"All right, stop now, Peter sweetheart," Eve advised.

Peter quit.

"Well, you think about it and let me know," Pinky said to my mother. After that, Peter said the word *Disneyland,* quickly and quietly, every thirty seconds, irrespective of the conversation in progress. The fifth time he did it, my mother stood up, came around the table, and grabbed him by the arm. "Get up," she ordered, pulling him out of his chair.

"Oh now, Leigh, he was just playing."

"I'll handle this, Pinky," my mother said.

"Let go of me." He struggled. She slapped him, hard, on the back of his head.

"Go up to your room and stay there, do you hear me? I will not put up with this behavior."

"What about your behavior?" Peter tried to wriggle free. "You're the loony bird." She hit him again.

"Be still," my mother yelled, "and get upstairs, now!"

He ran up the stairs, shouting, "I'm cuckoo for Cocoa Puffs, cuckoo for Cocoa Puffs," and slammed his door. Pinky and I locked eyes. I could see he was holding back a bronco of an opinion.

Peter stayed in his room the rest of the day. I knocked on the door around three o'clock and was told to scram. "I've got a surprise for you," I said.

"Yeah, sure."

"No, really. It's from Uncle Pinky." Silence. "I promise."

"Just a minute," he said, then the door opened a crack and Peter quickly wedged his body into it. "What?"

"Let me in, please? I'm sorry I ripped up my passport." He looked extremely tired. "Are you okay?" I said.

"What have you got for me?"

"You have to let me in and I'll give it to you. C'mon, Peter."

He sighed, no longer caring one way or the other, and opened the door all the way, shutting it again as soon as I was inside. He waited while I made sense of the situation.

"Oh my God," I said. Save for the bed, and a few items on the night-stand, the room was stripped bare of Peter's belongings. It was remark-ably empty-looking. Along the far wall stood a row of boxes stuffed full of Peter's things.

"I spent the whole day packing. I'm moving in with Dad as soon as he gets back."

"Does he know?"

"Not yet. I'm sure he won't mind. I think he's lonely." Peter sat on the edge of the bed. He looked so small in that barren room. I went and sat beside him.

"Oh, Peter."

"What do you care? You've got Kim."

"I'll go crazy if you move out."

He dropped flat on his back and said, bitterly, "I hate her guts." I joined him lying down, staring at the ceiling. "I miss Dad," he continued.

"Pinky gave me a handful of Liberty dimes for you." I dug into my pocket and handed them over. Peter studied one quietly for a long time.

"I wish Mom and Dad were like them," he said.

"Yeah, me, too." I scooched closer until our heads and shoulders were touching. "How will you possibly live without me? What'll you do for fun?"

He didn't say anything for a while, then wanted to know if there was any roast beef left.

..................

THERE WERE ELEVEN of us divided among three cars, all of them gas-guzzlers, all bound for Disneyland. I rode in Uncle Pinky's dark-green Jaguar with my cousin Elliot and his Canadian friend from college, Beth Ann. She had never been to Disneyland but was quite sure she wasn't going to like it. "Don't worry, you'll like it," I said, finding her truly bizarre. What I wanted to know was how she had endured childhood without the place. "I mean, you knew about Disneyland, right? Is there a Canadian version?" I continued my questions, but Beth Ann refused to concede she had missed out in any way. In fact, she seemed to think I was the strange one for caring so much, for loving the place as I did. Through her small, rimless glasses she blinked at me repeatedly, as though I were a spot on her cornea, and finally said, "Get over it."

Her refusal to smile, or be polite, or wear makeup were things I immediately envied about Beth Ann. She was beautifully plain, with cropped black hair and sun-starved skin—a brain, someone who knew who she was and would apologize for nothing. She was the kind of girl I would never be, precisely because of Disneyland, and Hollywood, and my mother, and the rest of it.

*Get over it.*

I pecked the phrase into my right and left thighs as though pressing the keys of a typewriter. The behavior, which had started as a way to practice typing, was now compulsory. I pushed myself to keep up during heated conversations, and movies, even when I knew a complete transcript wasn't humanly possible. Sometimes I air-typed until I made myself sick.

One last time I tried to make Beth Ann understand that for a child— which I was the first time I went to Disneyland—the place is completely magical, indeed the happiest place on earth. I told her when you grow up on Disneyland, you feel special about it the rest of your life. "Exactly." She smirked. "You can't see how phony and antiseptic it really is. Americans love Disneyland because it glorifies all the sentimental crap they like to believe about themselves."

I didn't know what sentimental crap she was talking about, but I knew she had to be right. She sounded right, and had the advantage of coming from another country. Her harsh words about Americans appealed to me instinctively. I recognized in them a brash new way to achieve sophistication, to be cool and intellectual. I thought I could become the self-aware American, critical of her country and its culture, and this excited me, but then Elliot spoke and my glimmering future as sharp-tongued cultural observer ended. He said, "No, Beth Ann. We like it because it's fun."

He was up front with Pinky, whose eyes had met mine more than once in the rearview mirror during the conversation. I'm with you, they shone. My uncle and I had a long history of such moments—knowing glances, well-timed pats on the back, and other imagined sympathies. We were pals who didn't really know each other, whose desire for connection exceeded actual closeness. "Pinky thinks the world of you," Eve often told me, so I thought the world of him back.

My aunt's white Continental was right behind us on the freeway, its cargo as follows: princess Caroline (my other cousin), Caroline's sidekick, Gigi, who dressed even nicer than Caroline, and my brother and his friend, Robbie. I was glad not to be in their car, where the mystery of Caroline's hair, combined with the glory of Gigi's clothes, would have undone me. How was it possible to have hair halfway down your back without a single broken strand? Caroline's was silky smooth, as though freshly shellacked, and hung with the opulence of full-length mink. All I had to do was move and my hair got caught in a nearby piece of furniture, or my own clothing or jewelry.

The Porsche zipped by with my mother and her new friend, Ron, inside. We all took notice, but they were too busy talking to each other to look in our direction. "Look! There goes Farrah Fawcett," Pinky joked. And he was right. In that car, going that speed, she could have been anybody.

The Matterhorn became visible ahead, rising over a bunch of trees. I could even see the specks that were actually Disneyland employees scaling the concrete mountain with their ropes and lederhosen like authentic Alpine climbers. "There it is!" I pointed. The dream you visited fully awake, where kids drove sports cars, and one could enter a building at noon and be waterborne moments later in a boat on the bayou at dusk; swamps and jungles; paintings that stretched into morbid tableaux as the walls they hung upon doubled in height; a pirate netherworld stinking of debauchery; a giant eyeball looking down at you through a microscope. How could I ever explain that life, for me, was largely a boot camp, a drab institution requiring near constant embellishment. The sun came up, the sun went down. Nine months of school, three months of summer. Monday then Tuesday, Wednesday, Thursday, Friday. Again and again and again. But once a year, if we were lucky, Disneyland—fantasizer's paradise, shrine to the imagination, a place as real as any other, and therefore a direct challenge to the suffocating sameness of daily existence. But I was in the wrong car. No one in Pinky's Jaguar gave a damn.

Kim, whom I'd invited, had come down with something at the last minute, leaving me the only one in our group without a buddy. I thought at first that I'd attach myself to Elliot and Beth Ann, hang out with the college kids, but as soon as we parked she started making cracks about the "fascistic" admission policies. "If I refuse to smile, will they still let me in?" I could see what a day with her was going to be like, and pitied my cousin, though he seemed to find her amusing enough. Perhaps the place would win her over eventually, but I preferred not to chance it. That left Peter and Robbie, who emerged from Eve's car arguing over which belonged first, Pirates of the Caribbean or Haunted Mansion. They'd actually put together a list of every ride they wanted to go on, in optimal order, taking into account park locale and thrill level. There was no way I was joining that nerd assembly. Caroline greeted me sweetly, but Gigi took one look at my matching pants and vest, purchased for ten dollars at Fashion Passion, and whispered something in Caroline's ear that caused the two of them to glow momentarily brighter.

"Guess it's you and me, kid," Pinky said, laying his hand across my shoulder. "Let's steer clear of the Canadian."

As we moved, packlike, toward the main entrance, Pinky folded a piece of Doublemint into his mouth. "What do you know about the character with your mom?" He offered me a piece.

"His name is Ron. He's okay." He was one of her Beverly Hills discoveries, an accountant with a head of silver curls and a belted, shiny-green leather sports jacket he wore with everything, apparently under the impression it looked good on him.

Pinky took a look over his shoulder. "Your mother doesn't have any problem meeting guys. She must have herself a boyfriend for every day of the week." I smiled, as though my uncle had made one of his usual witty remarks. I was aware of the muscles in my face, and knew holding them that way was a form of flattery, of making him think I agreed completely. With certain people, generally men, I discovered you didn't have to listen if you weren't in the mood. You just waited for the ends of their sentences, then smiled. It was all they required, for the most part.

Pinky turned around, suddenly. "Peter, I can hear you, buddy. What's in those pockets? You carrying a tambourine?" Everyone laughed, including Peter, who'd taken to keeping a fistful of loose change in his pocket. He'd somehow determined this was the height of cool. He even walked with a small limp to accentuate the chinkling coinage, and had started acquiring dimes and quarters minted prior to 1964, for their real silver, which he claimed produced a higher-pitched, more pleasing tone.

At the main entrance, Pinky approached the ticket window and pulled out his wallet. My mother reached for her shoulder bag. "I told you, this is on us," Eve said. Talk about nice. Pinky must have shelled out over a hundred dollars right there. I studied the effortless way he handed over the loot, joking with the cashier. I was sorry Kim wasn't there to see it. I wanted her to know I had classy relations.

Smelling of Jean Naté and breath mints, Eve wrapped her arms around me and rocked me from behind. "Your friend couldn't make it, huh? Well, then, I guess Pinky and I will have to lavish you with attention."

They were the relatives you wished you could go home with at the end of the day instead of your own implausible parents—instead of my mother and Mr. Green Leather Jacket. We passed through the hallowed gates, under the Disneyland railroad, and onto a flower-trimmed, litter-free Main Street.

Perhaps it was all the talking I'd done beforehand, the hyping for Beth Ann. Maybe I'd unwittingly set myself up for an extra-critical experience of the place. Whatever the reason, Disneyland was not as wonderful as I remembered. Everywhere I looked, I had difficulty defending its mythical status. I saw it through her eyes, or rather, through eyes infected by her proximity, her bad attitude. Even after she and Elliot went off on their own, as did Caroline and Gigi as soon as we neared Sleeping Beauty's Castle, I found myself privately lamenting things no longer there rather than enjoying all that was. I became one of those tedious people who can't stop comparing the inferior present to the superior past. Waiting in an obscenely long line to experience the new, for us, Space Mountain, I lovingly recalled a long-gone favorite, the Carousel of Progress. Once directly across from where we were standing, its domed roof was now home to something called America Sings, which I refused, in deference and protest, to try.

"Remember the Carousel of Progress?" I said, facing our group. The four adults and I had agreed to Peter and Robbie's itinerary, since my mother wouldn't let them go off on their own. "It was right over there." I pointed at the large white circular building.

"Honey, that's always been America Sings," my mother erred without conviction, which made me want to ram her.

"I thought that was a souvenir shop." Eve laughed. "Shows you what I know."

Ron raised his hands and mugged, "It's a souvenir shop *and* America Sings!" as though he were funny enough to be on *Saturday Night Live*.

"I remember it," Pinky said. "It was put on by General Electric. Meredith's right. It was right over there." He winked at me.

"The great Oz has spoken." Eve bowed, not entirely kidding.

"Why is it, just because he's got the penis, we assume he's the authority?" said my mother. "I say it was always America Sings." I saw Peter hide his face. Robbie's mouth hung open.

"Give it a rest, Leigh," Pinky flared.

"I will when you do," she practically sang.

"Look, wrong is just wrong, sweetheart."

"If you say so, honey pie."

"Children!" Eve stepped in. "That's enough."

"Just because he paid for my ticket doesn't mean he can buy my silence."

"For Christ's sake," Pinky said.

They hardly spoke to each other after that, unless the situation required it. (Him: "Iced tea, Leigh?" Her: "I can get my own if I want it.") Eve tried to remedy the situation once or twice. (To my mother when Pinky was out of earshot: "Go easy on him. He's on your side, you know." To Pinky when my mother was in the restroom: "I'm asking you to do it for me. She's my sister.")

My mother's ludicrous, convenient feminism had embarrassed me before, but that day at Disneyland I wanted nothing to do with her. I didn't even bother turning my head when she spoke. I wanted only that Pinky and Eve, and even Robbie, see how very separate I was from her, how uncontaminated, and not angry, and worthy of all the good things life had to offer. My uncle and aunt were the kind of people I wanted to be associated with, not this outspoken, difficult, and crass creature who just also happened to be my mother. Don't blame me, I wanted to say, one day I was born, and when I looked up, there she was, apparently my mother. If she minded the treatment I showed her at Disneyland, she gave no sign. She had Ron at her side, after all. I was ashamed of the way she acted, not like a mother at all, or even a nice person. She laughed at his lame jokes, squeezed his leather-clad arm, and ignored the rest of us, so I ignored her. I did my best to show Pinky and Eve how very much I appreciated them taking us to Disneyland.

The line for Pirates of the Caribbean was where we all converged again. Elliot and Beth Ann were at the end of the line when we got there, and Caroline and Gigi strolled up a few moments later sporting black plastic mouse ears on their fashion-model heads. I couldn't help it. There was something about Beth Ann's cool manner that made me want to shove my lack of hipness up her nose.

"How do you like Disneyland?" I said really loud, grinning at her like some nightmare mask straight out of Mr. Toad's Wild Ride.

"Oh, just what I expected." She hardly looked my way, moving subtly closer to Elliot until she'd almost disappeared behind him.

"I guarantee you're going to like this ride." I tilted in order to see her. "It's the best one in the place."

"I've heard."

Elliot smiled at me. "She just doesn't get it."

Had she asked, I might have likened Pirates of the Caribbean to the experience of falling asleep, into a dream. We all got into one boat and leisurely drifted into quiet waters, the oncoming dusk dotted with fire-flies and the hypnotic notes of a mysterious oboe. Then we were swept into cavernous darkness, descending twenty feet into a black ocean where, without the slightest regard for our presence, two huge, antique battleships were at war with each other, both sinking. Cannonballs flew, splashing into the water around us. Gunfire was exchanged over our heads. It was lunatic and grand, the animatronic captain taking swigs from a bottle and laughing at his own crazy demise. Pinky leaned in close and murmured, "If your aunt ever tried that 'male chauvinist' crap with me, she could start looking for a new husband, you know what I'm saying?" He straightened up and gazed off to his side of the boat. Before I had a chance to consider what he'd said, or even acknowledge my annoyance at being distracted from the ride, he leaned toward me again. "That mother of yours is a piece of work, let me tell you." He moved away, then thought better of it, coming back to press his lips into my hair. "How did your father take it for so long? Poor bastard." I went rigid, my face still bearing the look of pleased wonderment at the ride, but feeling like a captive of my uncle's sudden urge to share.

We left the dying ships behind and traveled on, plunging another twenty feet to surface in the belly of the ride, a living graveyard of pirate lore. "What kills me," Pinky confided, his arm stretched behind me, "is what she's doing to you and your brother. Does she give a damn about that?" What was I supposed to do? On my left, a skeleton in an evening gown was seated at her vanity, combing her dead hair. Treasure chests overflowed with jewels and stolen coins, and in the distance I heard song, merriment, laughter. "You and me, we've always known what she is. I see you watching her. I know exactly what you're thinking. It's the same thing I'm thinking." I started to feel physically ill, yet on and on the ride went, all the beloved scenes appearing more ghoulish by the minute. The pirate behind bars, trying to sweet-talk the dog with the key to come closer; solitary maidens being chased by groups of pirates; buildings on fire; drunkards, pistols, mayhem. *Yo-ho, yo-ho, a pirate's life for me.* The first tear launched itself down my cheek as Pinky said, "Someday your mother's going to get just what she deserves." When he spoke, he seemed to take big gulps of air away from me. I felt I was suffocating beside him, that I would have to jump ship if he didn't stop. "What really gets me—" he continued, but I turned sharply away, and refused to respond when he tapped my shoulder. He said my name once or twice, and kept on tapping me, but I offered him nothing more than my back. Finally, he gripped my shoulder, leaned over me, and asked if I was all right. We were passing under the final bridge, beneath the swinging foot of the lone pirate whose lower leg, I never failed to notice, even on this ghastly occasion, had been humanized to the last detail with what appeared to be real body hair. I pushed Pinky back with my elbow, and hunkered even farther away from him.

It was during our final ascent out of pirate hell that the situation became surrealistic. Pinky had let go of me and was now all the way on the other side of our bench, looking extremely agitated. I had straightened up, but was keeping my distance. Then, clunk—the boat abruptly stopped, marooning us at a forty-five-degree angle as we exited pirate central. "Now *this* I like," I heard Beth Ann say.

In all the years I'd been coming to Disneyland, no ride had ever malfunctioned. There was nothing to do, of course, but sit and wait, and listen—we had no other choice—as the magic of Disney undressed itself moment by moment. Sound effects meant to be heard once at precisely timed intervals were now heard again and again and again and again. Unable to see the ride any longer, we were forced to listen to its tedious tape loop, cycling every couple of minutes like canned laughter. I grew to know every gunshot, every ricochet. The pirate song became as tiresome as "It's a Small World." I could feel Pinky staring at me, willing me to make eye contact with him, but I refused, closing my eyes to listen to the sound of sacred unraveling.

When at last we exited and were back in the sunshine, I attached myself to Eve's side, managing, like my mother, to avoid direct contact with

Pinky for the rest of the day. Unfortunately, there was the ride home to endure. I couldn't think of a good reason for anyone to switch cars with me, so Pinky and I wound up side by side, as Beth Ann insisted on sitting beside Elliot in back. Their presence made all the difference, luckily. Pinky didn't risk conversing with me, and the two of them were in a talkative mood. I looked out the window, mostly, and said, when asked, that I didn't feel well. When we got to our house, and everyone said their good-byes, Pinky asked me, in front of everyone, for a hug. That's when he made his move. Quickly, clearly, and with a bit of menace, he said, "You don't repeat anything, all right? Our conversation was just between you and me." He released me, smiling innocently before turning his attention to Peter, then my mother.

Eve gave me a big hug. "My beautiful princess."

Beth Ann managed a chilly "It was nice meeting you" from five feet away.

"See ya," grinned Elliot, gently socking my arm.

Caroline and Gigi stayed in the car.

Soon all of them would be sitting around back home, criticizing my mother and pitying poor Peter and me. They'd have a good laugh, then go out for an expensive dinner. Even Ron wanted to get away from her. He declined her invitation to stay and order a pizza with us, addressed something Shakespearean-sounding to "one and all," got in his car and drove away, honking. Everybody hates you, I wanted to say as we walked to the front door. Not to hurt her, but to wake her up, make her see how desperately I needed her to behave a bit better. We all did.

During *60 Minutes* I contemplated speaking up. My mother was eating her mushroom pizza in the shifting TV light, enjoying the segment about a lady who paid to publish the memoirs of her pet poodle. She looked so defenseless, my mother—tired, vulnerable, a woman barely coping. The only reason she'd gone to Disneyland was to please Peter and me. She had no idea what people thought of her. She was bored and said provocative things to keep herself entertained. How could I crush her by revealing Pinky's betrayal? How could I *not* tell her, an even worse betrayal? The weight of it was becoming more than I could bear. Then she turned unexpectedly, and caught me staring. She saw the drama-in-progress on my face and it startled her.

"What's the matter?"

What passed between us in that moment was irrevocable. I averted my eyes but knew it was too late. She'd already opened the telegram that began with the words, "I have something bad to tell you . . ."

At the commercial she got right up and shut off the set in order to focus everything on me.

"What? Why do you look like that?"

Peter wasn't there to complain about the TV going off. He'd already gone to his room, so the silence quickly closed in around us. She seemed to be bearing down on me, pinning me in place with her insistent gaze.

"Tell me what's the matter, Meredith."

She could see how scared I was. My eyes reached out to her, full of words unspeakable. Still, she caught some of the gist.

"Did Pinky say something to you?"

"Yes."

"About me?"

I hesitated.

"You can tell me. I want to know." We sized each other up, assessing the odds that a conversation at that point could turn out well. Unfortunately, my mother and I shared an irresistible attraction to ruin.

"It was nothing," I stalled.

She came to the couch and sat right on the end closest to me. "You can tell me, Meredith. I promise not to get mad. Something your uncle said upset you very much, and I want to know what it was. That's all. Nothing earthshaking is going to happen if you tell me. What did he say to you?"

She seemed so strong and steady, so ready to receive her blows without injury. Still, I knew better than to believe in my mother's calm. Sensing this, she poured on an extra layer. "Do you trust me? Do you believe that when I say I won't get upset I'm telling the truth? Now, I want you to believe me, Meredith, and I want to hear what happened between you and Pinky."

"Okay," I said, softly. She waited for me to begin. She didn't interrupt. She even managed to keep a poker face for most of the story, which came out of me in fits of noisy tears. In the end I saw her jaw tighten, of course, and her eyes grow hot with fury, yet I felt relieved to be back in my mother's camp again, safe.

That night in my bed, I thought about the Carousel of Progress, not the precise details of the ride, which were lost to me, but the happy feelings it had always inspired. I saw and heard Father charming the audience as he talked about home life through the years. Even the kitchen appliances were under his spell, energetically demonstrating themselves on cue. Mother, Son, and Daughter, as always, were happily, wholesomely occupied in other parts of the house, illuminated behind transparent scrims. At the end of each era the stage went dark, the theme song came on, and the audience was rotated to a brand-new scene narrated by a brand-new Father, who was clearly the same man except that, like his home, he and his family now existed twenty to thirty years later, as evidenced by their clothes and time-saving General Electric appliances. The fact that all of them, including the family dog, were themselves electrical appliances only enhanced the wonder of the ride. Inside the Carousel of Progress, home and family were made to seem magical, imbued with a surplus of brightly lit order and good humor. It was a picture at once familiar and unattainable that we, the darkened audience, clung to while turning counterclockwise through the advancing century, ever closer to our own moment.

atherine Stone, the lone female from driving school a year before, held my father's hand in the Elbow Room, my favorite restaurant, as she told Peter and me how the two of them had been on the exact same plane from New York to L.A. without even knowing it. "Then we all had to get off and wait inside the airport. Engine trouble." She paused to roll her eyes, reliving the whole thing as she talked. "Flying, under the best of circumstances, makes me incredibly nervous, so you can imagine what this did to me." On her way off the plane she swiped an open bottle of chilled champagne from first class. "I needed it. Besides, I had something to celebrate. I'd just sold my first script to CBS."

In the terminal she recognized my father. He mentioned he was getting divorced, and so they spent the next two and a half hours drinking her champagne and getting reacquainted.

Even with her hand locked in his, and their unambiguous smiles, I couldn't accept them as a couple. It was like looking at a hen and a Labrador retriever some crazy scientist intended to cross-breed.

By the time they reached L.A., according to Catherine, my father had decided to rent her guest house in the valley. "It just made sense. Your dad needed a place to live. I had the guest house."

"There's a little more to it than that." My father winked. Then they kissed. We hadn't seen him in nearly two months and now this woman—she was waiting for us at the restaurant, though he'd said nothing about her in the car—was hogging all the action, eclipsing our reunion as though she were the central star of the solar system.

I'd never seen anyone talk to a waiter the way she did. "I'm looking for something simple, but not boring, you know what I mean? Maybe an egg dish, maybe the crepes. What do you recommend?"

The waiter suggested the crepes, whereupon she lost interest in them altogether. "How about the seafood salad? Tell me about that." Peter's knee rammed mine under the table, and I pressed back as hard as I could. I was counting on the waiter to shame her with a scowl or a ponderous sigh, but this was the Elbow Room and he was only too happy to lend himself.

"You got rid of your beard," I said to my father once the waiter was gone.

Catherine clapped her hands, startling me. "As soon as he got back, thank God." She looked at the ceiling and held her hands in mock prayer. "I couldn't stand it. I hate to see a good-looking man with hair covering his face."

She was exactly as I remembered her: pretty despite herself, overly talkative, plump, with that long gray hair and strangely heavy black eyeliner.

"And what do you like to do, Peter?" She heaped butter on a Ry-Krisp. She had the same effect on him as she'd had on me the year before. Peter went quiet, shrugged, and looked away, which only made her try harder. She popped the cracker in her mouth, seemed to swallow without chewing, and said, "Let me guess. I bet you're a creative type, like your dad."

He thrust his knee into mine again, deciding his only option was to fake a coughing fit, which required drinking a lot of ice water and appearing unable to speak.

"He belongs on the stage." My father frowned, but Peter insisted he couldn't help it.

"That's okay." Catherine buttered another cracker. "I can tell Peter and I are going to be friends." She was, without a doubt, the least self-conscious woman I had ever encountered. Specifically, she was unself-conscious about being a woman, about appearing pushy or unfeminine. She was just a person, just Catherine. That our father found her attractive was the hard part.

"How was Europe, Dad?" Peter mumbled, looking down at his empty bread plate.

"Oh, waiter! Anthony?" Catherine hollered across the dining room, until it seemed every customer was staring. "A large OJ, too, please." Then she turned to my father. "I forgot how much you like it."

Our father—was he sedated?—seemed not to notice the human brushfire holding his hand. "Europe was great," he said. A mysterious satisfaction emanated from him, made him appear quite impervious to his manic companion.

"You want to know what Europe is like?" Catherine said to Peter. "Well, guess what? I'm going to stop interrupting and let your father tell you." She got up. "All of you, visit. I'm going to lock myself in the ladies room for a while, give you a chance to hear yourselves think." As she clumsily extricated herself from the table, lugging an enormous shoulder bag and trying not to catch her billowing clothes on anything, she looked at me, not sweetly, not apologetically, but directly, and to my surprise I smiled, an attempt to put her at ease, if such a thing were possible.

"She's nervous," my father said, "so try to be nice. She's got a heart of gold."

Unlike you-know-who, I completed his thought. My mother was now someone he didn't talk about. She was history. He had picked us up a few blocks from the house just to avoid seeing her.

"Tell me what's new." My father sipped his just-arrived orange juice. Europe had done him good. His travels surrounded him like a buffer that clearly separated all he'd left, back in January, from the present.

"Can I come live with you?" Peter said. "I'm all packed. I've been waiting for you to get back."

Hands to the face. Face-rubbing. My father wasn't so changed after all. Through the spaces between his fingers, he looked at Peter. "What's wrong at home?"

"Nothing. I just want to be with you. I don't like living with only Mom."

My father turned to me. "Something going on I should know about?" I shook my head. Under the table I was nervously twisting my friendship ring round and round.

"I packed my room up. I can leave today."

My father emerged from behind his hands. "I wish I could, kiddo. Really. There just isn't enough room. I got no place to put you."

"You could move. She wouldn't mind. Her guest house was empty before you took it."

In that instant I knew, the way you just do without anyone telling you, that my father wasn't living in any guest house. He may have started there, but he'd progressed, swiftly, to the same bed where Catherine slept. The guest house was the version they'd agreed upon for today so that we wouldn't have to digest all at once the fact that our father was now living with Catherine's kids.

"Give me a little time." He patted Peter's hand. "We'll figure something out."

Peter pulled away. "I don't see what's so great about living in her guest house. You're not going to marry her. She's way too weird."

"Hey, there's no need for that." Peter was close to tears, so I excused myself from the table.

I expected to find Catherine in the restroom, in one of the velvet chairs, chewing her nails, but she wasn't there. Nor was she at the bar, quietly drinking. I found her hunched over a thick paperback in the waiting area. All around her people clustered and dispersed while the heavy doors repeatedly opened to blinding sunlight, then closed with a bang. Not once did she break her concentration.

I slid gently into the spot beside her. "Must be a good book."

The way she shrieked and started you'd think a cockroach had emerged from behind the page and mounted her arm. I had my own junior heart attack off hers. Then she was laughing and hanging on to me, pawing my blouse and burying her face in my shoulder. "Jesus, Meredith. Oh my God. Oh sweetheart. I'm sorry. You scared me."

I slowly, gently, removed her. Catherine's body disgusted me on some barely perceptible level of awareness. Her little hands were brutally crosshatched with lines that made them look dry and weather-beaten. Her long gray hair, rather than frame her face alluringly, seemed to dwarf her small head and sharp features. You looked at Catherine and longed to conduct a makeover, color her in, show her some Audrey Hepburn films. Yet she had chosen not to concern herself with such things. It was the gall inherent in that decision that seemed to lie at the heart of my disapproval. She dared to live a woman's life without acting much like a woman at all.

"Is the food down?" she said, readying herself to go back to the table.

"No. Peter and Dad got into a heavy talk, so I left."

"Is Peter okay?" She looked alarmed.

What business is that of yours, I wanted to say. She was the kind of person who lived to get involved, who assumed her participation was welcome, and why wouldn't it be? She hadn't been told all her life that good deeds would be punished. Surprisingly, Catherine was the one who dropped the subject.

"I wish I'd ordered a burger. God, that sounds good. I don't know why I bother with anything else. I'm a hamburger person, medium rare, with a slice of pickle. How about you?"

"Chinese food." This made her smile, as though I'd shared something deep.

She said, "You know what I like best about Chinese?"

I waited, again suppressing the urge to be cruel, to say, Ask me if I care, because clearly some part of me did.

"The fortune. I love the cookie, and the anticipation of breaking it open, and the fun of getting the little message, you know what I mean? I keep all my fortunes in a little bottle, except for the one I got in New York the day before I saw your dad at the airport. That one I chewed up and swallowed. Swear to God, gobbled it just like food."

It was easy to imagine paper dissolving on her tongue, entering her stomach, and becoming part of her bloodstream, as if eating fortunes explained the not quite normal aspect of her.

"It must have been a good one."

She looked at me, considering whether or not to tell. Behind her, I could see my father coming toward us from the dining room. Catherine closed her eyes.

"It said, 'Very soon and in good company.' "

"Ladies, lunch is served," my father announced, extending his hand. Catherine was off that bench in a heartbeat, her arm hooked firmly under his.

Peter stayed sullen the rest of the meal, but nobody bugged him about it. His hamburger sat untouched in front of him, where Catherine could mentally devour it while bravely chomping her salad greens. She went right back to dominating the conversation, telling us about the episode of *Wonder Woman* she'd written and sold, and her ambition to turn herself into a producer. She used insider expressions, though none of us knew what they meant. It wasn't until we left the restaurant and were heading back to the cars that she stopped speaking long enough for me to notice my ring was gone. I screamed.

"What ring?" my father calmly said. As usual, his lack of emotion only made me more hysterical. The impossibility of explaining about the ring, what it meant, where it had come from, made me want to cry, while the urgency of the situation kept me dry-eyed. Then Catherine took hold of my wrist and began pulling.

"C'mon. Let's go right back and find it."

My father reached for her shoulder. "Babe, it could be anywhere."

"This will just take a minute," she insisted. I was too overwrought to question why she wanted to help. I simply let her do this thing that for her was second nature, this giving thing I wasn't too familiar with but was starting to like.

Informed of our plight, Oscar went off to check the lost-and-found while we stormed the dining room. Luckily, the table, which had been reset, was yet to be occupied. Catherine walked around it, looking at the floor, while I kneeled and searched directly underneath. Nothing. Then I heard it, as sudden and startling as an earthquake. "Excuse me, everyone!" It was Catherine, addressing the patrons of that elegant room as though she were activities director on a cruise ship. I got up off the floor. "If I could have your attention for just a minute. This is Meredith, and she lost a silver friendship ring somewhere in this restaurant within the last hour. If everyone could just take a quick look on the floor around them, we would really appreciate it. The ring has enormous sentimental value." Mortified, I wanted to explain that it really wasn't important, wanted everyone to see they shouldn't bother over me, but then I noticed that almost all of them, at every table, were bending over and looking for my blasted ring. No one minded! "I've got it," a voice three tables away announced. Emerging from under a starched white tablecloth came a white-haired gentleman who hoisted my ring as though he were the proud winner of a treasure hunt. If I hadn't been there to see it, I wouldn't have believed it was my life.

Peter started making fun of her the minute our father dropped us off for the short walk back home.

" 'Oh, waiter? What's the best way to chew my food?' Man, what a fruitcake."

"She isn't *that* bad," I said.

"Yes, in fact, she is."

"Still want to live with him?"

"Sure. Why wouldn't I?"

"And see *her* all the time?"

He slipped into the Sanchez persona. "Let us just say that Beeg Mouth can be eleemeenated. Permanently."

"Yeah, right."

"Jes. You see, me and my asseestant, we gonna whip up some Welcome To Da Family cookies for da leetle lady, to es-press our especial love. Now, what ees dees? How did botchuleesm get in her cookies?" Without changing the plot, Peter inexplicably switched to his own voice. "Oh well, sorry you're dead, Big Mouth. Maybe you shouldn't have eaten so much, Piggy."

I went ahead and laughed, though my heart wasn't in it.

"Or, what about this: What's that in your mailbox, Horsehead? An anonymous gift? No, don't open it!" Peter performed the sound effects of a large explosion. "Aw, too late, she's blinded and disfigured and no one wants her now."

"I kind of like her, Peter. A little."

He moved his face really close to mine. "Are you feeling all right?"

When our mother asked how it went, we said nothing about Catherine Stone. She was having enough trouble, though she tried not to show it, accepting that our father wanted nothing more to do with her. He refused even to speak to her without his lawyer present. "You'd think I was a leper," she said, referring as well to Aunt Eve's recent disappearance from her life.

My mother had an uncanny ability to forget the part she played in her own troubles. For instance, the night I blew the whistle on Uncle Pinky, she yelled at Aunt Eve over the phone, "He's not welcome in my home ever again, do you understand? I'll never forgive him for trying to turn my child against me."

Eve apologized profusely, but apparently added, "You shouldn't have provoked him, Leigh. You can be very harsh sometimes." That only got my mother angrier.

"The two of you can rot in hell as far as I'm concerned!" She climaxed with her signature phone slam. Now the blinding indignation was gone, and in its place, as always, my mother discovered a great loneliness and sharp longing for those she'd pushed away. There were no men to distract her, either. She'd put an end to them, too, had told Judith she was sick of standing around bars making idiotic conversation with the opposite sex. "I don't even *like* men," she declared, as though just realizing it. "They're missing something, and I'm sick and tired of pretending not to notice." The last thing my mother needed was news that her husband, who wanted a settlement as quickly as possible, appeared to be living with his new girlfriend, and so we kept it from her, for our sake as well as hers.

---

I NOTICED MY MOTHER in the living room window, watching us, when Kim dropped me off after school.

"Nice of you to grace us with your presence," she said the moment I came inside. Her arms were crossed. "I notice she always drops you off without coming in. Obviously, your brother and I don't rate the time of day from Miss Kim Adamson."

"She comes over all the time," I whined.

"Not when I'm at home."

I was smart enough, for once, not to answer back. It was obvious she was looking for a fight. "I'm going to my room," I said, and headed for the stairs.

I'd cleared three steps when she said, "If you think there's dinner tonight, you're mistaken. Restaurant's closed. Permanently." I kept walking. "Do you hear me? I'm onto you, Meredith, Miss Drop-In-at-Dinnertime. Who do you think you are?" I didn't bother answering, just quickly, carefully shut my bedroom door. As expected, it opened seconds later, but, thankfully, was not my mother.

"Hi," Peter said, enjoying the look of relief on my face. He came in and lay down on the bed. After a moment, I joined him.

"She's worse than ever today," I said.

"Tell me about it." It was extremely nice lying beside him, our emotions as flat as our bodies.

"It's been a big day around here," he said. "Mom's been breaking stuff." As if on cue, there was a crash of some sort downstairs, quickly followed by the sound of our mother cursing. I got up, but Peter didn't flinch. He remained impassive, philosophical, as though he'd already outgrown my crude reaction.

"Holy shit." I opened my bedroom door. In the kitchen, my mother swept the cupboard clean of canned goods. You could hear them raining on the linoleum.

"Sonofabitch!" she screamed. I heeded my brother's suggestion and shut the door.

"What is going on?" I said.

"She needs a straitjacket, that's what."

My mother stopped making meals for Peter and me. She hung around the kitchen fixing herself whimsical snacks—eggs scrambled with Baco Bits and grape jelly, creamed spinach decorated with Fritos corn chips—then carried them off to her bedroom. From behind the perpetually closed door emanated a steady flow of cigarette smoke, television noise, and heated phone conversations with her lawyer. "Yeah, I know it's petty, but I don't give a shit," I heard one particularly sour afternoon. "He's in such a big hurry, let the bastard pay for it."

The bastard. The SOB. Somewhere along the line my mother's clear-cut rejection of my father had become his cold-blooded abandonment of her. When the door of her sanctuary opened, Peter and I went into a state of alert, scrambling to avoid her. We didn't breathe right until she was back inside.

She continued going downtown each morning to her job, but now she did it like the rest of the population: grudgingly. The novelty of employment had faded, giving my mother just one more thing to feel disillusioned about. She drank her coffee glumly as Peter and I hustled to fix ourselves breakfast and pack our lunches. "I guess I'll get dressed," she muttered, then stayed put. We found a way to turn the situation into a game, of course, referred to ourselves as the "Go Team" and pretended to be a precision-trained duo of no-nonsense, get-the-job-done professionals. No job, not even breakfast, was too small.

"Cereal."

"Check."

"Milk."

"Check."

"Bowls and spoons."

"Check."

"Commence mastication."

We'd sit down at the exact same moment and absorb our nutrients, like teen variants of our bionic heroes, Steve Austin and Jamie Sommers.

"If I killed myself, do you think your father would notice?" our mother said, dragging herself from the room.

I began spending more time at Kim's, yet another thing my mother harped on. "I just think you've seen her enough this week," she'd say, forbidding me to go. "You don't have to see each other every day. Do something else with your time." Of course, her meddling drove us closer together.

"Tell her to go bite a mailman." Kim gurgled with laughter.

"She needs one of those T-shirts," I said, also laughing, and pointing to my chest, "that say 'Bitch' right here."

Just calling home from Kim's to see if I could stay the night filled me with as much dread as being there. I had become my mother's way of staying in shape for her bouts with my father and his lawyer. "Don't give me that look," she'd say when I was around, "and don't act stupid. You know what look I'm talking about." She picked on me all the time, screaming, "I'm not the maid, you know. Pick up after yourself!" If I kept to my room, she walked right in without knocking and accused me of something or other. "You took the last banana, didn't you? Did you know I was planning to eat that in the morning?"

Even Kim's mother was on my side.

"She can be so rude, Mom," Kim cut loose. The three of us were standing in the kitchen at their house. "I'll be talking to Meredith on the phone and it isn't five minutes before her mother picks up the extension and says, 'Excuse me, but you're not the only person in this house. Someone could be trying to call me, so wrap it up and stay off for a while.'" I'd never heard Kim impersonate my mother before. Her voice was laced with a spite I hadn't known existed.

"You don't have your own line?" Diana said, as though this were a clear indication of my mother's inadequacy.

"Nope." I said it conspiratorially, joining in the mother-bashing even as I started to experience the familiar guilt that went with it.

Kim continued, "And then, before she even has a chance to say good-bye, her mother picks up again. 'Off!' she orders, then slams down the phone. Can you believe that?"

It was all true, yet hearing Kim reenact it for the enjoyment of her mother, her perfect, beautiful, ultra-cool mother, triggered a defensive loyalty in me. I had to go home when we were finished and see my mother trying to keep herself together, pruning the roses and wiping her brow with the back of her gardening glove.

"By the way," Kim pressed on, "do you think anyone calls for Leigh after she makes Meredith get off? Of course not."

It was all I could do not to ask Diana, by way of payback, "Had any orgasms lately?"

-----

> Whether you prefer to have a penis there or not at that moment
> depends on your own personal preference, of course. For most
> women, "vaginal ache" is not felt so intensely with a penis
> present; the penis seems to "soothe" and diffuse the feeling. . . .

I'd been enjoying *The Hite Report* for a long time when the doorbell brought me back to the lateness of the hour and the strangeness of my surroundings. Steve and Lisa, the couple whose toddler I was baby-sitting, weren't due back for an hour or more, so I went into a panic, returning the book to its place on the shelf, putting my shoes back on. I took my dishes into the kitchen, grabbed a very large knife from the block, and made my way to the front door. My mother was on the other side of the peephole, nervously chewing her fingernail. When she pressed the bell again, it startled the wits out of me.

"I didn't mean to scare you." She eyed the knife as she came inside. What a mess she was—lopsided hair, wrinkled clothes, blanched complexion. I expected some kind of explanation, but she took her time, surveying the room. "What were you doing?"

"I fell asleep." I rubbed my eyes.

She picked up a photograph of Steve and Lisa. "Cute couple. What does he do for a living?" Actually, I had no idea. Kim had got me the job. Steve and Lisa were friends of Natalie's, a good-looking couple with a two-year-old named Justin. That was all I knew about them, that and the fact that I was making five dollars an hour.

"Mom, what are you doing here?" She let out a little laugh, put the photograph down, then exhaled loudly and continued her inspection of the room, stopping in front of the bookcase.

"You know what I did this afternoon?" She studied the titles. *The Hite Report* was right in front of her. "I drove to the address where your father is living and sat in the car, waiting to see him. What do you think about that?"

I said nothing. There was no question whose daughter I was. My mother's behavior, at its very worst, was never less than understandable to me.

"I kept telling myself I should stop it, go back home, but forty minutes went by." She kept her back to me.

"I hope you had something to read."

"Ha-ha," she said, miserably, turning to face me. "Your father's car pulled into the driveway finally. He and a woman got out. She was talking and laughing, and took his hand as they strolled oh-so-happily to the house."

I stared at my mother, unwilling to offer her even a twitch of a reaction. She reached in her pocket and pulled out her cigarettes. "Did you know your father was seeing someone?"

"You can't smoke in here." She didn't say anything, just proceeded to light the thing and take a deep drag. "Great. Now Steve and Lisa will think I was smoking in their house."

"Did you know?"

"Mom, I don't want to talk about this now. I'm baby-sitting. This is like me coming to your job and—"

"Just answer the question!" she shouted. Justin stirred in his room, coughed a couple of times, then was quiet again. "I'm not leaving until you answer me."

I imagined an arrow piercing her forehead, its point striking the language center, bull's-eye, and turning her into a mute. She plopped herself on the sofa, at once defiant and baffled.

"Whose side are you on, Meredith?"

"No," I said. "I didn't know. All right?"

She studied me, taking another puff.

"Look, why are you doing this to me?" I was close to tears, waving my arms around to fan the smoke. She decided to take pity on me at last and held out the cigarette, which I took and put out in the kitchen. It was a chance to collect my thoughts, briefly, to figure out how to deal with the situation, only I couldn't think of any solution. When I went back to the living room, she was standing again.

"Well," she said, as though preparing to leave, "guess this was a shitty idea. Sorry I bothered you."

I held my tongue and thanked God.

"Just tell me one thing. Are you the slightest bit surprised to hear your father has a girlfriend?"

"Yeah, of course I am. I'm just too freaked out by you being here to think about it."

She nodded, unconvinced, but she made no progress toward the door. "I had lunch at the Elbow Room yesterday. Oscar asked about your ring."

My eyes shut. Why did I bother trying to beat her? My mother was like the sky. There was no getting out from under her.

"Naturally, I had no idea what he was talking about, till he told me about the woman with Mr. Herman who helped my daughter recover her ring. So why lie, Meredith? I know you know."

"It's all your fault." The words shot out in a clean spurt, pointing me in a surprisingly potent new direction. My mother was caught off-guard. "Yeah, if only you hadn't left us in Sonoma. Then none of this would be happening."

"Oh sweetheart, don't be ridiculous. If you think that's what—"

"That's where they met." I sliced into her with pleasure. "She's the one who drove us all the way to the San Francisco airport after you abandoned us." I could feel the power leaving her and coming to me. It was a thrilling, heady moment. "She flirted with Dad all the way. And, yes, I knew about her. She's been glued to him ever since he got back from Europe." My mother's face was turning gray. She was starting to set, like concrete.

"What else do you want to know? Go ahead, ask," I sneered, watching her. "Her name's Catherine Stone. I tried to tell you about her that night when we got home, but you were so mean to me! You're always so mean to me." Tears were pouring down my face, contradicting my apparent joy in attacking her. "Are you happy now? I tried not to hurt your feelings, stupid me, but you had to come here and make me look like a big liar. Well, I'm sick of it. I'm sick of you and Dad."

She reached for me, but I backed away like a wild, trapped thing. "Don't touch me," I screeched. "I hate you!"

For that she struck me, hard, sending me tumbling into a conveniently placed armchair, where I could receive more heartfelt whacks to my head and outstretched arms. "Bitch," she called me, her teeth clenched tight as she proceeded to explain how my contempt for her would never equal her hatred for me.

---

IT WAS ALWAYS the husband who drove me home, the dreaded finale to baby-sitting. I had to sit side by side with him in the dark car, not talking, being self-conscious about not talking, pretending to be completely at ease with this *man* whose aftershave I'd sniffed just hours before, imagining a husband of my own whose smell would someday surround me.

"Sorry you have to take me home, Steve," I said, as we glided through the late-night streets. How pathetic. I considered apologizing for apologizing, but knew once I got started I'd never stop prostrating myself in a tortured cycle of anxiety and regret. He turned on the radio a moment later. In my hour of self-contempt, it was the clearest sign he couldn't wait to get rid of me.

------------------

WHEN MY MOTHER CRIED, it wasn't sweetly or gently. Not a dainty, beckoning sound. It was more like retching, like someone beset by waves of a violent illness. No matter how hard I tried simply to exist alongside it, the sound inevitably pulled me into its shuddering, bleating vortex. That's right, I said to myself when I got home from Steve and Lisa's to hear her pealing away—cry your head off. You deserve everything you get. I sat on my bed and ate toast, confident I bore none of the blame.

As I brushed my teeth, I studied my callous face in the mirror, feeling older and more beautiful as I resisted a fresh bout of sobs from down the hall. The sound grew tendrils. They reached along the walls, desperately trying to invade my brain. *Save me, someone save me,* they sucked at me. In all the other houses, I imagined the people calmly, purposefully going about their boring lives, not asking for so much, just taking what life offered them without a lot of fuss. In the other houses the mother kept her problems to herself.

She was still going at it when I turned out my light. I went back over everything I'd said at Steve and Lisa's, and decided I had nothing to feel guilty for. Then I hummed to drown her out, stopping when I heard her door open. She walked down the hall to the bathroom and took a gushing piss, blowing her nose at the same time. I got out of bed and walked to the bathroom door.

"Mom?" She told me to go away. I went back to my room and stood around until she flushed, then listened to her go back to her room and shut the door. Moments later, I gently knocked. "Beat it!" came her response. I waited at least a full minute, then turned the knob like a prowler, and stepped inside.

My mother was flat on her back, one raised arm over her face to keep out the bright scourge of the bedside lamp. The TV was on, the volume nearly inaudible. I moved incrementally closer, a floating, incorporeal intelligence, until the arm quickly shot up and my mother raised her head with a gasp. It was like being caught and fixed by a sudden strobe, but just as quickly the head went back down, and the arm closed over it again. "What is it, Meredith? Tell me, and then go on to bed." Her voice was drained of all fight. I continued moving closer until I was standing next to her. She lifted her arm, revealing her hot, swollen face to me. She was so pretty, my mother, so real just then.

"Honey, I just need to be by myself right now." It was her sad, worn-out face calling me honey that started me crying. I dropped down next to her. She could have easily sent me away, but she pulled me to her chest and gently rocked me. I couldn't believe how good it felt, better than sleep.

"It's not your fault," I wept.

"Shhsh." She stroked my head. "It's no one's fault."

She had been the enemy for so long, but there I was, surrendering to her. I couldn't think straight anymore, couldn't keep track of who did what to whom, and why, and what it meant, and who was right. I was so incredibly tired.

"You're all I've got left, you and Peter," her voice trembled.

I was dissolving into her.

"We have to be good to each other."

Becoming one with her breathing, entering into her blue-black bloodstream, getting lost.

"My baby."

Nothing but an oozy dribble, a trickle of an idea, a zygote. Back, back.

My parents' divorce became final, and, in the end, my father contested nothing. A week after the final judgment arrived, we found out why when he announced his intention to marry Catherine Stone. My mother laughed, then she destroyed the one work of art in our house my father had asked for and won in the settlement: a simple line drawing of a woman's profile, signed by Picasso. It had been purchased by his father when my father was just a boy, eventually coming to hang, undisturbed, in my parents' bedroom for most of my life.

I don't know for a fact that my mother destroyed the Picasso. It disappeared shortly after she learned of my father's marriage plans. She claimed she took it down for him and left it in the garage so he could pick it up any time. "Maybe somebody stole it," she said when he showed up. She didn't even try to sound sorry. When he started yelling, she said, "How should I know what happened to it? I never even liked it." I thought he'd hit her. Instead, he started tearing apart the house, looking for it, but you could see from my mother's expression he was never ever going to find it. The incident marked a turning point for my mother.

Not long after the Picasso incident we found her waiting for us in the kitchen one morning with a cup of coffee in hand, an apron dangling from her neck. "I quit my job," she announced, brightly. "From now on breakfast around here is going to be fun! We're going to eat whatever we like." Citing *Vogue,* she explained the body's ability to know what it needed, especially first thing in the morning. Cravings, she said, were urgent memos sent by the brain to address the body's nutritional deficiencies. She waited. "So, what'll it be?"

After a brief discussion, Peter and I concurred that our bodies, though sleepy, were signaling for spaghetti with meat sauce.

"Terrific." My mother removed ground round from the fridge, and thirty minutes later we were twirling our forks and sucking hot spaghetti to our lips. It was seven-thirty in the morning. As she watched us, a fiery light caught her eyes. "What do you think you want tomorrow?"

I said, "But I thought the whole point—"

"Pizza," Peter interrupted.

"Oh, that's good." She picked one up later that day at the market and again watched us consume it the next morning, as though waiting for the food to work an immediate, visible change upon our lives. The day after pizza we had bacon cheeseburgers with all the trimmings.

"This is great!" Peter gorged.

Day four, expecting Shake 'n Bake chicken, we were confused by the bowls of glutinous, putty-colored oatmeal staring back at us from the table.

"Party's over. I'm sick of cooking for you brats," she said.

"Told you," Peter murmured as soon as she left the room.

----------

I HID MY PLEASURE at being told to buy a dress for the wedding, and acted as though my father had assigned me a chore. "How fancy?"

He turned to Catherine. "How fancy, Mac?"

She looked up from her yellow legal pad and held her hands about five inches apart. "That fancy." Her maiden name was MacNair, hence the nickname, which she encouraged us to use. I couldn't, not without turning her into a big rig.

"Does that answer your question?" he said.

I'd become used to them as a team. Catherine was my father's stronghold, the only place left to find him. To hate her would have been self-defeating.

"The cow will probably inspire him to write," my mother said when she first learned of Catherine's profession. It drove her crazy. "She'll get from him in a few months what I spent years hoping for. Watch him start writing just to spite me." In fact, my father now had an agent, thanks to Catherine. The two of them had been signed, as a team, for the fall season of *Vega$*. Though proud, I felt cheated of bragging rights, seeing as his sudden, glamorous rise was due entirely to getting the hell away from my brother, my mother, and me. His favorite thing was to talk about work as if it were a big bore, a never-ending headache, when clearly he thrived on little else about being alive. Complaining about "the industry," I learned, was a professional privilege, a way insiders covered their elation at their extraordinary good fortune while coping with the fear of losing everything. My father was so changed from the man I once lived with that the only place I still recognized him was my dreams. In all of them he lived in a small apartment up a dark flight of stairs. There was no Catherine. Catherine didn't exist. He lived by himself, surrounded by photographs of my mother, hundreds of them, like a hall of mirrors. "I will always love her," he would say, looking sadly, deeply, into my eyes.

---------------------

IN THE SUPERMARKET checkout line, my mother and the man behind her struck up a conversation about the scanners, and how much faster everything had been before, with cash registers. They watched the checker pass the same box of spaghetti over the reader three, four, five times before finally typing in the code by hand. The man asked what she did for a living and I almost lost it when my mother said she was a screenwriter. It was the sort of gag Kim and I might have pulled.

"No kidding." He was feeding himself tortilla chips from an open bag in his cart. "I'm a producer." He rubbed his salty hands together, wiped them on his jeans, and extended his hand. I could tell she didn't want to, but she politely shook it. "Nick Gervis," he said.

"Leigh Herman."

He noticed I was looking at him, and said hi. I checked out the contents of his cart, deciding from the small thick steak and bottle of expensive wine that he might be for real.

"So, what are you working on right now?"

She came up with this amazing story about a script she was working on. "It's kind of a female version of *The Odd Couple*."

"Uh-huh." He didn't get excited. He seemed to be assessing its commercial potential.

"How about you?" she said. "What are you working on?"

"This and that. Right now I'm trying to get a flick off the ground with Diane Keaton in the lead."

"Great."

There was a lull in the conversation. It stretched into a chasm. The man reached for *Time* magazine. "Do you believe it? We've got a B-movie actor running for president." He wasn't really talking to her any longer. He was looking at his magazine.

I watched the prices blink on and off the display. It seemed my mother was trying to act detached from me and from our groceries, as though shopping were something she, the busy writer, rarely had to do.

"Well, Nick, good luck with your project," she said before we left. The checker was already ringing his items.

"Hey!" He joined us at the end of the checkstand. "Take my card." It was already propped between his fingers like a cigarette he wanted my mother to light. She took it.

"Give me a call. I'll buy you dinner. We'll talk about your movie."

"Sounds fun." Even she knew how to put on the professional cool, the Hollywood face.

"Think he's really a producer?" I said on the way to the car.

"I don't know." She looked at the card. "This says Financial Consultant, but that doesn't mean anything. What's a card going to say, Movie Producer?"

That night, my mother bought a screenwriting manual and a squeaky highlighter pen. Over the next few days, from the sound of things, I'd say she underlined the entire book. She used Nick's card to keep her place, and began telling people there was a producer interested in "optioning" her script. She sounded serious and knowledgeable about the movie business. The only problem was the writing itself. She didn't seem to be doing any.

"I can't sit still long enough to write," she complained. "As soon as I try to work, I think of five other things I should be doing." We were in the kitchen. She was meticulously frosting a two-layer cake.

"What's this for?" I said.

"What do you mean? It's a cake. You eat it."

Two weeks after meeting him, my mother called Nick Gervis to say she appreciated his interest, but had abandoned the project. She asked how things were going with the Diane Keaton film and was told Keaton "passed." They had dinner anyway, during which Nick confessed he really worked for Merrill Lynch. My mother, who persisted in calling herself a screenwriter, was appalled by his deception and never saw him again.

The dress I chose for my father's wedding was the last thing anyone, including me, expected. I was going to buy myself something gorgeous for the evening ceremony, something dark-colored and sexy enough to turn a few heads. I had one hundred dollars in my wallet and planned to carry it around all day, see as many dresses as I could before making the final decision. That's why I even bothered to enter Better Sportswear, the most conservative department at Bullock's. It was next to the entrance, and so I thought I'd "warm up" a bit. I was just sliding hangers from right to left, moving dresses into and out of brief consideration when it appeared in the middle of a rack, halting me with its utter simplicity and pale lavender color—a dress as unremarkable as a brown paper bag. It was terrible, for me, for the occasion. A long-sleeved, knee-length sheath someone's mother—though not mine—would dress up with pearls and a cloud of sweet perfume. I held it at arm's length. Someone named Mildred would wear this, I thought as I put it back on the rack.

My day was already ruined, but I continued to shop several more hours, my thoughts kept returning to Bullock's and the strangely calming lavender garment.

My father married on Saturday, the seventeenth. At the appointed hour I changed into my lavender smock, nude panty hose, and ugly gray pumps, all acquired specifically for the occasion, never to be worn again. Peter stopped by my door and said I looked like an old lady. I thanked him, feeling deeply criminal. It was like dressing for an assignment, reporting for duty on my own impossible mission.

In the end, I had stuffed the dress, on an impulse fluid and intuitive, into my purse while watching myself in the dressing room mirror. No thought was involved, only instinct. I knew I was following the course suggested to me by the dress from the moment I'd first seen it: to attend my father's wedding in disguise and deny his guests, who were all Catherine's friends, any hint of my true self, while also keeping the money from going to that event. Even now, when I look at the pictures from the wedding, I take comfort in my matronly appearance. I didn't really go to my father's wedding, I congratulate myself, she did. Mildred. Millicent. Run-of-the-mill.

It was at Cottage in the Elms, a pretty restaurant high up one of the canyon roads, once a large, two-story home that had been converted into a candlelit hideaway. At five P.M., Peter and I took a cab from our house to the restaurant, sitting far apart from each other in the backseat so the driver couldn't see us in his rearview mirror. Our mother had gone to see *Kramer vs. Kramer,* then out to dinner with Judith. Peter and I didn't speak. We kept our faces turned to the houses going by along the curvy road. Sunlight flickered from behind the tall trees as they whipped past us. We were going to our father's wedding. He was marrying Catherine Stone, the lady who talked too much and wasn't half as pretty as our mother.

"Meredith, look at you!" She swooned as soon as she saw me, without even bothering to truly look. "That dress is stunning." She was out of her mind, of course, running her wedding with the same chaotic energy she brought to every situation. That day, she was the happiest woman alive, and I was there to hand him over, to say, Please, take my father, you need him more than I do.

It's like, you think your life is the world. You think it's you and your family for so many years, and then the wheel, which you never realized was turning, suddenly stops, and you find yourself on the sidelines watching the biggest part of your life go spinning off. It was their life now, Catherine's and my father's. She had snatched him up like a fallen five-dollar bill, face-up on the pavement.

The ceremony took place on the upper level of the cottage. After a swirl of introductions to smiling strangers who wanted Peter and me to know how lucky my father was, we were called to stand beside him. Catherine's daughters, Melody and Jennifer, stood next to her. In my lavender dress I played the good daughter. I understood what was expected of me, but behind my beatific smile and shining, firelit skin, I saw my stepsisters' naked joy, read the healthy sparkle in their eyes as they watched their mother, long lonely, at last claim a new husband. Did my father love Catherine Stone? He didn't act like someone in love, but then I'd come to the conclusion I didn't know my father very well. I knew Catherine was crazy about him, and maybe that's what he loved, or wanted, after my mother. He hadn't even dated anyone else. It was like, Hi, how are you? I'm getting a divorce. Would you like to marry me? Like a game Peter and I might have invented. We'd have called it Divorced for Five Minutes, a True Story.

1980

The trick to going fast around curves was in abandoning the accelerator beforehand. You took the first part like a wave, feeling the motion and aiming the wheels before accelerating on through. That's what I learned on Sunset Boulevard, stretches of which were like a snake on the move. I learned to chase that snake past drivers whose hearts were all brakes and no bravado. For my sixteenth birthday my father got me a new red Fiat sedan. I drove around singing, "I'm special, so special, I gotta have some of your attention," as though I'd turned immortal. Life was suddenly better than Disneyland, and all because I no longer had to ride the RTD, or stare out, passively, from the passenger seat. I kissed my baby-sitting days good-bye and got a part-time job at Paris Jeans, in Westwood.

Our jeans weren't from France, they were just "French cut," which was another way of saying sexy, which was what we sold: sexy jeans, and everybody wanted them. We had jeans that laced up the front, jeans with a sailor flap that unbuttoned at both sides of the pelvis, stovepipe jeans that fit so tight you needed help undressing—all to be worn with the other popular item at the boutique: cling T-shirts bearing the insignias of expensive cars. I was supposed to wear the merchandise to work, which meant I got to pick a few things to keep every time a new shipment came in.

"Watch out!" Kim howled when she saw me in my candy-striped Ferrari "chemise" and high-waisted, hip-hugging tuxedo jeans (they buttoned up the front with a little cut-out area at the navel). "Meredith's on the loose!"

For my birthday she'd given me musk-scented body lotion, a key ring that said "Hot to Trot," a bottle of glittery nail polish (color: Temptress), and a gold anklet. The time had come. All I needed was the guy. Plenty of attractive candidates came through Paris Jeans, but they hardly noticed me. I got the crazies from the Veterans' Administration, who would never wear our clothes but had nothing better to do than wander around the village with their haunted faces. There was one, "Edweird" I called him. He liked to touch everything, and mess up my neatly folded stacks, and peer at me from the back of the store. Sometimes, to get my attention, he'd take a T-shirt into one of the changing stalls along the back wall and just stand there doing God knows what.

One night I was alone in the back of the store, where I'd been helping a customer, when he appeared by surprise.

"Hi, Lisa." I'd told him my name was Lisa.

"Oh, hi." Somehow I managed to turn panic into the sound of pleasant surprise. Edweird had taken a pair of scissors to his hair and the results were rather disturbing.

"I brought you something." He produced an object wrapped in crumpled newsprint.

"Oh, no thanks," I said, and charged past him to the front. I took pains never to show him how much he scared me. I knew from movies the dangerous ones were sharper than average, and more touchy. Your fear just made them angry. You had to be nice, at least superficially, had to act as though you hardly noticed their excessive interest.

Edweird stayed in back awhile, looking at his rejected offering, then gradually made his way to the front counter. "I had a dream about you and me." His voice was agitated now, and insistent.

"Oh yeah?" I stared at my sales report as though hard at work, hoping he'd take the hint and go. It was better than being a bitch. On TV, serial killers always came back for the bitches.

"We were horseback riding in the forest." His face twitched. "I'm pretty sure it was Ireland. I made you laugh."

Except for stuff like that the job was great. I helped people shop, got to see their bodies in the clothes, and played whatever music I felt like on the tape deck. My first week I sold clothes to Goldie Hawn and Kurt Russell while listening to Steely Dan. I was good with celebrities. I gave them their space, let them think they were the same as anyone in my eyes. If I stared, it was only when they weren't looking. If I told someone, "Take a look at Robert De Niro, he's right over there," I made sure De Niro couldn't hear me. If I simply had to make contact, like a big jerk, at least I was clever about it. Valerie Harper came in once, and, after some thought I decided to say, "Great belt. Can I ask where you got it?" (It was always interesting to watch their surprise at being addressed, not for their celebrity, but for something small and unrelated to it.) She had to look down to see what she was wearing. Then it was just me and Valerie Harper, eye to eye. "Oh, I've had this belt for years. I think I bought it in Italy."

I always expected there to be more, hoped they might wonder who *I* was and why I wasn't in awe of them, but it never happened. My moment on-the-level with someone famous invariably came to a quick end. They went back to being recognized and fussed over, and I went back to being a nobody to whom nothing happened and no cute guys were attracted. I was sixteen three months before someone finally came along willing to help me out.

He entered Paris Jeans on a Tuesday night around six, a tall guy with all the best qualities of a slept-in bed. My kind of guy. Full, sensual lips. Irresponsible hair.

"Hi," I said. He was examining a pair of black denims, or rather, staring intensely at the label. "Do you need some help?" Hearing me, he slowly turned, pulled his glasses just enough down his nose to peruse me over the heavy black rims, and, without a word, took me in, all of me, with pale, blazing blue eyes.

A naughty smile blossomed at the corners of his mouth. "What did you have in mind?" Then he changed. He started to chuckle, as though embarrassed. "God, I'm not usually such a jerk." There was a thin gap between his front teeth, and spectacular dimples appeared in the hollows of his cheeks. "Guess I wanted to know if that sort of thing actually works with girls."

"Worked on me," I offered, eagerly.

He hid his obvious pleasure behind a look of pretend reproach. "And your parents had such high hopes for you." The guy had the gentle reassuring voice of a brother, the bone structure of a model, and the eyeglasses of a scientist from the 1950s. Running his hand through his long, dirty-blond hair, he asked my name.

"Pretty," he said when I told him. "What kind of underwear are you wearing, Meredith?"

I went away, temporarily, without actually moving. I know this because I was unable to account for the time between the end of his question and the start of my laughter, but in my absence, George Benson's voice had become louder on the stereo, and the room, suddenly warmer.

"Did I say something funny?" He cocked his head sweetly to one side, like a dog, his eyes roaming up and down my body. I was so unaccustomed to being looked at and talked to this way, I wasn't sure if it was okay to enjoy it.

"All right, that was in bad taste." He raised his hand. "I'm sorry." After a brief look away, he said, "Just tell me what color it is."

There was the feeling of being a human punching bag. Each new and surprising comment sent me reeling, yet there I remained, dangling in front of him. I felt idiotic. "Let me know if I can help you find anything," I said, returning to the counter.

"Hey, I thought you liked it," he called out.

I assumed I'd left him behind, but there he was a moment later, slapping those black jeans hard enough on the glass to startle me. "I'll take 'em." His eyes were bright and devious.

"You didn't even try them on."

"Oh yeah." He snapped his fingers. "Okay, forget it. My name is Andrew, by the way." His voice was his greatest asset. It was enormously soothing, gently angelic. He began humming a pretty tune, then moved his face so close I could practically feel the smoothness of his cheek against mine. "Would you like to get a bite to eat after work, Meredith?"

--------------------

"PEPPY'S PIZZA, name your pie." My mother's new boyfriend answered the phone. I had hoped he would. He was at our house a lot.

"Hi, Leo, it's Meredith."

"Meredith who? Do I know you?" I heard my mother half-complain, half-laugh in the background. Leo Fields, "Number One Closer on the Westside," according to his realty company advertisements, was hard at work selling my mother the idea that she loved him, or could, or should. That was his talent, according to him. He sold ideas, not property. He said he decided what people wanted, then made them want it, too. "I'm your man," he'd say whenever my mother needed someone to lend support. He was intense about her in a way that made me uncomfortable, but for once I was relieved to hear his voice because his presence tended to mellow her.

"Let me talk to her," my mother said. I waited while he handed over the receiver.

She was in a good mood, had probably had a glass of wine or two, maybe something stronger. I told her Kim made a surprise visit to the store and that we wanted to go out for a snack if it was okay with her.

"Do you think you should, on a school night, I mean?"

"Tell her to get her butt home right now," Leo hollered, then raucously laughed from somewhere in the room. I was grateful for him. He was so obnoxious most of the time it distracted my mother from thinking too much.

"Use your own judgment, I guess." She sighed. "But I want you home by eleven."

Was two hours enough time to lose your virginity? The store was empty, so I called Kim and we got to giggling and squealing about my impending moment of truth.

"I don't know if I can go through with it," I said, flirting with the long telephone cord, winding myself in its tight embrace.

"Of course you can. How old is this guy?"

"I don't know. Twenty-five?"

"He's a baby, Mere."

"Yeah, well, as long as he brings his pacifier."

It wasn't that I was fearless. Far from it. It just never occurred to me *not* to go through with it. That would have been like deciding not to see *The Exorcist* or *Jaws* when they first came out, just because I was scared. Kim had convinced me losing your virginity was a necessary rite of passage, like getting your driver's license. You did it at sixteen if you were lucky, so you could go on and get wherever you were going that much sooner.

I twisted myself tighter in the phone cord, away from the sheltering wall, and discovered I wasn't alone any longer. There was a guy standing near the entrance holding a long-stem rose, watching me closely over the lowered rims of his black eyeglasses.

"I gotta go," I said, struggling to get free of the cord.

Andrew's pursed lips and predatory eyes told me he'd heard plenty. I had to think fast. As he stepped closer I said, "I'm so embarrassed. That was my best friend. We were talking about this guy I know."

"You're really cute when you're nervous." He held out the rose and waited for me to take it.

"Well, I just hate to think that you—"

"Actually, I was hoping you were talking to your friend about me."

Our eyes hooked and it seemed everything that would happen between us was contained in that moment. He was going to unmask me and both of us knew it. I lifted the rose to my nostrils, needing its good scent, but there was nothing, no sweet perfume buried in the coiled petals. If anything it smelled slightly bitter, had the faint tang of something cut too soon from the bush.

"That's a peace offering," he said. "I have bad news about our date."

He'd remembered an appointment to meet a friend at nine-thirty. "He's someone who gets me jobs sometimes, but—and I don't know if you'll go for this—I was thinking you could come with me, meet my friend, then you and I can do whatever we want after that. I'll even spring for dinner if you come."

In the little employee bathroom in back, I peed. You can still get out of this, I told myself. You can give him your phone number and do it when you're more prepared, when you've showered, brushed your teeth, rubbed on body lotion, given yourself a facial, investigated the douche market.

I came out and switched off the lights in back, then joined Andrew. He was softly singing to himself.

"So?" he said.

"Sure, why not."

As I pulled the accordion gate across the storefront and locked it in place, I noticed the sporty white convertible at the curb. "That's mine," Andrew said. I'd never heard of an Austin Healey. When he saw how excited the car made me he said he'd let me drive it someday. "But don't go getting the idea I'm rich, young lady. That jalopy's older than I am. It was a hand-me-down from my father."

On Wilshire Boulevard I dropped my head back to look at the sky, my private sky. This is how you do it, I thought. This is how you live. The woman in the passing Oldsmobile looked at me and I realized that, for the first time in my life, I, Meredith Herman, was the girl beside the sexy guy in the convertible. In the open air, the longest blondest strands of Andrew's hair flapped gently against his face.

"So, what kind of jobs does your friend get you?" I had to yell.

When he turned, the hair wrapped his cheek like a veil. "I'm not sure I should tell you."

We were coming to my favorite stretch of Wilshire, where the road opens into eight sweeping lanes that all but beg you to press down on the gas and storm around the curvy pass into Beverly Hills. Andrew didn't seem to notice. *American Gigolo* fresh in my mind, I said, "Are you a male prostitute or something?"

"Meredith!" His jaw dropped and his voice went up high. Then he laughed. "Well, maybe. I do some acting, modeling, bartending, house painting—anything that comes my way. I'm really a songwriter." His hand left the steering wheel and rested on my thigh. "I want to know more about you. What do you do when you're not selling jeans?"

It was hard, at first, to respond with his hand heavy on my leg. It changed everything, the way I talked, my ability to think, to listen. I hurried through a lie about being a UCLA student majoring in photography, and wondered if I should lay my hand on top of his, or pat it, or give a light squeeze. I was trying to make up my mind when we came to a red light and Andrew's hand left me for the stick shift. I waited for him to bring it back as we continued eastward, and the longer I waited the more forlorn I felt, ugly and stupid. Other girls knew the right things to do, I told myself. Andrew belonged with one of them. Then he smiled at me with such affection I knew I was losing my mind. "You look like a dream, Meredith."

We zoomed left onto Santa Monica Boulevard and I turned to watch the world rush by. Was this how love began? Did you set out to do one thing only to have fate mark you for another? Did trying to find out what sexual intercourse was all about lead you instead to "the one"? I saw our future together, the songwriter and the schoolgirl, going from parties to recording studios, arguing passionately, making up with great sex, having babies, winning Grammys.

---

THE HOSTESS AT Café Figaro flashed Andrew a sexy smile the moment we walked in. "Robin's on tonight," he said with pleasure. "I'll be right back."

I watched him thread his way through the small crowd waiting ahead of us, then tried to decipher the meaning behind their eye and lip movements. All around me, older, sexually experienced faces conversed beneath sophisticated haircuts. Even the waiters and waitresses carried themselves with knowing flair. When I braved another look at my date I discovered he was no longer with Robin, the hostess, but was making his way back to me, so I prepared to act charming and magnanimous.

The first words out of his mouth were "She is such an angel."

"Oh?"

"She hasn't seen Billy come in, but she said she'd try to get us something here pretty fast."

"Great." My eyes found the large neon clock above Andrew's head.

Nine twenty-two. I kept my eyes on it so as not to seem overly interested when I asked how he happened to know Robin.

"She's the assistant manager." He was too busy grooving on her to be more helpful. "God, I used to have the worst crush on her." He nodded, in case I doubted it. Wasn't he breaking some rule of the universal dating code? Or was it the kind of thing people meant for each other are supposed to share?

I looked into his eyes and smiled. "Maybe tonight will be your lucky night. I get the feeling she likes you, too." There was no triumph in appearing *that* aloof. My impenetrable façade only made me feel more miserable.

"I think you know I'm not interested in Robin anymore." He leaned in close. When he saw I wasn't convinced, he said, "Don't tell me you're jealous!" I shrugged. "If you only knew what was going through my mind right now. It's all I can do to keep my hands off you, Meredith."

At our cramped corner table, the waiter, Gil, showed Andrew photos of a party he'd recently attended. He and the other party guests, all men, were in dresses and garish makeup and wigs. The two of them gossiped about people I didn't know, while I studied the walls, which were covered with varnished sheets of the French newspaper *Le Figaro*. It was nine forty-five and the guy we'd come to meet still hadn't shown up.

"Well, I suppose I should be getting back to work," Gil said. "Do you know what you want?"

Andrew turned to me. "There's a little matter we need to discuss." He winced. "Someone forgot to go to the bank today. I'm a little low on cash, so I'm afraid it's going to be soup and bread for us. Is that okay?"

"He uses that line on every girl he brings here," Gil said. "If I were you, sweet pea, I'd make him show me his wallet."

"Gilbert!" Andrew howled, then started for his back pocket. "All right, I'll prove it."

"Oh please," Gil said, "I believe you." He blew two kisses at Andrew. "I was only being contrary. You know it's on the house."

"How come you know so many people here?" I said, once Gil left. It turned out Andrew had tended bar for a year.

"Gil's been trying to get me in bed ever since we met."

I couldn't tell if that amused him or actually held some appeal, so I shrugged and said, "Hey, why not?" pulling my Miss Worldly routine, as though I encountered bisexuality in all my men. Rushing by, Gil dropped off what looked like a tall stack of bread and some butter, but turned out to be just two very thick slices, one of which Andrew began preparing immediately.

"Because, sweetie," he said, "I'm straight. Gil thinks one night with him will change that. In the meantime, I get free food." He folded the pillow of bread and butter into his mouth, which appeared to double in size around its large load, then he picked up the other piece. "You didn't want any, did you?" He grinned as he spread it with butter. "We can get more, but, actually, I'd prefer you to be hungry." He leered. "I shouldn't have let you order anything. Oh well, next time."

His eyes had this way of fastening on me whenever he alluded to sex. They were full of foreboding yet brilliantly blue, vividly explicit. Then their sharpness softened. "I could really fall for you," he said. I was fully under their spell. "I could see myself coming home to you, or traveling around the world and writing you long, soulful letters."

The problem was the perpetual twilight zone I lived in. I wanted desperately to believe in impossible things. People in movies and fairy tales fell madly in love the moment they met. Why not Andrew and me? I was convinced he really cared when I got on the subject of my parents' divorce. For once he listened without trying to distract me, nodding knowingly and becoming upset when I attempted to excuse them. "I'm sorry, but what they did to you and your brother is tragic." He launched into a whole deal about the way children are mistreated by adults. "I mean, where do they get the right?"

At ten twenty-five, when Gil lifted our plates and asked if we wanted dessert, Andrew closed his eyes, then said, "Fuck." He turned to me. "I just realized today's only Wednesday."

"And, don't tell me, lambchop, you're supposed to meet Billy Thursday night." Gil smiled, facetiously.

"Jesus, I am such a flake."

"You said it, not me." Gil turned and left.

Just as quickly as he became upset, Andrew relaxed and tapped the tip of my nose. "If you and I are going to start seeing each other, you might as well know I can be extremely absentminded. This has been known to get me in trouble with girlfriends." His breath on my face caused a quivering somewhere near the pit of my stomach, a sort of gentle spasming not far from my genitals. "Do you realize what you're getting yourself into, Meredith? If I were you, I'd think twice."

How glassy-eyed I must have been. How adoring. Buoyed by my evident pleasure at being termed "girlfriend," he suggested we get the hell out of there. When Gil handed him a bill for two cups of coffee, Andrew took a five from his wallet and said, "I owe you, Gil."

"You certainly do, and one of these days I'm going to see that I get paid." The two of them made eyes at each other. "But for now, how about calling me once in a while?"

Andrew stood up. "No phone, remember? But as soon as I get one I promise yours will be the first number I call." I got up, too, and thanked Gil for dinner, then carefully walked in front of Andrew toward the door, as though we'd gotten away with something the other diners musn't discover.

"I have something to tell you," I said when we got to the car. "Only, I'm pretty sure you're not going to like it."

He opened the door for me and told me to get in, then crouched on the sidewalk, his head and arms resting on the window frame close to my face. "I have something to tell you, too, but first I'd really like to kiss you. May I, Meredith?" When I nodded, his head came forward and my head helped a little by moving closer, then our lips pressed softly together for a sweet second.

"If you're going to tell me you're not a college student, save your breath." He studied me, tenderly, from an inch or two away. "Probably want to stay away from acting when it's time to pick a career. You're a lousy liar, sweet Meredith. I'd say you're about sixteen." He brushed my cheek with the side of his finger. "And I'd also say you're probably a virgin." He kissed me again—a shorter, harder pop this time—before circling around to the driver's side. I felt my pulse clanging in my head. My face was hot with humiliation.

"There's something else," I said, turning to see his eyebrows inch up as the glasses came down once again so that I might have a better look at his unremitting eyes. Pure sex was what I saw in them. He was the professor of sex wondering how much longer I was going to squirm out of taking my exam.

"I, um, have to go now. I told my mother I'd be home by eleven."

"I'm afraid that's impossible." He restored his glasses to their intended position and put the key in the ignition. "We're going back to my apartment now." Then he started the car.

"I can't." I raised my voice for the first time all evening.

"Sorry, darlin'," he said, pulling away from the curb. "You don't have a choice."

"Andrew," I complained, pretty sure he was kidding but realizing he could take me anywhere he wanted. "C'mon," I said. At the first side street he made a shrieking left turn onto a dark block that was a throughway to Santa Monica Boulevard. Before we got there, he jerked the car to the curb.

"Were you scared?" He grinned, his voice playful, his eyes shining in the light of the dashboard. I refused to answer. It had dawned on me, finally, just how vulnerable I was. Then he softened into that other Andrew, the one you could trust like your brother. "Meredith? What's wrong? I was only goofing around."

"It wasn't funny."

He turned off the motor and we sat there, not speaking, for what seemed a long time. "I'm really enjoying your company. I just want the evening to continue. I admit I thought about kidnaping you for five seconds, but I'd never do a thing like that. It was a stupid joke, sweetheart. You don't know me very well. I'd never make you do anything against your will. That's a complete turnoff for me. I want you to be completely comfortable. Otherwise I couldn't enjoy myself."

I looked at him finally. "Well, I really do have to go. Dinner took all the time I had. I'm going to be late as it is."

"One more kiss, okay? Your lips are *so* irresistible." I turned my head away so he wouldn't see me smile.

"How did you know I was a virgin?" I faced him again.

"Come home with me, Meredith, and I'll tell you."

"I can't," I said, more teasingly now.

"I can read your mind," he murmured, following the outline of my mouth with his finger. Then he pressed gently on my lower lip until it separated and let his tongue in. "You're a good kisser." He smiled. "You sure you want me to take you back to the store now?"

I leaned back, eyes closed. "What time is it?" My voice poured out like syrup.

"I want to make love to you," Andrew whispered in my ear. Then it was my own voice privately informing me that I was an idiot if I went home now. Luckily, I didn't have to say a thing. Andrew saw my caramelized stupor for what it was and started driving. Before we had a chance to say anything else we were at his apartment, a one-bedroom in West Hollywood, just south of Sunset Boulevard.

"Oh my God!" The furnishings, like the car, probably belonged once to his parents. They certainly weren't the accoutrements of a struggling songwriter. There was a strikingly beautiful painting of summer squash hanging over the antique sofa.

"I'll be right back," he said, and went into what had to be the bedroom.

"It's nothing like I expected," I shouted after him with delight. All around, a stately sense of comfort and taste prevailed. On the mahogany coffee table, *Artforum, Architectural Digest, Rolling Stone,* all with his name—Andrew Peyton—on them. He'd made it most of the way through a large book with the intriguing title *Gravity's Rainbow.*

"What did you expect?" he shouted back. "Or maybe you shouldn't answer that." Then I saw it, on a small end table hidden by the sofa: a white dial phone.

Andrew returned thrumming a guitar he'd strapped over his shoulder. He was no longer wearing his jacket, or glasses, nor anything on his feet, and looked the part of a luscious, wild-haired rock star.

"How come you told Gil you don't have a phone?"

"Oh, that," he said, looking at the strings. "That just looks like a phone." He thought he was being cute. "It's actually a very expensive piece of conceptual art." Satisfied that he'd answered my question, Andrew drifted in my direction. "I promise never to lie to you, Meredith, if you promise not to believe anything I say." He held out his hand. "C'mon, let's go into the bedroom."

There was another guitar, just like the one he was holding, on the bed. And a shiny red electric one in a stand on the carpet. "Why so many?" I said. Andrew was going around the room lighting candles, setting the scene for my seduction.

"I had another one but I sold it last week," he said without turning around. "I could have deep, meaningful relationships with twenty guitars."

His bedroom was spare. It felt colder than the living room, but purer, too, with just the bed, the guitars, and at least a dozen candles all around.

"Have a seat." He gestured to the bed. Once he'd lit the last candle he went to the wall and switched off the overhead light. Then he reached behind the bed, and on came a ceiling garden of little white Christmas lights, directly over the mattress. The effect was beautiful, magical, yet a stab of fear caught me at the thought of what was coming.

"So," my voice was high and tight, "you're saying you can tell the difference between this guitar and this one, even though they look exactly the same?"

He picked up the one lying on the bed and sat beside me with it in his lap. "Of course." Without any introduction he began playing a very pretty song, looking at the neck and strings mostly, but breaking away now and then to sing directly to me. It was a quirky love song about a girl who's gone and all the things, good and bad, he misses about her. Andrew slipped up here and there, missing a note or coming in late with a chord change. He even forgot the lyrics once, but he didn't seem the least bit self-conscious. The whole bumpy, endearing performance gave me an excuse to look inside his unbuttoned shirt at his chest, which wasn't hairless and smooth the way I liked but furry, like my father's. Another stab of anxiety shot through me.

"I can't believe I forgot the rest." He suddenly stopped. "Oh well."

"What a great song."

He put the guitar aside and stood up. "Yeah. Wish I'd written it."

"Oh, you didn't?"

"Wait here," he said, and left the room, returning a minute later with a dish of chocolate ice cream. "Just one bite."

He brought the spoon to my mouth and I didn't resist, trying to relax and enjoy the silky chocolate.

"What's the difference between a woman and a guitar?" he said, preparing another spoonful for me. "Open up." When he withdrew the spoon he began kissing me, his hot tongue seeking the cold ice cream. He probed and provoked until I completely forgot myself, lost my shape and ideas and anything else that made me distinct. Kissing him was like going to sleep, like multiplying into a hundred different constantly changing characters.

He ate a few spoonfuls, watching me. "Lie down," he said, patting my tummy, then put the dish out of the way. I was on my back, squinting at the dozens of lights, turning them into flowers, starbursts, when Andrew's beautiful face appeared over mine. He stroked my hair. "The difference between a woman and a guitar is that a guitar doesn't mind if you leave it to play another guitar for a while. It waits patiently for you to come back."

*It* was starting, and every moment seemed terribly important. There were details to be memorized, sensations to be experienced, all manner of data to be recorded on the way to the Big Event.

"Would you wait for me, Meredith, like a loyal, patient guitar?"

I didn't know what he was talking about. I just smiled. Andrew unbuttoned my tuxedo jeans and slid his cold hand over my underpants. Then the same hand pulled up my T-shirt, exposing my bra. I felt so many things: like an astronaut about to leave everything behind; like a life-size Barbie in the hands of a devious child.

Propped on one elbow, Andrew admired the view. "You're beautiful," he said, his index finger playing lightly over my rib cage.

"They're kind of small," I apologized.

"Your breasts?"

"Uh-huh."

"No," he purred. "They're just the way I like them."

"Really?"

He stood up to remove his shirt. "You have no idea how much." I was watching him, feeling pretty sexy with my underwear hanging out, but when he began unbuttoning his jeans, I had to lie back down and close my eyes and tell myself, You can do this. It's going to be all right. Andrew returned to the bed in his glowing white briefs, and, reclining on his side next to me, fastened one hand to the inside of my thigh as though poised to pry it open any minute.

"Do you want to go fast or slow, sweetie pie?"

"Slow," I instantly responded, practically pleading. I was counseling myself almost incessantly. You're here because you want to be. You're here to do away with idiotic virginity once and for all.

"Are you okay, Meredith?" Andrew's hand left my thigh and sweetly brushed my cheek.

I opened my eyes, finally, and looked at him. "Will you play me another song?"

He wasn't as clumsy this time, though he still played faster than he could, preferring to stumble and slip rather than slow down. But his voice was tender and reassuring, as always, and the music was so pretty I once again got hold of my fear.

"Did you write *that* one?"

"If I could write songs like that, I'd have it made." He laughed. "Neil Young wrote it."

"Would you play me one of yours?"

"Maybe a little later." He put the guitar away, and as he did I felt the butterflies return to my stomach. Courage.

"What are you using for birth control?" he said, standing over me.

"I didn't have time. I mean, we just met today and, I figured you—"

"Uh-uh. I don't wear rubbers."

"Oh." What else could I say? Not only didn't he wear them, but it was clear from his tone he found any man who did downright offensive. It was a moral position beyond argument.

"I've got an idea." He took my T-shirt all the way off, then unhooked my front-closing bra. Searching my face like a worshiper at the altar, he said, "Will you lend me your body, sexy Meredith?" I whispered yes.

"Don't move." He left me then, with my bra hanging askew, like something broken. I thought of the hell I was in for when I got home, imagined my mother and Leo pacing and fuming, worrying and sighing. Andrew came back carrying a big cushion from the sofa and told me to sit up. Placing it at an angle against the wall, he then had me rest my head and shoulders against it. "Are you comfortable?" When I asked what he was doing, he said "You'll see." For the next minute or so he adjusted my position and the position of the cushion, as though organizing objects for a photographic composition. When everything was at last in place, he took off his briefs and showed me how to hold my mouth without exposing my teeth, so they wouldn't hurt his penis as he shoved it in and out.

"Oh God," he moaned, using my face like a hole in the wall. I had to keep my eyes shut unless I wanted to look at his hairy stomach gyrating forward and back. It didn't occur to me he was doing anything ugly, not for a long time. He was teaching me about sex and I was trying to be a good pupil. "You're doing great," he panted. "It feels so good." But my throat was getting sore, and I couldn't breathe well, and still he kept on. "I'm almost there," he promised, after I started to gag.

"I can't take it anymore." I pushed him away, gasping.

"Just another minute." He tried to enter me again.

"Wait," I pleaded, turning my face.

"Okay, okay." He dropped down on all fours and gave me a quick peck on the mouth. Then, rising back up, he placed my hand around his penis and, guiding it with his own, managed to jerk off, ejaculating over my stomach.

"Not very impressive." He examined the disappointing trickle he'd produced.

Postejaculatory bliss lasted ten seconds, then he got up and went into the bathroom, where he switched on the light and started running the water. I didn't feel a thing, not even confusion. Everything was sharp and clear, just like the glowing wire centers of the Christmas lights above me.

Andrew was washing off my saliva while a blob of his semen grew cold on my stomach. I turned to watch him through the door crack, only to discover, in horror, that his back was a carpet of brown hair from his shoulders to his butt crack. It seemed impossible yet perfect, the one thing that grossed me out most in the world.

When Chewbacca returned, I was fully dressed and sitting on the edge of the bed. "You okay?" He rubbed my shoulder, taking a break from buttoning the sleeves of his shirt. Too late, I wanted to say, I already saw your sickening body.

At twelve forty-five the telephone rang. The one he didn't have. I walked into the living room to watch him speak to "Kev," someone he cheerfully agreed to meet in half an hour at a nightclub. It occurred to me his voice was exactly as it had been earlier, before I'd let him fuck me in the mouth. How was that possible when I myself was so very altered, unable, in fact, to speak a word?

"Want to come?" he said when he hung up. "I think you'd like Kevin." For a minute I actually considered it, tried to resuscitate the dream that we would go on and become a happy couple.

"Nah, I need to get home."

Andrew talked the entire drive back to Paris Jeans, about his prospects in the music industry, and his dreams of world travel, and overnight stardom, and all the rich, beautiful women he hoped to make it with. All I could think about was how much I wanted him to shut up, how very quickly I'd come to despise the sound of his voice.

He wrote down his phone number when we got to my car. "Birth-control pills are best, but I wouldn't take them, personally. That leaves a diaphragm. I'm not opposed. Give me a call when you decide, okay? I think we need to try again." He didn't ask for my number. He didn't kiss me good-bye.

Driving home, I sideswiped a parked car. I was busy trying to get a tape unstuck from the mouth of the car stereo when it happened. It was

one-fifteen, there was no one around, and I had no chance in hell of fig-
uring out which house the car, a Cadillac, belonged to, so I kept driving,
not wanting to know the damage to my own car until morning.

No one was waiting up for me, by the way. No one wanted any explanation. The house was bedroom dark, slumber quiet. No one had even
noticed I was gone.

---

MY BEDROOM DEVELOPED like a Polaroid print in the gradual morning light. For hours I'd lain awake, eyes unblinking, remembering a car I
once owned, a perfect red Fiat bought just for me. I had secretly planned
to keep that car twenty years or more, in perfect condition, until it became one of those classics you admire on the road. I so wanted to be the
kind of person whose possessions told of a certain care and easy longevity.
Instead, I'd shown exactly who I was in just three short months of own-
ership. I was one of the other people, who couldn't take care of anything.
All night I'd wrestled against that truth, obsessively replaying the moment I began messing with the tape deck instead of watching the road.
What if. I imagined a dozen other ways I could have handled things—
pulling over, patiently waiting, ignoring. I tortured myself, as if doing so
might telepathically reverse events. Thoughts of robbing a bank followed, of becoming a one-day prostitute, anything to get money so I
could erase the damage before anyone saw it.

I looked surprisingly normal in the bathroom mirror, no bags under
my eyes, no marks around my mouth. Pretending Andrew hadn't happened would be a cinch compared to dealing with the car.

Over breakfast, I envisioned a kindly older man of limited income
walking out to the street that very moment, finding his Cadillac bashed
without so much as a note of apology. As he reached out to examine the
Fiat's red paint, smeared like blood on his pale car, he would curse me.
Damn hit-and-run driver. I was sick with guilt.

Peter looked equally miserable across from me, gloomily submerging his Cheerios with the back of his spoon. "What's with you?" I said. He pulled a bunched-up sheet of paper out of his back pocket and placed it between us on the table. It uncrumpled itself, gently, breathing a bit of life into the room.

"Check it out," he mumbled.

In blue ballpoint my mother had composed an ominous set of lists.

| Pro | Con |
| --- | --- |
| Doesn't care about sports | Crass, obnoxious, can be |
| Admits when wrong | embarrassing to be with |
| Will probably be a millionaire | Only 5'10" |
| by 40 | Bad temper, though never violent |
| Very loyal, always takes my | Ruthless |
| side | Not "in love" with him |
| Crazy about me, no matter | |
| what I say | |
| Beach house | |

"Where did you get this?" I said.

"The wastebasket in the den."

I tossed the paper back. "Excuse me while I go kill myself." The thought of living under the same roof with Leo Fields was more than I could bear at that moment, though the beach house did sound pretty great.

"He hasn't proposed, as far as I know." Peter picked up the evidence. "I think she's just doing her usual fantasyland, what-if routine."

"I thought Sanchez retired."

"I never said that." Peter shoved the paper back in his pocket, then asked if I could give him a ride to school.

"Sorry."

"Why not?"

"I don't have the time."

"Yes you do."

"No, Peter, I don't." He was giving me a look of incomprehension.

"Why can't you ride your bike?"

"I blew a tire yesterday."

"You want to take mine?"

"No."

"Why not?"

"Just forget it." He got up and left the room.

He was going to find out sooner or later about my car, like everyone else, so I started putting together a believable story. Once I felt its construction was sound, I climbed the stairs to my brother's room. He was stuffing his backpack quite full for the day.

"I can give you a ride," I said.

He was surprised.

"But you have to promise not to freak out when you see my car. I scraped it against a concrete parking lot pole last night." It sounded good, casual. Peter's eyes burned with sudden urgency.

"Your car? You hit your car?" He bolted for the stairs.

"It was dark when it happened." I quickly followed him. "I don't even know how bad the damage is yet."

We crossed the street to where I'd left the car so my mother and Leo couldn't see anything from the house. I braced myself, joining Peter on the curb. "There go Dad's insurance rates," he said.

It wasn't too bad, just wavy beige streaks along the midsection and a long shallow dent near the front. All in all, the evidence accompanied my explanation rather well.

"Now I'll never get a car when it's my turn."

"I'm planning to fix it with my own money, Peter." I wasn't chancing getting caught by the insurance people, who could probably tell in one glance I'd hit another car.

On the way to Peter's school my sense of dread at last lifted. So what if Andrew had turned out to be the worst kind of human imaginable? What did that, ultimately, have to do with me? The thought of his penis, choking me, instantly brought back the heaviness in my chest, so I blocked it out and swore I'd get the car fixed as soon as possible.

"Thanks," Peter said. He got out and quickly became one of the hundreds of faceless bodies marching into that chain-link-bordered place. I watched them for a moment, then assured myself that people who drove Cadillacs and lived in Westwood could afford to have their cars fixed. I sat up straight, put my hands on the wheel at ten and two, and took a deep breath. "Today is the first day of the rest of your life," I said, then headed for school.

By the time I saw Kim, after first period, I was able to smile and roll my eyes when she started in with her questions. What was it like? How long did it last? Was there any blood? I promised full coverage at lunch, which we decided to have off-campus, "to celebrate." I didn't give it another thought after that. I was unusually attentive during my next three classes—relaxed, receptive, and remarkably wide awake.

-------------------

IN THE SEVEN MONTHS since losing her virginity, Kim had gone from a size one to a size ten, from gauntly appealing to voluptuous, almost chunky. When we got to Mort's Deli, she ordered a chef's salad with blue-cheese dressing, a side of avocado, and a blueberry muffin. She surrounded herself with food now, becoming momentarily disappointed at the end of meals, when all the plates in front of her were empty.

"So," she said, her eyes eager, "give me all the details."

I wished I could have made what happened sound colorful and sardonic, done my usual twist. She was waiting, hungry for it. "It was bad."

I smiled, watching her closely so I wouldn't miss the change on her face. "A total waste of time."

She picked up her diet soda and sucked a third of it through the straw. When I didn't continue, her sparkle began to dull. "Did you *do* it, at least?"

The night before already felt incomprehensible. Turning it into a story that involved my willing participation was beyond me. "Let's put it this way: he put his dick in me but I'm still a virgin."

She considered the riddle, looking into my eyes while turning over the possibilities. I lifted my soda and sucked a piece of ice into my mouth, manipulating it provocatively for Kim's benefit.

"Oh my God! You gave him a blow job?"

I knew I hadn't done anything as active as "give" Andrew a blow job, but the conversation felt like a negotiation, so I went ahead and accepted her terms.

"Uh-huh." I was aiming for a kind of deadpan smile, a try at dampened self-satisfaction. Whatever I was doing, it made me feel sophisticated and in control.

"And?" Kim said. I wasn't sure what she was fishing for. "You know . . . did you swallow?"

I told the truth, that he came on my stomach using his hand to masturbate. I didn't mention the assistance provided by my own hand.

Kim didn't look happy. Then our beautiful food arrived, heaps of it, and she busied herself getting ready to consume.

"He wouldn't wear a rubber." I felt defensive. "That's why we didn't get around to you-know-what. The whole thing was a disaster." Having managed to tell her the hardest stuff, albeit by rearranging certain facts and omitting others, it seemed safe to go back and make her understand why I'd bothered with Andrew in the first place, so I began at the beginning, keeping the story's end from my mind as I described his entrance into Paris Jeans. The food helped a lot, felt very good going down, and the story I told was exactly as I hoped to see it someday: light, amusing, a touch sarcastic. I just had to hurry and finish my chicken salad before my stomach seized up.

Being a senior, Kim didn't have any classes after lunch. I had geometry, but decided to ditch when she suggested going to the beach. It was less than a mile south of school. The surfers did it all the time, were conspicuously absent when the waves were high. Their teachers showed surprising tolerance. For me the penalty would probably be detention. That was how it was. Some people got away with everything, and other people—myself apparently among them—paid one way or another for every go at illicit pleasure.

During the short drive to the beach I provided the final piece of the story—the part about my car. Kim, sucking on a peppermint, listened carefully without turning to me. I didn't know if she was concentrating on the story or thinking thoughts of her own, so I finally said, "What? Do you think I'm scum for not leaving a note?"

She parked the car and finally turned to me. "Please. Don't be ridiculous. Of course I don't think you're scum."

"I do."

She pressed her lips together as though hesitant to say what she *was* thinking. "Andrew's scum. Right?"

We stared at each other and I felt a massive crumbling begin. She'd understood, though I'd done my best to spare her. "Yeah," I whispered. Then Kim put her arms around me and I found myself weeping, going back and forth between laughter and tears as I admitted, once and for all, how truly awful my experience had been.

At the water's edge we strolled north through packed, yielding sand, our feet repeatedly washed by the rushing-in waves. We didn't talk. We listened to the hovering seagulls instead, and the force of the waves drawing back, then crashing down. Their gentle reach erased our footprints, sent pebbles sliding to and fro in perpetual indecision. In the far distance the cliffs of Malibu jutted into the ocean, curving the landscape into a sweeping bowl.

"Any word from Washington?" I broke the silence.

"Nope. I'm hoping today's my lucky day." She would be accepted, of course, though I didn't understand how or why she'd decided on Seattle for college. It was so very far away. I imagined her classmates in Pendletons and logging boots, saw guys with bushy beards huffing and puffing through pine forests each day. It sounded scenic and dull, and nothing like Kim.

We sat for a while on a sandhill, staring at the water. I mentioned the list Peter had found in the wastebasket.

"You're the most beautiful, intelligent, fantastic person, Meredith. And so am I, and we should never forget that, you know?"

I lay back, shielding my eyes from the sun, and looked at the sky. "Extra, extra, read all about it." With tears in her eyes, Kim burst out laughing.

Thirty minutes later I was in a darkened, near soundless room with one other person, making a test print of Kim's face. It was a close-up I'd shot some weeks before in the library. She was deep in concentration, copying information about capital punishment for a political-science report. It was just the kind of picture they might put in the yearbook to balance all the zany shots of people with their mouths wide open—mid-scream, mid-bite, mid-laugh—many with their tongues stuck out; or guys in cheerleader outfits and wigs, their bustlines grotesquely over-stuffed.

I set the timer, exposed a fifth of my printing paper, and waited while five seconds of light graced the room, trained downward through the negative onto the shiny white strip. I uncovered two fifths of the paper and invited another brief interval of light. When the fifth and final section of paper had been exposed for five seconds, I took my test print from the easel and slid it into the tray of developer in the center of the room. This was the magic part, where the image gradually appeared, ghostly, from underwater as I gently rocked the paper with my tongs. After a minute and a half I moved the print along to the stop bath, then the fixer. Then I carried the wet print, which was a rainbow of black-and-white exposures, ranging from too light to too dark, into the next room to determine, under strong light, the best exposure.

There were quite a few prints I wanted to make that afternoon in my bid to be a yearbook photographer. I'd been snapping away, trying to capture the cliques in their distinctive habitats. I had a shot of a black girl and her friends over by the cafeteria, where most of the bussed-in kids congregated. She was wearing fuzzy bedroom slippers and a shower cap over curlers. I also had a great shot of four girls from the all-black drill team practicing their routine. I caught the surfer guys standing in a loose lineup in front of their favorite brick wall, hands stuck deep in the pockets of their corduroy Levis. They looked at the ground, or the quad as they spoke, instead of each other. The theater people formed a circle, gesticulating like mad, touching and slapping each other. I had tried to photograph every group, even the misfit loners who somehow always managed to sense my presence and turn away.

Printing had always been my least favorite part of photography. I generally felt entombed in the darkroom, a restless victim of sensory deprivation. The strong smell of the chemicals irritated my throat and lungs, so that I could take it for only so long. Yet something was different that afternoon. I didn't resist the blackness that swallowed me, or the quiet. For once I didn't count the minutes passing, separating me from the world. I lost awareness of the outside altogether, and found comfort in the small, sheltering space. My work ceased to be a separate activity from my thoughts. I was the room and the activity inside it. There was no room. I wasn't me. It was fantastic. When the bell ending sixth period rang, I kept right on working, something I'd never done before. Mr. Dorion stuck his head in and asked was I staying after. "I'd like to," I said. Then I was joined by a couple of other people, full yearbook staffers.

Norman Tamigawa, Mr. Official Hotshot Photographer, worked right next to me and I wasn't even intimidated. His pictures of hang gliders at sunset and seagulls in flight were just like the ones on calendars and greeting cards. He also took most of the official portraits for the yearbook: Most Likely to Succeed, Best-Dressed, Class Clown. He looked a little too old to be in high school and I imagined he kept flunking so he could stay back and be Mr. Cool forever.

For an hour no one spoke. Familiar faces emerged in the scarlet dim, passing through the trays of pungent, magical chemicals. Unfamiliar faces, too. Pieces of our personal lives. There was a picture of Peter, a surprise "gotcha" kind of photo I snapped one morning at his bedroom door. Even though he'd said, "Wait just a minute," I'd pushed it open and caught him in his underwear, which he barely managed to pull on before I took my picture and ran away, laughing. I decided not to crop it, liking the way the up and down stripes of his wallpaper accentuated my brother's hobbled form. Only his face confronted the lens full-on: gaping mouth covered by upraised hand. Eyes as awake as they could be, showing disbelief and a trace of the pain of violation. I looked at this face projected on my printing easel and absorbed my brother's astonishment for the first time. What I'd done wasn't the least bit funny. In fact, it sickened me, and so I removed the negative from the holder and, using scissors, cut it to pieces over the trash bin.

It was a quarter to five when Norman told us to wrap it up. He began dumping the trays and running water into them. I'd been in the darkroom three hours and felt remarkably pleased with myself and the work I'd accomplished. Then I got to my dented car. The sight of it took me right back to Andrew's bedroom and all that had occurred in it. I raced home, eager to crawl into bed and go to sleep.

Across from our house, nine-year-old Mikey Waller said something as I got out of the car. He was in his front yard, his bratty voice aimed in my direction.

"Did you speak to me?" I said.

"Yeah. Why don't you park in front of your own house?" He had a smirk on his face. Years before, Peter and I had created our own version of the famous Life cereal commercial, the one with little Mikey. Our cereal was called Death, but we kept the same slogan: "Mikey likes it."

"The street is public property, Mikey. I can park anywhere I like."

"Yeah? So, how come you stopped parking in front of your own house?" He was looking at the gash on my car, then our eyes met.

"How come you care, Mr. Know-It-All?"

"Someone's scared," he said, importantly. "I saw you and Peter looking at it this morning. I bet you're in trouble if your mom finds out."

"Wrong." I started walking away. Leo's car was in the driveway, one more annoyance. "She already knows, dork."

"Oh really? So you won't mind if I ask what she thinks of it?" he shrieked after me. I kept walking. I had no doubt he meant business. Occasionally, Peter and I imagined new ways to murder him.

My mother and Leo were in the kitchen. He was wearing her apron and dribbling white wine over a sauté pan of cut-up chicken. When I said hello and commented that it smelled great, my mother, who was leaning against the counter with a Bloody Mary in hand, gave me quite a look. Had Mikey already done his dirty work?

"Something the matter?" I made a sharp turn for the fridge to get myself some apple juice. As I reached for a glass, she poured on the sarcasm, addressing Leo.

"The matter? Now, what could possibly be the matter? Leo, do you know of anything?" I sipped my juice and waited. Leo smiled awkwardly.

"Let's see." She let out a long sigh. "Someone named Eric called from Paris Jeans around four-thirty, wondering where you were."

I ground my foot into the floor and stuck my chin all the way out. "Shit."

"Oops." Leo laughed, grinning at me. "Looks like someone forgot to go to work today Hey, at least you're okay. Your mother was worried." He went back to reading his recipe and cutting up mushrooms.

"I was in the darkroom. I completely forgot." I started for the phone, but she asked me to wait, said they had something else to tell me, about Peter.

"He wasn't where he was supposed to be today, either." My mother smiled, sourly. I didn't like her when she drank. Alcohol gave her a floaty detachment that she depended on when things got difficult. She preferred it to showing real concern. "Instead of going to school your brother rode the bus to Sherman Oaks and showed up at your father's doorstep demanding 'asylum.'"

All of us smiled. "You gotta love the sense of humor on that kid," Leo said.

"He begged your father to take him in, said he didn't want to live with me anymore, especially with Leo around."

"Who can blame him?" Leo roared.

I decided not to call the store after all, for fear they would tell me to hurry in. There were three and a half hours left until closing and I was in no state to work.

"He begged Dad to take him in a year ago," I said. "So it's not about you, Leo."

"What happened that time?" He munched a piece of fresh parsley.

"Dad was wishy-washy, said he didn't have room, but maybe later. He was just back from Europe, living in Catherine's guest house." Both my mother and Leo were staring at me, listening intently. It shut me right up.

"Well, anyway," my mother said, "your father's coming over to talk. He's bringing Peter back. Time to set the table, Leo?"

"Yeah, this is ready. Let's eat." He looked at me. "You going to call your boss?"

"I guess I'll wait till tomorrow."

He continued staring at me. "You look like hell, darlin'. Let's get some food into you." I wanted to hug him for noticing.

Leo, who was thirty-seven, like my mother, was good-looking at a glance. Dark hair, blue eyes, ruddy skin, big smile. You put it together and handsome was the first idea that occurred to you. But if you looked at him awhile, or found yourself, say, at the same dinner table with him, something happened. That smooth red skin turned out to be a bit slack, pulpy and soft, like raw meat. Those bright blue eyes were actually somewhat bloodshot. His hair was either slick with gel or wet from the shower, and his mouth was overlarge for his face. But it was Leo's style, more than anything, that called his good looks into question. His swaggering speech, his deep and rasping voice, his overexercised laugh, his mistaking loudness for authority. All through our short meal he argued with my mother over what sort of participation he should have in the coming discussion with my father. He felt he had every right to be there and to speak his mind freely.

"Who knows how you're going to feel once he starts in about Peter and all? You're going to need someone in your corner and I'm going to be there looking after your interests, and Peter's, too." He was holding his chicken with his fingers, getting grease on his face and enjoying himself immensely. "You know the way I am," he continued.

"That's what I'm afraid of," my mother said.

"You know I can't just sit there when I've got something to say, especially if it concerns you."

He had these ideas about being united with my mother against the world. He was already talking about "when you get your realtor's license, Leigh," like he was going to teach her and groom her. He seemed utterly unacquainted with insecurity or self-doubt, a human bulldozer.

At seven o'clock the doorbell rang. Leo was in the bathroom and I was finishing up the dishes. When I turned off the water Peter and my father were coming inside, dour expressions on both their faces, so I sent a friendly wave from the kitchen. Then Leo stepped into the foyer and introduced himself to my father.

"I guess you've heard plenty about me. Isn't that right, Peter? Why don't we all go into the living room so we can shout this thing out. Who wants a drink?"

That was Leo's talent right there. It wasn't that he knew how to make people comfortable. He knew how to make them *uncomfortable* just as quickly as he possibly could, before they got their bearings. While strangers were on their best behavior he set things instantly off-balance, daring them to tell him off, knowing they wouldn't. People were sheep, he often said. All he was doing was capitalizing on it.

I almost invited myself in on the discussion but settled instead for a patch of floor in the dining room, where I could hear every word. My father was talking.

"Peter started calling me a couple of weeks ago from a pay phone at school." His voice had its now standard postdivorce air of exhaustion. "I'm mostly at home now, writing. Anyway, I started getting these calls from the kid here, and he didn't sound too hot, said he hated school and begged me to come pick him up and take him the hell out of there, et cetera, et cetera." Every sentence strained for emotional flatness. Nothing phases me, his tone insisted, but I knew his act too well to be convinced.

"He cried and told me school wasn't the only problem, said there were problems at home, that Mom's new boyfriend did things he didn't like. He wanted to move in with me."

My father released a big sigh, resting momentarily, then resumed his story. His controlled delivery began to have a lulling effect on me. I flattened my body on the dining room floor and the drone of his voice began to mingle with the wonderful chicken and dinner rolls in my tummy. I hadn't slept in thirty-six hours, and fell quickly asleep.

"Look, excuse me," a voice shouted, jolting me awake. "I'm not clear. Do you live here?" It was my father, and all pretense of self-control had gone out of his voice.

"Do you?" Leo fired back. He was probably grinning, his skin redder than ever.

"Okay, look. I don't see how this concerns you, pal, but if you want to sit in I can't stop you. But for Christ's sake, have the intelligence to stay out of it. This is about Peter, not you."

My mother suggested Leo let them talk privately.

"Can't do it," Leo said. He'd heard a lot about my father and wasn't impressed. "This concerns you, sweetheart, which means it concerns me, too. If I have to step on a few toes, so be it." He was from Texas, and fancied himself some kind of cowboy. "Maybe Peter *should* live with his daddy if he wants to. I mean, why the hell not?"

The living room went silent, then Leo's big, Evinrude voice started up once again. "Hey, he doesn't like it here? Maybe he doesn't like me? I know I'm tough to get along with. Let him live at your house for a while, see how he likes that. I happen to like that kid. He's got spirit. I'd like to see him be happy."

"What do you think, Robert?" my mother said. I sat up, petrified I was about to lose my brother.

My father sighed. "I don't see how it would be possible. My schedule right now, the house—"

"But you said—" Peter whined.

"Here we go!" Leo clapped. "I knew it."

"Listen, whatever your name is, if you don't back off—"

"C'mon, I'll meet you outside. You can show me and your son you've got more than lame-ass excuses up your sleeve. Your schedule? What kind of BS is that?"

"That's it." My father stood to go. "I don't know where you found this jackass, but this is pointless."

"Uh-huh. I didn't think so," Leo said, as my father left in a fury.

I was up now, standing with my back pressed hard to the wall. Peter, in tears, stormed the steps on the other side of that wall, up to his bedroom, where he slammed the door.

"Jesus, Leo," my mother said.

"Pretty good, wasn't I?"

She thought about it. "Yeah, actually, you were." Then she kissed him and said, "I always wanted a personal attack dog."

"Let me tell you, you're going to need one with that guy coming round."

"Robert's not a bad person."

Leo growled like a dog. "But you like me better, right?"

"You're my Doberman." They snuggled and cooed, then my mother said she wanted to talk to Peter, privately.

"I'm going to head on home tonight. I'll call you when I get there," Leo said.

"All right." She walked him to the door. "I'm so glad you were here tonight, Leo Fields."

"I think maybe you like me just a little."

"Maybe a little."

When I was finally in bed with my eyelids shut, I found my mind unwilling to quit for the day. I had more worrying to do, this time about my job and how I was going to redeem myself. I was amazed I'd forgotten to go to work, but there it was. Now I'd have to be perfect, always on time, no more lazing around the counter. I needed every cent from that job to fix my car.

Then it came to me, like a gift from the gods of simplicity: pretend. Admit nothing. Play dumb. Show up Saturday as if I never got the message from my mother, as if I definitely called Wednesday morning and spoke to someone to say I couldn't make it in. Deny, insist, accuse. With every breath, I felt my brain's enfeebled, depleted reserves at last begin to shut down.

--------------------

I WALKED INTO Paris Jeans and was instantly greeted by Craig, an assistant manager who had never liked me. "What are you doing here?" He was sincere. He honestly wasn't expecting me.

"I'm supposed to work."

"Didn't someone call you?"

"No."

He smiled, sadistically. "Well, then, let me be the first to tell you you no longer work here."

I started right in, acting all surprised and devastated. It wasn't hard, because the sense of loss was genuine. I had to fight a lump in my throat, and felt tears in my eyes. Craig thoroughly enjoyed himself, smiling unabashedly as I pled my ignorance and begged for a second chance.

"You're fired," he sang, waving good-bye once my dance of desperation lost its novelty. All I could think about as I got back in my car was how I would ever manage to fix it. I'd grown accustomed to the money from that job, and the free clothes. I drove past Edweird, of all people, holding hands with a girl who looked pretty normal. They were talking and looking at the ground. For five seconds, I was actually jealous.

When I got back home, my mother was just closing the garage door. "I thought you'd be at work," she said.

I looked at her, gloomily. "How was the beach?"

She'd spent the night at Leo's. "Interesting." She gave me a look that threatened big news. I pretended not to notice and we proceeded to the front door.

"And how are you?" she said, brightly, as we went inside.

"Lousy. They fired me."

"Well, how about some iced tea?"

I wanted to scream, Did you even hear me, you stupid twit? I got fired. I lost my great job that I loved.

"We can sit in the living room and have a nice visit. How does that sound to you?"

"Okay." I lacked the energy for a fight.

For some reason she wanted to wait on me, so, while she got our drinks, I sat in the other room in Kamran's bright-blue chair and let myself imagine having a real conversation with my mother, one in which I got to share my feelings and receive actual comfort and guidance. Maybe I'd even tell her about my car. Things had been going well for her. It wasn't inconceivable she might offer to help.

She carried a tray into the room and placed it on the coffee table. "There's sugar, and I cut up some lemon, so you can help yourself." I scanned the tray, idly, wondering how to begin the conversation, when I noticed the huge pear-shaped diamond in the little black velvet box.

"Oh my God." I reached forward and lifted it to my face. It was the most beautiful thing I'd ever seen, like holding a star.

My mother's expression was that of someone who had just sat on a tack but was trying not to yelp. She bit her lip. Her eyes bulged slightly.

"Can I put it on?"

"Just be careful."

They'd only been dating a few months, yet it wasn't much of a surprise. I thought of Craig's sadistic enjoyment in firing me less than one hour ago, and my own humiliating pleas for another chance. Now I was wearing a diamond a man with a beach house had given my mother. I removed the ring, about to ask what she was going to do.

"What should I do?" she said. I put the ring back on the tray. She'd quit smoking two months earlier and taken up a new bad habit: digging her fingers into her scalp. The self-assaults varied with her state of mind. At that particular moment her right hand was like a small animal nervously grazing at her head, feeding itself from the skin and oils under-neath her hair.

I said, "Don't decide if you're not ready."

"I'm never going to be any readier than I am now."

"And? How do you feel?"

She let her hand fall from its busy work and picked up the ring box, then her face took a sour turn, her eyeballs rolled, and her lip, in con-junction with her nostril, faintly snarled. "Like a failure, how else could I feel? Like a big, fat zero."

"You're not a zero," I said.

"No?" This seemed to perk her up momentarily, but then she slipped right back into her seething pit. "Tell me one thing I've done with my life that's been a success. Tell me something I'm good at. Nothing. I'm noth-ing. I don't know how it happened. I wanted to be something. I wanted to be more than someone's wife."

"You're good at Scrabble." I meant it in all sincerity but she let out a bitter laugh, as though she were an empty can I'd just kicked farther down the road.

"Gee, thanks."

"No, I mean, you're smart. Maybe you should go back to school."

"I'm almost forty, Meredith. It's a little late for that."

"A lot of women are doing it."

"And study what? That's the problem. I don't care about anything. I just want to be a natural at something." She put the ring on, and placed the empty box on the coffee table. Looking at it, she said, "It's so osten-tatious." The diamond disappeared into her favorite patch of scalp. I oc-cupied myself trying to come up with a good profession for her.

"Anyway." She let out a sigh that turned into a moan. "You got fired, those shits. You going to look for another job now?"

I shrugged. "I guess I have to if I want to fix the damage to my car." She ceased her digging while I described the inconveniently located pale yellow concrete base of the parking lot lamp I'd hit four days earlier. Every time I told the story, the details got sharper, more complex. It was to the point where I could actually remember being involved in this entirely made-up accident. I dealt with her inevitable question about insurance by explaining there was a deductible, for one thing, and I didn't want Dad's rates to go up, for another.

"I got an estimate from the body shop. Five hundred bucks. I was going to pay for it myself, which is why I didn't tell anyone, but now I don't know what to do."

"I can talk to Leo. He knows a lot of people. He's always cutting deals and trading favors. And he likes you, you know."

"I like him, too," I said, automatically, the feelings arriving at the thought of his help.

"You do?" She became suddenly hopeful.

It was the wrong time for such questions. She was wearing that ring and looking at me as if my vote counted double. Then the transformation began, the one I was so familiar with yet never prepared for. Whatever held my mother's face up began to collapse, reminding me of an avalanche. First came the rumbling and loosening, the falling out of the bottom, followed by a colossal downpour of tears.

"My life is shit!" she cried. "I wake up in the morning and I have no idea how I got to this point. I can't believe your father is married to that woman. It just isn't real. I need someone to take care of me, too. I can't do it alone. I'm not strong. I'm weak. I'm a coward." She dried her face with the back of her hand, and sniffled. "Oh, Meredith, you're so lucky to have your whole life in front of you. You're wise and bright."

She could be a little child, my mother, so lost and frightened. The problem was, I didn't feel the least bit sorry for her. That was always the problem. I could sit and watch her weep, I could listen to her pleas for help, and what I felt—strangely, consistently—was anger.

My mother dropped to her knees then, right in front of me. "Tell me,

Meredith. You're so clever and capable. What should I do?" Her face was soaking wet again, her nose running. "I just want someone to tell me." She shivered, then laid her cheek on my knee, wrapping her arms around my calves before giving herself over to wordless, eerie wailing.

Three days later I was sitting in Leo's Mercedes-Benz outside the office at Alex's Body & Paint on Pico Boulevard, squinting. All around me were cars that had once been right and straight, waiting to be restored to their earlier condition. Dimpled, punched-in, twisted and split open, each had acquired a certain grandeur. Mine just looked stupid with its set of cream-colored streaks. A chicken at the game of crash and burn. Thanks to Leo, who was friendly with the owner, the work was only going to cost two hundred and fifty dollars, and, thanks to Leo again, I was going to pay it off by working weekends at Leo Fields Realty, answering the phone.

After ten long minutes Leo came out and got in the car with me. "He'll have it for you a week from today."

"Thank you so much, Leo."

"Don't worry about it. It's all in the family, right?" He was turned toward me, his face looking out the rear window as we backed into traffic.

"Uh-huh." Monday my mother had accepted his proposal of marriage. He had no idea how wrenching her decision had been.

"Your mother is a beautiful person." Leo turned north on Twenty-sixth Street. "I'm talking on the inside, you understand. God knows, she's gorgeous on the outside."

His arm was resting on the open window, the sleeve of his blue silk shirt billowing noisily in the breeze. I'd been tired for days but was only just becoming concerned. My fatigue seemed to emanate from deep within my bones.

"The reason we're good together is that your mother doesn't know what she needs. I look out for her, and I'm going to look out for you and Peter, too."

I smiled. Who the hell were these people, anyway—Leo and Catherine—and why did they insist on winning my approval? Catherine had made it her project, lately, to get to know me. Now Leo wanted to protect me?

"Your mother and I are straight with each other. No bull. We show it all, the good and the bad, and I mean the very bad."

I simply couldn't understand why my parents had decided life with these people was better than life with each other.

"Let me tell you something, Meredith. All that BS about falling in love and finding the one true person who's meant just for you? Crap. Don't waste your time on it. Rule number one: life is messy. Why do you think there's so many divorces? Relationships are like houses. You can have any kind you want. Shop around. Don't buy the first one you see. And watch out for guys like me. I could sell you a Porta Potti if I decided that's what I was going to do. Ha-ha!" Leo poked me in the leg.

I was thinking that all four of them—Leo, my mother, Catherine, and my father—were like human leftovers, when my finger pressed into a surprisingly hard little bump protruding from my neck, just below my ear.

"Am I boring you?" Leo said, watching me.

"Ouch!" I fingered the bony swelling. "My gland's really big."

Leo reached over and felt it. "A little swollen, maybe."

At Broadway he turned right and parked a few blocks later. "I have a little business to take care of. Come with me. It'll just take a minute." We got out and started walking.

I hadn't known there was a restaurant at Twenty-second and Broadway until Leo came to a stop in front of the small, pleasant-looking patio full of diners. "See this place?" He raised his voice loud enough to collect several startled looks. "Don't ever eat here. It stinks, it's just god-awful!" He pretended, convincingly at first, to be talking to me, but it became obvious as he went on that his intended audience was the restaurant's patrons, several of whom became visibly alarmed, not by his claims but by the possibility he might be dangerous. "The kitchen is filthy, the food is rank, and, on top of that, it's overpriced. I think the health department's been out. I wouldn't eat here if I was starving."

I was too shocked to know what to think. A few diners, I noticed, found his performance amusing. Then it was over. His business concluded, Leo took my arm and guided me back to the car.

"I can't believe you did that." I pulled away from him. "You totally embarrassed me."

"Why? What's the big deal?" He calmly unlocked my door, then went around to his own and got in. He'd been irate a moment earlier, angry enough to beat somebody up in front of that patio. Now he was Leo again, acting as though the entire incident hadn't happened. What I didn't know was that Leo repeated this exact routine about once a week, or whenever he was in the area and had someone in the car with him. That day it happened to be me. It would come to be known in our family as Leo's "Broadway Café Disease." We could be on our way to the movies, or coming back from the airport. It didn't matter. Leo would park for five minutes and pretend to be strolling by the restaurant just so he could do his part to hurt business. That's what it was all about. Payback. The owner had screwed Leo out of a big commission once upon a time, and this was his revenge: years of steady and vociferous bad-mouthing. I came to enjoy it. "Let's drive by Broadway Café," I'd say, wanting to see Leo in action. He was a great nut, howling at those people trying to have a nice meal. It didn't matter how rich or busy Leo became, and he became both. He didn't quit cursing the Broadway Café until it burned down in 1987.

Mononucleosis. Strange name for a disease you got from kissing, or being penetrated in the mouth—I would never know which, only that the cure was sleep, and so, sleep is what I did. When I wasn't sleeping I thought about Andrew, not me and Andrew, just him, alone, driving his car from place to place, parking his penis wherever a space opened up. I had trouble accepting his version of me: the stupid high school girl who would let any guy have his way. I couldn't stop thinking about the power I had possessed before playing everything so terribly wrong. I was sure I could have made him fall for me if I'd only acted differently. Sometimes I imagined he was there, sitting at the edge of my bed, smiling sweetly at me and stroking my cheek with his soft, gentle hand. How lovely that would have been.

Peter knew nothing about my escapade, yet made it his personal goal to cheer me up. He brought me little treats, like the *National Enquirer*, which he read aloud using a hard-news, businesslike tone of voice. One afternoon, near the end of a riveting story about a woman who walked on all fours, ate only dog food, and slept in a little wooden house, my brother suddenly threw the *Enquirer* down, announced "dance break," and did a ridiculous number for my amusement, rotating his hips wildly, then pulling off his shirt and whipping it around above his head.

I gasped, hurting from laughter. "Stop! I'm supposed to be resting! Peter!"

Grinning, my out-of-breath brother fell on the bed as the tingly call of tired blood enveloped me. "Will you stay while I take a nap?" I said. Peter found the comic book he kept under my bed and was still there, reading, when I changed positions.

How to Spend the Evening Alone in a Beach House: 1. Pour yourself a vodka tonic, courtesy of your stepfather's bar. 2. Drink it and wash glass immediately. 3. Locate Billy Joel LP *The Stranger.* Turn off lights and put record on turntable, using the aqua glow of the amplifier as your only light. 4. Position headphones, turn volume up. 5. Lie down on carpet in front of sliding glass door overlooking Pacific Ocean. (Especially nice if you can see the blue glow of amplifier reflected in glass, superimposed over ocean in front of you.) 6. Feel alcohol anesthetize you. Let music shoot through your cortex like a gleaming silver pinball. 7. Accept the voice of Billy Joel as your personal savior. 8. Turn album over. Consider second drink. Replay as needed.

Our house had sold in July. Just like that, like everything, it was lost to us. Then, in August, my mother sold the vestiges of our lives in that house, first at an estate-, then a yard sale. I had only to conjure *The General*, a treasured oil painting from our living room, to recall it bobbing away in the arms of a neighbor.

Never again would those doleful eyes follow me and Peter across the room. Gone forever was the exquisite blue vase with red cherries my mother had sold for six dollars to a complete stranger, even though I offered to buy it for eight.

"Forget it," she said. "I want to get rid of everything." She was wearing one of those change-makers around her waist, and stood behind a table with a sun visor on her head, yelling, "Everything goes. Make me an offer!" She saw everyone except me, right in front of her, trying to stop the hemorrhaging.

Away went the turn-of-the-century sideboard, the set of sweet antique chairs with tie-on cushions, our crushed-velvet sofa, and on and on, piece after piece, until the blows eventually lost their power and I gave up. After that we moved to the beach, where Leo and my mother got married on the sand in their bare feet, and our new lives began.

Of course, you don't live somewhere your entire life without it coming to live in you. You can sell everything you own but that doesn't mean you get rid of it. It was inside me now—the rooms, the objects, the way the light from outside graced everything. I moved through that house at will, opening cupboards, walking to the backs of closets, whenever I needed to, so as not to forget.

Leo's house felt like Leo's more than I expected. When he was around I acted especially polite, moved about carefully, and ate less than I really wanted. I pretended not to know my mother well, not wanting my presence to remind her that I knew she had chosen him out of desperation, to get back at my father and the rest of the world.

I liked Leo, surprisingly. He was aggressive and outrageous, but there was something unbridled and innocent about it. I found him theatrical rather than arrogant. He didn't waste time wishing he were anyone else, or attempting to learn from his mistakes. At home and in the world, he behaved as he liked, regardless of the opinion of others. "Fuck 'em!" he roared.

There were times I found Leo hard to take, of course, like the day Kim left for Washington. I took a long walk up the beach that day, and when I returned, Leo was standing on the deck, a towel wrapped precariously around his waist. His towels always seemed loosely fastened above his manhood, though none had ever come undone in my presence. He was fresh from a shower, holding a drink in one hand and letting the clean ocean air give him a final blow-dry. Leo took about five showers a day. What coffee breaks were to other people, showers were to him. They cleared his head between projects, refreshed him, changed his channels like nothing else. I'd become used to him dripping wet, half-naked and reeking of Irish Spring.

"How about that sunset?" he said, as I came up the stairs leading from the sand. "Wasn't she a heartbreaker?"

I wasn't in the mood for conversation. I felt melancholy and wanted to continue the quiet of my walk.

"Sit down and have a drink with me. Go on in and get yourself a Coke or a tomato juice."

One of the problems with the beach house was its open, up-and-down design. The common rooms were largest and made one feel onstage, the audience being anyone outside on the sand. You couldn't get to the bedrooms or the kitchen without passing through the common rooms. Consequently, privacy, or the feeling of it, was hard to come by.

I stood in front of the open refrigerator and stared at the choices. Heineken, Mr. & Mrs. T, Coke, V-8, orange juice. I considered nonchalantly wandering off to my bedroom, saying, if asked later, that I had gone to the bathroom and forgotten all about Leo waiting on the deck. Instead, I poured some Bloody Mary mix over ice and stuck in a piece of celery—a Virgin Mary for the virgin—and went back out to face my fate.

"Have a seat," Leo said. He was relaxing on one of the loungers. We looked at each other briefly, then out at the sea.

"Well," he sighed, "it's sunset, you take a long walk by yourself.

Something's on your mind, that much I know. What it is—now that's where I need a little help."

He waited, as though I owed it to myself to tell him my thoughts. It was pure Leo. The whole point of conversation, for him, was to prove he was good with people, extra-insightful, a combination mind reader/ guidance counselor. I figured what the hell, it might be amusing to watch him in action.

"Kim left today, that's all."

He didn't say anything right off, just sipped his drink and looked in the distance. Then he turned to me. "Here's to Kim." We toasted. "I know you're going to miss her, but I also know something you probably don't know."

Yeah, yeah, yeah. I was just practice for him, his mental calisthenics for that next big home sale. "And what might that be?"

"It was time. The two of you needed a break from each other." He watched for my reaction.

I felt myself turn unexpectedly angry. How did he do it? He got right under the skin every time. Even when his amateur mind-games were ludicrous, as this one was, he managed to tap a vein for even daring to make the suggestion.

"Oh, really?" I said. "And how did you come to that brilliant conclusion? You don't even know what we're like when we're together."

"Sure I do." He turned back toward the ocean and stretched, closing his eyes and arching his head way back. I imagined throwing my ice-cold drink in his lap, upsetting the towel.

"I see things, Meredith. I understand people."

"Uh-huh." I started calming down. He was returning to a tolerable, laughable size.

"You don't have to believe me. I know what I know. And I know you're going to be better off without Kim."

"Fine. Whatever you say." I emptied my drink and got up. "I have some stuff I need to do."

Summer had been a blast with Kim. When I finally recovered from mono in June, she was obsessed with an older man named Marcus Ferraro. He was the first guy she ever liked who was also my type: long-haired, temperamental, creative. Marcus—she wasn't allowed to call him Marc—was directing a play at the Rustic Canyon Playhouse, where she'd gone to audition. He'd given her a garter belt and frilly lingerie, and she demonstrated the way he pinned her arms above her head when they made love.

Though I loved hearing her stories, I couldn't help feeling that during my long bed rest, Kim had mistakenly been granted the fulfillment of *my* fantasy life. The secrecy thing—Marcus forbade her to acknowledge him in public—was right out of my erotic imaginings. And the glamour aspect, Marcus being a noted local director, and ten years her senior, was like *All That Jazz,* one of my favorite, favorite films.

"We need to find you someone," she often said, after telling me about their torrid afternoons. "Maybe you should give Vince a try."

Vince waited on us at Luciano's, our restaurant of choice that summer. He probably thought we came in for him, but it was the Pizza Special we wanted. For $4.95 you got a cup of minestrone and a dinner salad, a small pizza, a side of spaghetti marinara, and a dish of spumoni. With all those trips to and from the table, you also got to know your waiter.

"He's really more your type," I said. Vince was a brawny, mustachioed hunk. "How about we trade? Vince for Marcus." The truth was, I did find Vince attractive, more and more as the summer progressed. I loved the respectful, admiring looks he reserved just for me.

"He's crazy about you," Kim said one night in August, after we ordered. "I think you should go for it. Summer's almost over."

I watched her scarf up every morsel. She even ordered a side of garlic toast. By that point the Pizza Special was *her* meal, not mine. I'd quit ordering the parade of food when it started showing up on my hips and thighs. I marveled at my beautiful friend's ability to eat like a linebacker and stay thin. "Where do you put it?" Kim had actually lost weight that summer, trimmed back the bulky softness that in spring started accumulating, even in her face. She was angular again, though not too skinny. Her body kept its new curves and womanly contours while somehow resisting excess weight completely.

"How about when he comes to clear the table we ask him what he's doing after work?" she said.

"Don't you dare."

She wiped her face and hands, then abandoned her napkin. "Well, I'm going to the loo." As she headed off, she commented, with pleasure, "I almost forgot I still have spumoni coming."

Vince brought it as soon as she got back, two dishes, even though I reminded him I hadn't ordered the Pizza Special. "Yes, I'm aware of that. I thought you might like some anyway." He stood over our table, beaming at me with arms crossed like the King of Siam.

"Meredith wants to ask you something." Kim spoke to him directly. I cracked up.

"No, I don't."

"She's kind of shy."

He didn't look at me, thank God, at least not right away. He stood there with one of those awkward smiles on his face until I couldn't stand the situation any longer.

"We just wanted to know what you're doing later, after work." I glared at Kim, who didn't care. She was delighted with herself, and waited for Vince's response. I don't suppose either of us will ever forget the slow, fluid way his smile transformed into a look of distaste.

"Excuse me, ladies," he said, curtly, "I'll be right back with your check."

"What did we say?" Kim was genuinely spooked.

"What's *his* problem?" I added. Mostly we were silent, understanding, somehow, that our feminine wiles had just been rebuked, practically spat upon. We pretended confusion, but I, for one, felt vaguely ashamed.

Our check was delivered for the first time ever by the busboy. We quickly got out our money, left it on the tray, and got up. Vince was standing in the lobby with his arms crossed over his chest. " 'Night, ladies," he said, the way he would to anyone.

" 'Night," we called back, miffed.

On the sidewalk Kim burst out laughing. "What a freak!"

"He *is* Catholic," I joined in. For some reason, this caused her to laugh even harder. "I mean, in his religion we're probably sluts."

"What a creep. He probably can't even get it up."

"What a schizo," I said. We carried on like that all the way to the parking lot.

"I'm sorry." Kim hugged me good-bye. "He was so adorable all summer. Who knew?" The whole episode had already become lore, another wild story in the epic of us.

"Hey, I'm glad we found out," I said. Then we got in our cars and headed for the exit. I didn't mind the long drive ahead of me, out to Malibu. It was my first week in Leo's house and I still enjoyed speeding up and down Pacific Coast Highway.

At the first red light a few blocks from the restaurant I noticed Kim's car ahead of mine in the other lane. She was eating potato chips from a bag on her lap, one after another, as though she were famished. It was like watching a complete stranger. Then the light changed and she turned left and drove away.

I continued west on Wilshire, maintaining thirty miles per hour, and discovered that at that speed one never hit a single red light. They kept changing as I approached—green, green, green. I couldn't get the episode with Vince out of my mind. I was sorry the flirtation was over, that

I'd taken it further and spoiled it. That seemed to be my big mistake: showing guys I was interested. It turned them off.

The night before Kim left, I gave her a back rub. I'd never done that before, to anyone, but she looked so sad and scattered standing among the boxes in her bedroom. No wonder. She'd been dumped that morning by Marcus Ferraro, who had promised to make the long drive with her to Seattle. The little shit backed out over the phone, ending their summer-long affair with one sentence: "It was good while it lasted, but I think we're mistaking lust for something deeper."

She cleared off one of the beds and lay on her stomach, her head turned sideways, eyes open. I climbed on top, seating myself on her butt. "It's for the best, I guess." She exhaled, releasing her frustration. "I knew he wasn't in love with me, but I was crazy for him."

What would I want if I were the one lying here? I asked myself, then placed my hands between Kim's shoulder blades, my thumbs stretching down into her back while my other fingers held on near her neck. I would want it deep and sure, strong but not too hard. Right away, Kim moaned that it felt amazing. "Let me take off my shirt," she said.

I was relieved not to be the disappointed one, for a change, to know that even girls as beautiful as Kim got used and discarded. She may have gotten to live my fantasy that summer, but now that it was over the despair was all hers. We were even.

Her back settled beneath me again, a patch of perfect earth for my fingers to turn and cultivate. I brought my thumbs in line over Kim's vertebrae and alternated the pressure between them, moving leisurely up from her tailbone, pressing the edges of the little circles. I drew feather-light patterns that radiated to the far corners of her skin, then dug in deeply where I imagined it felt best. I didn't know where my ideas were coming from, only that I was capable of variation after variation. After twenty minutes I was finally emptied, satisfied my fingers had said it all.

Kim was in a state resembling sleep. I lowered myself next to her, close on the bed, and felt very strange indeed.

---

"JUST THE WAY YOU ARE" was pouring from the headphones, all deep and reverberating. I tried to experience the song as if for the first time, but excessive radio play had killed it. Besides, if you thought about it for any length of time, Billy Joel was really saying *don't* be yourself. Don't change your hair, your clothes. Don't try to please me. I don't like it when you do that. I don't love you just the way you are. It went either way, depending on how you looked at it. "Scenes from an Italian Restaurant" came after that, clattering up and down my tracks like a giddy roller-coaster car.

> Brenda and Eddie had had it
>    already by the summer of '75.
> From the high to the low
>    to the end of the show
>    for the rest of their lives. . . .

It was so good to be inhabited by sound, surrounded by water, pacified by alcohol. I wanted nothing and smiled at everything, sensuous slip-sliding world. I loved its silent turning. Drunk. Happy. I was. Then I felt the incursion of harsh light all around me. Leo, my mother, and Peter were back from their movie.

"What are you doing here in the dark?" my mother said as soon as she saw me, though the answer was perfectly obvious from the headphones I was removing. I asked how the movie was.

"It was great," Leo decreed, at the same time that Peter condemned its stupidity. They'd gone to see Robin Williams in *Popeye*. "This moron didn't think it was funny." Leo pitched his thumb in Peter's direction.

"This moron laughed nonstop through the entire movie." Peter applied the same gesture to Leo.

They liked each other now, thanks to the Doctors Nogel, as Peter and I had called them all summer, though their names were really Charles Nogel and Elizabeth Fischer. They were child psychologists my mother found after Peter's attempt to move in with my father. For his first visit, my brother was taken down to the first-floor coffee shop and bought something to eat.

"That was the whole visit?" I asked, later the same afternoon.

"Uh-huh."

"What did you order?"

"Apple pie à la mode." The two of us grinned in contemptuous dismay.

The second visit was the same, but the third brought a little surprise. After Peter and Nogel had eaten and taken the elevator back to the fourth floor, Nogel walked him to the door of the other office in the suite, the one with Elizabeth Fischer's name on it, and knocked. "Dr. Fischer is my wife," Nogel said.

My brother described a large open room, three times the size of Nogel's office, with multicolored toys and a blue mat on the floor, and very bright fluorescent lights.

"How come I'm in here?" Peter said pretty quickly, which made her ask if he was uncomfortable. When she offered him a seat and explained that she and her husband often worked as a team, he said, "Well I've already had chocolate cream pie, so I doubt there's much you can do for me."

She said he sounded angry. "Would you like to hit me, Peter? You can if you want to. Maybe that's what we should do. Maybe we should have a good old-fashioned fight." According to Peter, she went to the big mat in the middle of the room and held out her arm for Peter to join her. "I'm pretty strong. You won't hurt me. I bet I can wrestle you to the ground."

He took the bait and they quickly became serious. She was a strong opponent, tugging him forward and back, left and right. He tripped her once and messed up her hair pretty good. She grunted and showed her teeth. Eventually they stopped in a draw, smiling and panting.

My brother's subsequent appointments were divided between fights with Dr. Fischer and treats at the counter with Dr. Nogel. The treatment took three months, exactly, after which he was cut loose, a happier, healthier person.

"Well, I still say the movie was dynamite," Leo hollered on his way to take a shower.

My mother said the room was stuffy and slid open the glass door. I followed her onto the deck, where we gazed at the black ocean. "What did you think of the movie?" I said. I felt small and luminous as I waited for her answer, connected intimately to the universe that held us. After too much silence she exhaled, loudly, the sound of someone fed up.

"I wanted you and I to be close," she said, her eyes on the far distance. "I remember when you were a little girl, everyone said you'd bring me the most joy in life. Well, I'm still waiting. Do you think we'll ever be close, Meredith?"

My stomach tightened. An incongruous smile dominated my face. "I don't know." But I did. I just couldn't imagine telling.

"Anything's possible, right?" She smiled back, bitterly, and went inside.

1 9 8 1

JANUARY

My father pulled the car to the side of the narrow mountain road—there was *snow* right outside the window—and said, "From now on, your mother is your business. I don't want to know about her." I'd only mentioned that she and Leo were going away for the weekend, too.

"You don't want to know anything?"

"I don't care if that asshole she's with wins the Nobel Prize."

Catherine complained about his mouth. Asshole, I recalled, was a name my father once despised, but I decided not to mention that as I studied the scads of gray hair he had acquired in the past year. Melody and Jennifer stayed out of it. They were kind, friendly girls, but us kids had yet to become more than acquaintances, so it was embarrassing to be having this discussion in front of them.

"So," Peter clarified, somewhat indignantly, "you're saying me and Mere are not allowed to talk about our own mother in front of you ever again?"

"Yeah. Can you handle that?"

"What if we forget and accidentally say something?" I said.

"Hey, relax, okay? You're taking this the wrong way here. Just try to remember that I don't want to hear about your mother or that crazy maniac she lives with."

"Leo?" Peter said.

"Right. Loco." My father pulled back onto the zigzagging road. We were roughly halfway to Mammoth, where a rented condo awaited.

"Be careful," Catherine touched his arm.

He didn't speak for another hour. Once or twice, she tried starting a conversation but her efforts were met with unanimous silence. (Example: "I wonder how many people will be there this weekend.") I don't know what the others were thinking, but I was psyching myself up to do well on the slopes, possibly astonish all in our party. Only Catherine and her daughters had skied before. This gave them, their bloodline, the advantage. If I could do well on my own, they'd know our side of the family was tough stuff, too, that we didn't need anyone's charity.

"I can't believe you're a beginner!" Jennifer would say, once she saw me in action. She was seventeen—my age in another month. "You ski like you've been doing it all your life!" Melody would gush.

The three of them had been talking about the "rush" of skiing since we left L.A., extolling the fresh powder we'd have all weekend. They meant to excite Peter and me, of course, but their enthusiasm only made me competitive. They seemed to be flashing their lifetime membership cards in some exclusive Winter Sports Achievers' Club.

"So, Meredith"—Catherine suddenly pivoted to face me in the backseat—"have you decided where you're going to apply to college?"

"No." I sounded curt, then worried Catherine might think the attitude was for her instead of college.

"Melody loves San Diego. You two should get together and talk about it. There's a lot of outdoorsy stuff to do down there."

The University of California. It was an obvious choice because it was affordable for state residents and had a good reputation, as well as several campuses in appealing locations, but I had no interest in going there.

"That would be nice if both of you were at the same place. You'd have someone to show you around," Catherine continued.

"You should come check it out," Melody said warmly.

"Let's talk about something else." I cushioned my remark with a laugh. "I don't even want to think about college yet."

The car was slowly filling with subjects we couldn't talk about. College was mine. My stomach knotted when I thought about it, because I knew no one was going to cheer when they found out I wanted to put it off awhile.

Our condominium was ugly, though I was probably the only one who felt that way. Brown carpeting, white walls, beamed ceilings also painted brown. The main room was open all the way to the ceiling, where a dirty skylight added some light to the dingy interior. While we kids investigated the upstairs, my father hauled in most of the gear. Peter and I immediately dubbed our room "the chalet." As usual, I postponed practical matters such as unpacking, or checking out the surroundings so I could lie on my bed and adjust. It had been a five-hour drive. We'd gone from city to mountains, from warmth to cold, from the familiarity of home to temporary cohabitation with our *other* family. I needed to close my eyes and be still for a while.

Just as I began to relax, there was a gentle knock at our door, then Catherine stuck her head in. "I'm sorry. Are you feeling okay, Meredith?" I told her I was just resting, and she chuckled. "Same thing your father's doing. Can I talk to you guys a second?" She was inside before we answered.

Catherine sat on the edge of my bed, her words aimed at me and my brother, who was on his own bed. "Your father loves the two of you very, very much, I want you to know. It's because he cares about you so much

that he doesn't want to hear about your mother or Leo, can you understand? He's not too fond of Leo, so, naturally, he doesn't like the thought
of you having to live with him."

I watched her as if she were a puppet, as if her hands and the movements of her head were being controlled by invisible strings. Had she
honestly forgotten Peter's attempt to come live at her house? If Leo bothered our father so much, how come he didn't do something about where
we lived?

"It drives him crazy!" she stressed, earnestly. "The doctor said he'd
give himself an ulcer if he didn't cool it, so that's why he asked you not to
mention her anymore."

She wanted to be a bridge, and I could appreciate that. For the most
part, I'd stopped thinking of Catherine as some arbitrary lady my father
married when my mother didn't want him anymore. I genuinely appreciated her goodness and intelligence, but I had a problem with the very no-
tion that a grown man required a spokeswoman to explain him to his
children. She was too new on the job to be telling us how it was. Never-
theless, we mumbled our agreement when she finished, said we understood, would cooperate, blabbity smiles, blabbity arm squeeze, blabbity
bye-bye.

By dinnertime my father was in good spirits again. Catherine sat next
to him and rubbed the back of his neck as we discussed handguns, and
whether they should be legal. This led to a debate about TV violence that
soon turned into a forum on the superiority of British television, ending
in a comparison of Europe and America in general.

I hadn't known that police in England didn't carry guns, that they
didn't need to because no one else had them, which is probably why I
said I wanted to live there, with that exaggerated forcefulness people use
during frivolous conversations. Europe just seemed better all around. In
my mind it was one big country, not a collection of countries. A compos-

ite place made up of all the good things I'd ever been told about it. I had the impression the clothes were better, the food was better, the people were given better educations, the kids were given wine, dogs ate in restaurants, movies were more like art, art was more like art, people took longer vacations, the buildings were prettier, the driving was faster, they didn't give tickets for jaywalking, heroin addicts didn't have to steal, and prostitution wasn't a crime. Based on these things alone, Europe symbolized, for me, enormous personal freedom and quality of life and greater wisdom and better safety. And so I said it, longingly, jokingly, when I found out cops didn't shoot people and people rarely shot each other. "I want to live *there.*" As soon as it was out of my mouth, I realized to my deepest surprise it was true. I didn't want to go to college right away. I wanted to see Europe, like Chester, to live there and experience it for myself. I wanted to know if people were different in Paris, if I might be different among them. All of this came to me at that noisy table with my father and Catherine, and Peter and my stepsisters, as their voices passed instantly out of personal relevance. They went back to discussing the right to bear arms. I touched the handle of my fork, held it up and studied the fine layer of scratches that caused its dull, worn appearance. Europe was going to be just like the nose job, I realized. Convincing them would be misery. I'd have to cry before it was all over, maybe a lot.

"Meredith, don't you like your lasagna?" Catherine had noticed something was keeping me from my food. Now everyone took an interest, so I said it was delicious and forced myself to take several bites, though my stomach was already tight with new excitement and dread.

"What's the big deal?" Peter said when we were back at the chalet, seated on our beds.

I'd chosen to confide in him, had sat him down and explained my secret desire to travel instead of go to college. "It is a big deal." I was near tears, but that was the first step. You had to try it out on someone, so you picked the person who was sure to take your side and bolster you for the fight ahead. At first he was surprised by Europe, then he didn't see the problem.

"Why are you getting so bent out of shape?"

"Because," I agonized, trying to keep my voice down but wanting to scream, "why would they want to pay for me to go to Europe? It's not normal. Parents want their kids to go to college. They'll never let me do it." I threw myself across the mattress, aware that my prostration was self-inflicted, almost ritualistic. What I really feared was Europe itself, doing this thing I'd latched onto during dinner. Paris was way far away, totally foreign. What if I ended up a street urchin, dirty and in rags, a beggar-expatriate-photographer-drug-addict? I began to cry, because I wanted it but was also terribly afraid. All Peter could do was look on quizzically.

"You think I'm silly." I blew my nose.

"No." He shrugged. "I just don't understand."

Melody tapped on the door and invited us to take a Jacuzzi with her and Jennifer. Slowly, like a flock of pigeons, Europe lifted from my mind and scattered in fifty different directions, making room for more pressing American considerations. I had seen them in their bathing suits before and they had seen me, so there wouldn't be the usual here's-my-lousy-body routine. And, as I recalled, my body looked damn good compared to theirs. Jennifer had that pinkish, freckled skin so many redheads were burdened with, and she hadn't been given enough height to carry her large breasts gracefully. Melody was a little taller, had silky, light brown hair, and a more evenly proportioned figure, but I looked most like someone in a magazine, so I quickly agreed to go along. (Peter, outnumbered three-to-one by females, claimed he wasn't in the mood.)

There were two Jacuzzis down at the pool. One was already full of people drinking and visiting. The other, at the opposite end, had only a man and woman sitting close together, drinking from martini glasses. I followed Melody in their direction.

She said hello without being overly friendly as she stepped into the steaming, aquamarine circle. Jennifer and I were right behind her and each of us said hi. The man and woman turned their smiles to us, not appearing to mind the intrusion one bit. That was Jacuzzi etiquette. You had to be prepared for company and act gracious about it when they showed up, because, more than anything, the spas were for relaxing and mingling with fellow guests, for soaking tired bodies and dissolving boundaries by way of bubbles and booze. If you wanted a hot scene with your companion, you excused yourselves and went back to your condo. That's what I hoped Mr. and Mrs. Martini were going to do. I flunked Jacuzzi etiquette. I wanted us to have the circle to ourselves.

"Ladies." The man raised his glass in our honor. His haircut turned me off, as did her powder-blue eye shadow, and so I snobbily decided I knew all I wanted to about this couple.

Jennifer and Melody were much kinder, engaging with the nobodies, who showed no sign of wanting to get back to their condo. They were all talking about conditions on the slopes, describing their various skiing levels. When asked, I politely said it was my first time. The woman—we'd learned her name was Bobbie—very sweetly offered that it wouldn't take but one quick lesson for me to be on my way. I think she was slightly cross-eyed. "My favorite part of skiing," she confessed, "is this right here." She indicated her martini, which was almost gone.

Hubby, Rex, reached around for a large thermos and refilled their glasses. When I realized they were there for the duration, I began to relax. I heard Rex say something about the fact that we weren't drinking, but I released myself from the obligation to respond, delegated that role to my stepsisters, and delivered myself with closed eyes to the action of the swirling, foaming water. Why did humans require themselves to make conversation, I wondered, willing myself to dissolve like a cube of ice in the boiling, chlorinated soup. Why was it so hard to be silent in the presence of strangers, to be quiet without being judged rude or peculiar?

I leaned my head back, resting it on the hard ledge. The hiss of breaking bubbles filled my mind like music. They were all talking about sunglasses now, comparing the best brands for maximum protection, using terms like *ultraviolet, snow-blind, fiberglass.* When I opened my eyes I had the startling sensation of falling into the black sky as though pulled by the force of the many stars splattered across my vision. My stomach dropped away and I panicked, quickly grabbing the plaster ledge beneath my knees for reassurance.

Stars were something you forgot about when you lived in Los Angeles. The word itself meant only one thing: celebrities. Yet there they were, nearly forgotten. The longer I looked, the harder they were to fathom, appearing to quiver slightly, to turn and vary from moment to moment. Their spell was broken when Bobbie and Rex dredged themselves, like sea creatures, out of our cozy cauldron and said their goodnights.

"Check out lift seven tomorrow. It's awesome," were his parting words to my stepsisters. We watched them amble away, then Melody complained, through teeth locked in a phony smile, "I thought they'd never leave."

The three of us spread out, forming a triangle in the round pool. We performed our own private water ballet as we talked, twirling our hips and outstretched legs over the powerful, uplifting jets of air.

"There's something we wanted to say to you." Melody's brown hair had gone limp in the rising steam, and her skin glistened. "It's about that rule Robert made today."

Robert. Of course that's what she would call him, just as Leo was Leo to me, but it caught me off guard, as if my father and her Robert were separate people.

"Oh, that made me so mad," Jennifer said, arching the small of her back over a roiling blast of bubbles that held her aloft and bounced her gently up and down.

"Yeah," Melody continued, "we thought it was wrong of him, and we just want you to know that around us you can talk about your mother whenever you want."

"We *want* to hear about her." Jennifer laughed. "Right, Mel?"

I told them that their mother—I called her Catherine to see how they liked it—had followed up the scene in the car with the later explanation about my father's health.

"Good ol' Mom," Jennifer said, getting out of the Jacuzzi to cool off on the rim. She and Melody exchanged a knowing look. "She's such a caretaker."

"Total caretaker." Melody let herself slip under the water all the way, so that every inch except her face was submerged. She was staring at the sky when she said, "We love our mother, Meredith, we really do, but it kind of makes us sick the way she bows down to anything Robert wants."

"Imagine what they're like in bed." Jennifer began to shiver slightly. Goose pimples stuck out on her breasts and thighs.

"Oh please," Melody groaned, "I'd rather not."

I didn't tell them I'd tried imagining the very same thing more than once, myself, in my early quest to understand how anyone could be attracted to their mother.

Jennifer said, in a breathless voice, "Just tell me what you want, Robert, darling. I'll do anything."

"Stop it!" Melody stood up, mock angry at her sister.

"You want me to put it in my *mouth*?" Jennifer continued.

"Please." I joined the protest. "It's too revolting."

I instantly recalled the sound of my parents "doing it." For years, there had been nothing but a wall between my bedroom and theirs, and some nights I had wrapped my pillow around my ears and hummed "The Star-Spangled Banner" until they concluded their pleasure throes, which sounded like two people being fatally stabbed.

"Your mother is this humongous mystery to us," Melody said.

"We don't even know what she looks like." Jennifer got back in the water, which seemed to sizzle as it accepted her newly chilled body. My father would have been pleased. I had no desire to talk about my mother.

..................

"HOW WAS IT?" Catherine said, wandering out of the bathroom to intercept me at the top of the stairs. She was in the middle of brushing her teeth with a big, buzzing electric toothbrush.

"It was great."

"I'm so glad you kids are getting to know each other, finally," came her garbled words. She was blocking me from going to my room, which made me want to get there even more, but this didn't seem to occur to her. "We played Scrabble," she said. "Your father won, of course."

Foamy white paste oozed from every crevice of her open mouth. I didn't offer that my mother had always won in the old days. I just nodded and smiled agreeably, and found myself captivated by the tempest in her mouth. The toothpaste was assuming a life of its own, doubling in volume every few moments, pullulating with an almost fluorescent virulence.

"Oh Jesus!" She laughed, catching the runoff with her hand, then hurried back to the bathroom.

..................

SNOW IS A GREAT SILENCER. Even Peter and I became mute as we watched it come down through our chalet window. It was nothing like rain or anything I'd experienced before. It was delicate and sneaky, and oddly, unexpectedly, soundless. The turmoil I'd put myself through the night before—lying wide awake, worrying about the future—seemed silly as I watched the snow accumulate, turning the landscape suddenly dormant. The condo was quiet, too, except for someone in the kitchen downstairs. We went out to the railing and saw Catherine in her bathrobe, putting a pitcher of orange juice on the table. Melody was down there, too, assisting her mother while Jennifer sat on the couch nearby, reading.

"Ever get the feeling you're being watched?" Peter's newly deep voice filled the air with the force of a crashing object. The three of them looked up.

At breakfast, my father complained about pain in his lower back. "I probably twisted it carrying in all our crap." He buttressed the spot with his hand. Catherine poured him coffee, to which he immediately added milk without thanking her. It was embarrassing, her servitude. I watched him chew as though it were tedious work, then swallow when chewing got old. Was he afraid he'd be accused of hunger if he showed a bit of pleasure? There always seemed to be an invisible KEEP OUT sign behind my father's eyes now, past which nothing could be confirmed. He could smile or grimace. It didn't matter, because there was a stiffness to him, a refusal to play his hand. He used dismissive terms, like "crap," to talk about our belongings, and called the executive producer of his show "What's his face." Why? Even I knew the guy's name was Gary.

"Enjoying your breakfast?" I asked him. He was catty-corner to me, at the head of the table, so there was no doubt who I was addressing with my raised eyes and focused voice. After a beat, he gave me an appraising look.

"Uh-huh." Then he resumed loading the food in, grinding it up, and dispatching it to his stomach.

"What do you like about it?" I couldn't look at him this time, but spoke as casually as possible into my scrambled eggs. Up to that point, the others had been talking. Now, it seemed, they were listening in.

"Well, it tastes good for one thing, and it doesn't ask me questions."

I smiled. "What's wrong with questions?" It was starting to feel like a game, like flirting, and I liked that. When he didn't answer, I said, "Which do you like better, the eggs or the bacon?"

He stared at me. "The bacon," then bit the piece he was holding. He was impenetrable. He gave answers, yet I failed to learn anything new about him. I took a big gulp of juice.

"Can I ask you something?" This made him laugh.

"Oh, now you're asking permission?"

"Okay, fine. What would you say if I told you I might not want to go to college?" My stomach tightened and I stopped breathing as I waited for some kind of emotion to arrive on his face. The response surprised me, coming as it did from the other end of the table.

"What do you want to do instead?" Catherine said. I noticed Peter was the only one not looking at me.

"I don't know." My heart was pumping fast. "I haven't thought about it. I mean, very much."

"Have you talked to your mother about this?" That was the end of the hot seat for me. We all looked at my father. "Oops." Catherine froze. "I'm sorry, honey."

Because he could never resist, Peter said, "Talked to who? Our mother? Uh, we don't know anyone by that name."

"All right, look." My father raised his voice. Pissed-off was one sentiment he freely permitted himself. "Let's talk about this some other time."

The cat was out of the bag. Europe had come one step closer.

---

TO BE OUTSIDE in snow is entirely different from watching it through the window of a heated condo. Even in my padded gear—I was insulated as if by bubble-wrap—I felt the weight and dampness of the cold, which hurt my face. What a lot of work skiing was. Rugged stop-at-nothing types saw it as a "challenge," no doubt. My father, Peter, and I pretended we belonged to that group as we trudged forward with our skis up over our shoulders, heading for the beginner's run.

The sun had come out and everything sparkled in the clean, crisp air.

Get with it, I told myself, trying to effect an attitude adjustment. The lyrics from "I Am Woman" came to my aid, accompanied by a mental picture of me in my red outfit, sailing over the snow, my hair flying behind me. Strong. Invincible. Sexy speed demon all the guys had their eyes on. With a snow-spraying flourish, I'd end my run like the girl in the Close-Up toothpaste commercial, just in time to receive a kiss from Mark Kapp (latest fantasy guy from school), who would be waiting at the bottom.

"What time is lunch?" Peter said. I looked at him and my father, and hoped this would be one of my last family vacations. Sexy fun didn't happen with your family around.

Patrick, our instructor, began by telling us how fortunate we were to be learning on "champagne powder." The light, fluffy snow would yield to our skis, he said, allowing greater edge control. He had a yummy Australian accent. I had to force myself not to fantasize kissing him, the two of us clinking champagne glasses in a steaming Jacuzzi, because I intended to learn something for once in my life.

There were twelve of us on Icebreaker, the gentlest run. From the bottom, it didn't look too intimidating. My father exhaled impatiently as Patrick had us practice stepping in and out of our skis. He was anxious to get on the lift, to start moving. The rest of us were happy to do things right.

Once the skis snapped on, your feet became four-and-a-half-foot-long sticks, difficult to stay upright on, let alone walk with in any direction, and the boots were little caskets that prevented your ankles from moving. I looked at the others in our group and wondered why they appeared so balanced and in control. I felt extremely wobbly, cut off from my body in all that clothing. It was as if, below the neck, the rest of me were partially numb.

We rode the little lift to the top of Icebreaker and suddenly it didn't look so gentle anymore. It looked big and scary. Patrick explained that there were two ways to ski, with your feet forming a wedge or held parallel to one another. He demonstrated, calling one "pizza" and the other "french fries." I heard Peter chuckle as I took in the dizzying miles of white all around. Obviously, it would be a while before I went racing confidently down any slope.

I started down Icebreaker in a wedge, the outside of my right ski pressed into the snow, my fists closed tightly around my poles. I sort of stopped and started, slid a few inches then stalled, terrified of falling. I heard Patrick shout my name. Ease up on the right ski, he suggested. I was scared to, of course, but I did it and all of a sudden I was in control, skiing! Then I was out of control, falling. When I got up, there was snow inside my coat, and in my pants and boots. Champagne powder. Patrick skied over to me and helped me get back in my skis, ready to go again. Don't lean too far forward, he said. Try to loosen up. You're looking a bit tense. He slapped my back as he waited for me to go. I began again, and again I fell almost immediately, only this time I tumbled down the hill several feet, ending up flat on my face. When I looked up my skis were gliding on without me. It wasn't that it hurt, falling, but it was exhausting, mentally more than physically. "You're okay," my father called. "Keep trying, kid." The humiliation was excruciating. I spent the next thirty minutes concentrating everything I had on getting it right, on learning, with Patrick's help, how to correct myself so I wouldn't fall. I fell anyway, though I managed to stay up longer and longer.

My father skied up beside me, stopping without difficulty. I said, "I'm starting to get it, I think."

He patted my head with his big, clumsy glove. "You will. Look, we've got an hour till lunch. I'm going to cut loose."

We were both wearing sunglasses. What I saw in his was me standing in a field of white, looking back at a man reflected in my sunglasses. Suddenly I understood the art of M. C. Escher.

"But the lesson isn't over," I said.

"I got the basic idea. I'm going over to the next level." It was the final insult. He was deserting me and my brother for his more graceful, agile family. I watched him ski away. He looked rough and ungainly in his technique, but full of determination. "See you in an hour," he called, looking back.

........................

AS WE WAITED for my father in the cafeteria, I noticed Catherine and her daughters had acquired more than just color that morning. They looked invigorated, like people in an ad for breath mints. For every minute he didn't show up, Catherine's exuberance faded a little.

"He probably just lost track of time, Mom." Jennifer rolled her eyes. "Why don't we eat?"

We'd been there nearly fifteen minutes. Catherine suggested waiting five more, then asked me to repeat his exact words before leaving Icebreaker. She quizzed me as to the direction he'd gone.

"Okay, you kids eat." She handed Melody a twenty, still searching the crowd for the one face she couldn't locate. When we got back with our food, she stood and said she was going to the condo to see if he was there. I watched her outside the café, uprooting her skis from the snow. She balanced them over her shoulder, then marched off. As soon as she was out of sight, I expected my father to show up. Every time the cafeteria door swung open, I looked up, drawing the eyes of the newcomers to mine through sheer will, then losing them on account of my disappointment. It seemed I couldn't wait to tell my father he'd just missed Catherine, that she had set off in search of him, but I never got the opportunity.

After lunch, Peter and I returned to Icebreaker. I already felt some stiffness in my muscles, and weariness regarding the effort of it all, but our stepsisters had given us a few pointers and I wanted to try them out.

I reduced my reliance on the poles, which Patrick had told us to hold at a ninety-degree angle, as though carrying a serving tray. Melody and Jennifer said they were crutches, and recommended putting them away. The improvement was immediate, liberating. My weight shifted instinctively to the inside of my right leg as my skis straightened out for the very first time. French fries! I began skiing with my whole body, and it felt much better. Then, plop—I hit the snow, belly down. That's how it was the rest of the day. I fell when I least expected, berating myself constantly. *Ski, you idiot. It's easy. Everyone can ski but you. Don't look at your skis. Think graceful. Think winner. Show these people what you're made of.* I was so imprisoned by my thoughts, I hardly noticed how close I was to crying.

---

WHEN CATHERINE GOT BACK to the condo she found my father flat on the floor, moaning. "I can't move," he said. He meant without pain. The muscles in his back had gone into spasm. By the time we returned, she'd helped him to bed, called the doctor, and gone into town to pick up muscle relaxers. These had made him dopey and sweet. We took turns bringing him ginger ale, and fluffing his pillows, and keeping him company.

"S'no fair," he pouted, changing channels with the remote control. The muscle relaxers loosened all his strings, not just the ones in his back, so that his words came out as soft as melting ice cream. "Now I wohn gedda ski," he whined.

But he wasn't truly unhappy. There was too much sweetness behind the grumbling. I suspected he was secretly pleased to have landed in bed for a few days with the remote control and no need to apologize. There were people around to baby him. His only responsibility was to rest. I knew I was right when I saw him the next afternoon, asleep. I had come back from the slopes before the others and was about to ask if he needed anything, when the sight of his head thrown back, and his gaping, aspirating mouth, halted me. The TV was on low, and the room was flooded with late-afternoon sun, which fell across his face and hands. As I watched those hands, pale and folded on his heaving chest, the sound of his breathing filled the air.

"Dad," I whispered, nearly inaudible. The sleeping man kept on sleeping, and the peeping daughter kept on peeping, taking in her subject with tenderheartedness, with amazement.

"Dad." I moved my lips again, feeling the idea of him in the word. That sentiment sleeping people evoke in their observers—compassion—suddenly overwhelmed me. I felt an outpouring of love for all I imagined he'd ever gone through, for how tired he was, and how hard he worked himself.

"Dad," I murmured a few more times, until it came to sound like "dead," an association, once it got hold of me, that frightened me back down the stairs.

That night, after dinner, we tried to console Catherine by inviting her to the Jacuzzi. "He's just going to sleep," Jennifer said.

"You kids have a good time. Maybe I'll come down in a while." But we knew she wouldn't. We soaked for nearly an hour, and smoked pot, courtesy of Melody, and talked about life after death, while gazing at the star-studded sky.

"What about life after parents?" I said. I'd hoped for a laugh, or some kind of recognition, but it was very quiet. Around us, soft white flakes gently began descending, disintegrating on contact with the steaming water, seeping cold into our heads. I assumed everyone was looking at me. "What?" I said, then realized they'd all floated away, each to a private, unknowable planet.

Before sleep that night, as I slipped, half-gone, into unconsciousness,

I saw myself skiing, thought I understood it finally. I was by myself under the blue sky, turning, traveling, without a sound or thought in my way. I saw it was about control *and* letting go, about making shapes while surrendering to the pull and play of gravity. And I knew, even as I was inventing it, that this wasn't just another fantasy born of loneliness and desire, but progress.

ACKNOWLEDGMENTS

Several people supported me, in one way or another, through the long, occasionally black tunnel that led to the completion of this novel. They are writer and teacher extraordinaire Jim Krusoe, who got me started and whose early lessons kept me company throughout; the Ladies' Penmanship Society of Austin (Miriam Kuznets, Robin Bradford, Mimi Mayer, Jane Thurmond, Martha Boethel, Sara Stevenson, and Karol McMahan), aka my Texas writing group; my sister Diana Tanney, my grandparents Stephen and Ethel Longstreet, my ex-husband Glenn Morgan, and my friends Gary Schwartz and Gary Stewart. I'd also like to thank the Millay Colony for the Arts for granting me a residency at a crucial point in the process.

On the publication end of things, people to thank include attorney Carla Roberts and agent Jonathon Lazear, whose patience and good counsel I relied upon; my enthusiastic and supportive editor, Kate Niedzwiecki; and, finally, Ann Godoff, whose faith in me I appreciate more than words can say.

ABOUT THE AUTHOR

KATHERINE TANNEY was raised in Los Angeles and
attended the California Institute of the Arts, where she
received her B.F.A. She was a nationally exhibited video
artist and worked in the film industry before getting her
M.F.A. in creative writing from Warren Wilson College.
Tanney has been an artist-in-residence at the Millay
Colony for the Arts, a *STORY* magazine award finalist,
and the recipient of various awards and grants for her
work. She lives in Austin, Texas.